SISTER BENEATH THE SHEET

It is springtime in Biarritz—and playtime for Edwardian Society. But that fast and fashionable world is suddenly shaken by the death of a high-class prostitute—and by the extraordinary contents of her will. Topaz Brown, hostess to royalty, rakes and roués, has left her considerable fortune to the suffragette movement. Nell Bray, committed suffragette but no stranger to society, is sent to Biarritz by Emmeline Pankhurst with instructions to claim the money. But on arrival she becomes involved in a mystery surrounding Topaz's death . . .

SISTER BENEATH THE SHEET

Gillian Linscott

ATLANTIC LARGE PRINT

Chivers Press, Bath, England.
Curley Publishing, Inc.,
South Yarmouth, Mass., USA.

Library of Congress Cataloging-in-Publication Data

Linscott, Gillian.
  Sister beneath the sheet / Gillian Linscott.
    p.   cm.—(Atlantic large print)
  ISBN 0–7927–1103–3 (pbk. : lg. print)
1. Large type books.   I. Title.
[PR6062.I54S58   1992]
823′.914—dc20

91–36356
CIP

British Library Cataloguing in Publication Data available

This Large Print edition is published by Chivers Press, England, and
Curley Publishing, Inc, U.S.A. 1992

Published in the British Commonwealth by arrangement with the
Macdonald Group and in the U.S.A. with St Martin's Press

U.K. Hardback ISBN 0 7451 8355 7
U.K. Softback ISBN 0 7451 8367 0
U.S.A. Softback ISBN 0 7927 1103 3

SISTER BENEATH THE SHEET

CHAPTER ONE

The story began for me in the middle of April, only nine days after I was let out of Holloway. I'd been relaxing at my home in Hampstead, enjoying being able to take baths when I wanted to and getting to know my cats again, until a cab drew up outside and Emmeline Pankhurst stepped out of it.

'Nell, my dear, I want you to go to Biarritz at once.'

'Oh,' I said, 'I'm not really so bad. Two days at Cookham will do very well.'

I can never resist teasing Emmeline a little. She has many strengths, but a sense of humour is not one of them.

'It's a delicate situation. A woman has died there, in distressing circumstances, and left us a great deal of money.'

'How much?'

'Possibly as much as fifty thousand pounds.'

'Wonderful. That would mean we could support fifty suffrage candidates at the next election. Who was she?'

For once Emmeline seemed at a loss for words.

'It's not easy for me to tell you, Nell.'

'Surely we know her name.'

'Apparently she was a Miss Brown.'

1

I waited.

'She had a *nom de guerre*, so to speak. Topaz.'

I waited again.

'She was a ... a ...'

I took pity.

'If she was the Topaz Brown I've heard of, she was a highly successful prostitute.'

Emmeline nodded, colouring up like a débutante.

'She's dead?'

'It seems she killed herself. Worn out, I suppose, by her degraded way of life.'

'And left us all her money. Was she one of us?'

'I don't see how she could have been. The question is, should we take it?'

'Fifty thousand pounds? Of course we should take it.'

I knew the state of our finances better than Emmeline did.

'I thought that would be your attitude. It makes you the most appropriate person to go to Biarritz and look after our interests. You even speak French.'

I didn't relish the prospect of weeks of French and English lawyers and probably litigious relatives, but fifty thousand is fifty thousand. Also, curiosity is one of my favourite vices and I was already very curious about the legacy of Topaz Brown.

'How did we hear about this?'

2

Emmeline looked grim. 'I received a long telegraph message yesterday from Roberta Fieldfare. It seems she's staying in Biarritz. Goodness knows why.'

'Bobbie? I shared a cell with her mother, Lady Fieldfare.'

She was serving three months for throwing horse dung at a cabinet minister. Her sister Maud, who's sixty-nine years old but has a sounder aim, actually hit the target and got four months. The Fieldfares, aunt, mother and daughter, are as enthusiastic as they come in our cause of votes for women, but all of them as wild as hares. They are not Emmeline's favourite allies.

'I'll call on young Bobbie as soon as I get there. Did she say where she was staying?'

'I should prefer that you didn't, Nell. In fact, I think it would be best if you keep your activities as discreet as possible while you do what has to be done in Biarritz.'

In other words, ease the legacy quietly into the bank account of the Women's Social and Political Union without creating any additional gossip about its source.

I promised to do my best, made arrangements with my neighbour to take care of my long-suffering cats and looked up timetables. I left Charing Cross at ten o'clock on Monday morning. At seven twenty-seven on Tuesday morning I stepped on to the sunlit platform of Biarritz station after

3

travelling through the night from Paris. It was six days since Topaz had been found dead. I'd consulted my *Baedeker* on the journey and found a reasonably priced pension, the St Julien, listed in the Avenue Carnot, away from the sea but not far from the town centre. I took a cab there, secured a room, deposited my suitcase then breakfasted off coffee and croissants in the café next door. As I ate and drank I considered what I should do first.

One of the few things I'd been able to find out before leaving London was that Topaz Brown was found dead in her rooms at the Hôtel des Empereurs. I decided to take a stroll and look at the place. I'd never been to Biarritz before and, although I knew the King's visits had helped to make it fashionable, I was struck by the luxury and gaiety of it, especially after the greyness of prison life. Most of the grand hotels were clustered around the casino and main bathing establishment, behind a rocky headland called the Atalaye. Long sandy beaches stretched away to the north, more beaches southward to the Spanish border. The waves thumped in with shattering force against the headland and a stiff Atlantic breeze blew, but the early strollers parading in front of the hotels looked as if they'd come straight from Mayfair. Manservants pushed elderly invalids along in bath chairs, women struggled to hold on to hats with decorations of bird wings and silk streamers that seemed designed to make them take flight, uniformed nursemaids clung to the hands of children in sailors' suits. In another few years, probably, the fashionable world would move on and Biarritz would be left to the waves and the fishermen. Meanwhile the grand hotels towered along the parade like a line of great ships at anchor.

The Hôtel des Empereurs was easy to find, one of the largest and newest in the resort. It was built in a modern baroque style with wrought iron balconies bulging out from every floor, its frontage a surge of garlands, gymnastic nymphs and sea horses in terracotta. Two caryatids stood left and right of the front steps, stretching to the first floor and supporting a balcony on their heads. At either end, seven or eight floors up, were round turrets roofed with copper domes, the shape of inverted egg cups. There were rooms in each turret with windows facing north, south and out to sea. In the one on the right the blinds were down. I stood for a while, watching people going in and out of the hotel, wondering what it would feel like to be so tired of it, or so disgusted with it all that extinction would seem preferable. I was as eager as anybody to take Topaz's money, but thought I owed it to her to find out something more about her.

*   *   *

'Speaking for myself . . .' the solicitor said. He got up from his desk, fidgeted with a pile of papers, walked over to the window, as if reluctant to commit himself. 'Speaking for myself, I can only say that I found Miss Brown a very affable and businesslike woman. In fact, until this business of the will, we found her the ideal client.'

Topaz's lawyer had turned out to be English, and to have an office in the same building as the consulate. Apparently with so many rich and influential English people spending several weeks of the year in Biarritz, their professional advisers migrated with them.

'She'd been a client of yours for some time, then?'

'For some weeks. We were engaged in a property transaction on her behalf.'

He was being rather more forthcoming than I'd expected. There'd been just the suspicion of a wince when I introduced myself to him, but lawyers tend to be cautious when faced with people who've served prison sentences for throwing bricks through the window of 10 Downing Street.

'Was her will drawn up recently?'

He looked surprised, suspicious even.

'You haven't been told?'

'We know none of the details.'

6

'Last Wednesday afternoon.'

He said the three words very quickly and turned away to the window, as if disclaiming any responsibility for them.

'But ... I thought ... didn't she?'

'Miss Brown was found dead by her maid on Thursday morning.'

'So she made the will only half a day before she died? Did you see her? Did you have any idea...?'

The lawyer walked heavily back to his desk. He was quite a young man, but bald, and the sun glinted on his pink head.

'Miss Bray, I am in an awkward position. You may not know that Miss Brown's brother is challenging the will on the grounds that she could not have been of sound mind when she made it. I assume that your organisation may find itself contesting this in court. You will therefore appreciate that, in the circumstances, there's nothing more I can say to you.'

I did appreciate it. I thanked him for his politeness and told him that he'd be hearing officially from the Women's Social and Political Union in due course. As he showed me out I said: 'You mentioned a maid. I suppose there'd be no objection to my speaking to her.'

'None that I can see. You may find her a little ... er ... embattled. She was very loyal to Miss Brown.'

7

'Do you know her name, or where I can find her?'

'Tansy Mills. She's still at Miss Brown's suite at the Hôtel des Empereurs. Miss Brown had paid for the suite till the end of the month, and somebody must pack her things.'

'When is the funeral?'

'That is yet to be arranged.'

From the way he said it, I gathered there were difficulties there, but he wouldn't be the one to tell me about them. It was mid-morning by then. I made my way back to the Hôtel des Empereurs and, at the reception desk, asked for Topaz Brown's maid.

I got some curious looks, but a boy in a pill-box hat and gold-braided uniform took me up in the lift from the back of the foyer. The gates opened at the seventh floor. He led me along a crimson-carpeted corridor, and knocked at a pair of double doors painted in white and gold.

'Who's there? Who is it?'

The voice, speaking English with traces of an East London accent, came sharply from inside. The boy shrugged and walked away.

'My name's Nell Bray. Are you Tansy Mills?'

'Yes. What is it?'

'I'd like to talk to you about Miss Brown.'

'Did the lawyer send you?'

8

'Yes.'

It wasn't far from the truth and seemed to be the only way I'd get in.

'Wait a minute.'

There was a pause, the sound of a key turning, then one of the doors opened. The woman on the other side of it couldn't have been much more than five foot two in height, but broad shouldered and with a sense of pugnacity about her. Her nose was long, her eyes brown and angry. She was wearing a plain black dress and her hair, already showing signs of grey, was pulled back into a tight pleat. She looked a most respectable little body.

'You're English? Thank goodness for that. I'm tired to the bone with all of them jabbering away in French to me, except that lawyer, and he's not much better even if it is in English. And none of them listening to a word I say.'

She'd closed the door behind me and we were standing in a wide entrance hall, with doors leading off it, in the centre and to the right. To the left I noticed a small lift cage.

'Well, what do you want to know? Are you going to listen, or do you just want to jabber like the rest of them?'

'I want to listen.'

She looked at me and pushed open the door in front of us.

'You'd better come in and sit down, though

9

it's all a muddle. I've been trying to pack up her things. Mr Jules is helping, but the more you pack the more there is.'

It was an enormous round room, with windows looking out over the promenade and up and down the coast. I realised that I was inside one of the two towers I'd looked at early that morning, the left-hand one. Islands of good furniture were scattered round it, armchairs and chaise longues with small tables beside them. Almost every available surface was heaped with gleaming piles of dresses, cloaks and shawls, or piled with papers, envelopes and leather cases. Tansy swept an armful off a chair for me.

'I suppose you want a cup of tea.'

'Yes please.'

As she took a spirit lamp from a cupboard, I tried to explain myself.

'Miss Brown left our organisation a very large sum of money. We know almost nothing about her.'

She put down a small tea kettle and stared at me, fists on hips.

'You're the ones who've been causing all the trouble over votes?'

'Yes.'

Feeling the anger radiating out of her, I decided not to add to it.

She walked across the room, trying to stamp her feet, hindered by the thickness of the carpet.

'Of all the silly things she ever did . . . Still, it was no use arguing with her once she'd made up her mind.'

She filled the kettle, with much clashing of metal and china. It was obvious that if Topaz Brown had been an unlikely convert to our cause, she'd had no success in convincing her maid.

Once the kettle was on, Tansy plonked herself down opposite me, sitting on the edge of a chair crowded with guides and railway timetables.

'What do you expect me to tell you, then?'

'All you can remember about the day before she died.'

It was clearly no use beating about the bush with Tansy, and it looked as if our claim to that fifty thousand pounds would hinge on Topaz's behaviour on that last day. To my surprise, Tansy seemed almost pleased.

'I'll do that. I'd tell anybody, only they won't listen.'

'I'm listening.'

She took a deep breath. 'The whole day before? Well, it was ten o'clock on the Thursday morning when I found her. If you go back a day from that, that's ten o'clock on the Wednesday. I'd taken her breakfast on a tray as usual, jug of chocolate, thick and creamy, those little twisty French rolls she liked. I tapped on the door and said, "Your

11

breakfast ma'am." I always started the day formal.'

'In this room?'

'No, in her bedroom, of course. Where else would she be?'

'On her own?'

The question had to be asked, but it annoyed Tansy.

'Of course she was on her own. I wouldn't have disturbed her otherwise, would I?'

'I suppose not. How did she seem?'

'Just like she always seemed in the mornings, curled up in the sheets like a big sleepy cat. Naturally lovely, she was, and don't let that woman on the other side or anybody else tell you different. Like that, only better.'

She pointed to a picture on the wall. I hadn't noticed it when I came in because the light wasn't on it, but when I looked at it, it seemed to glow with its own light. It was done in pastels, in tones of tawny, gold and apricot and showed a woman lying back, hair loose, among gold draperies and smiling a kind of lazy, satisfied smile. A replete cat rather than a predatory one.

'That was done by one of her artists. She liked being painted. You asked me what she was like that last morning, and it was just like that. Anyway, I put the tray down on the table by her bed and drew back the curtains to let the sun in, like I always did, and she asked me if the post had come.'

'Did she seem anxious about anything in the post?'

Again, she seemed aggrieved at the suggestion.

'No, she did not, and I'll tell you how I know. I'd got the post ready on the table outside the door, so I brought it in to her. It was much the same as it always is, all those square stiff envelopes with the crests on them and the foreign gentlemen's smells . . .'

'Smells?'

'You know, the oil they put on their hair and their beards and so on. She just glanced at them, put them to one side without even looking at them properly and said to me, "Have you heard from your little sister?" That's the kind of lady she was. A handful of European nobility and she puts them aside to ask after my sister, a ten-bob-a-week seamstress in a sweat shop off the Mile End Road.'

She glared at me as if challenging me to contradict her. I kept quiet, realising that I must let her get on with it in her own way.

'So I said no, I hadn't heard anything from Rose, and she said, "Do you think she'll come?" You see, two weeks before she'd caught me looking down in the mouth and got it out of me that I was worrying about Rose. Even then, though, I only told her the half of it, that Rose wasn't strong, not a work-pony like me, and I was worried about

13

her working all hours, lodging in a fleapit of a place. Topaz said, without even stopping to think about it, "Well, you must write to her and tell her to come over here. I'll pay her to keep my underwear in good order." I thought she was joking, but there was no satisfying her until I'd written a letter to Rose and sent it off, with a ten pound note that Topaz had given me for her fare. And that last morning, she wasn't asking about Rose because she was worried about her ten pounds, don't think that.'

I said I was sure she wasn't. Tansy got up and poured a jet of boiling water into a silver teapot, swished it round, poured the water into a basin. She was angry with the world, with me, with everything including the tea kettle, but she still didn't forget to warm the pot. She was silent while she finished making the tea and I thought of what she'd told me so far. If Topaz had killed herself in a fit of madness or self-disgust, there'd apparently been no signs of it at the start of her last day. That is, if Tansy was to be believed. She poured the tea and put a white and gold cup on the table beside me, pushing papers away to make room for it.

'Anyway, when I told her I hadn't heard anything from Rose, I must have let too much of what I was thinking into my voice, because she put down her cup and said, "What's the matter, Tansy?" And, God forgive me, I went

14

straight over to the bed and told her. "I'm afraid she's going to get herself into trouble with the police, ma'am."

' "What sort of trouble?"

'So I told her Rose wasn't bad in herself, only she'd been taking up with a bad set, giving her ideas she shouldn't have, wanting things she's got no business to want. She gave me one of her straight looks and said, "Are you trying to tell me your little sister's gone on the game?"

'Before I could think I blurted out, "No, ma'am, it's not that bad. At least . . ." Then she laughed and I felt myself going hot and knew my face was redder than a beet. I could have bitten my silly tongue out. But she only lay back there on her pillows and laughed, that deep laugh that a man who wrote a poem about her said was like a lioness purring.

' "Oh, my poor Tansy. There's a big difference between street corners in the East End and all this, now isn't there?"

'I nearly tripped over my silly tongue saying yes, of course there was. She gave that laugh again.

' "The difference is that this is so very much more comfortable. Now, what are these things your sister's got no business to want?"

'I blurted out: "Votes for women, ma'am."

'This time she laughed until I thought she'd never stop, and I stood there starting to get annoyed with her, as I did sometimes. At

15

last she said, "Are you trying to tell me your little sister's a suffragette?"

' "That's about the size of it, ma'am." '

Tansy stopped for breath and took a gulp of tea. Her face, from embarrassment or indignation, was as red as she'd described it. In spite of the need not to annoy her, I couldn't let this pass.

'But why were you so concerned about it, Miss Mills? There are women from all walks of life in our movement. I've just been sharing a prison cell with a woman with a title.'

Tansy glared at me. 'It's all very well for the likes of them. They can afford to be political.'

'Afford?'

'If lady this or countess that hits a policeman and gets put in prison, it doesn't matter to her, does it? She doesn't have to worry about losing her job without a reference and ending up in the workhouse. Girls like my sister who've got precious little in the first place—they're the one's who can't afford to lose it.'

'Has Rose hit a policeman?'

'Not yet, as far as I know. But she's been on a big march to the Houses of Parliament, so it's only a matter of time.'

It was not the time or place to begin the political education of Tansy Mills. Instead, I asked how Topaz had reacted. Had Tansy,

16

for instance, guessed her employer was interested in women's suffrage too?

'The papers were full of it before we left London, but that was two months ago, back in February. We always had more important things to talk about. Anyway, that last morning when I told her about Rose she just stretched her arms, in the way she had when she was waking up properly, and said: "It's all such nonsense."'

'She said votes for women was nonsense?'

'Votes for anybody. She said politics was half greed and half gossip. She said she'd known a fair number of politicians, and there wasn't one she'd vote for, not one.'

And yet, within hours of that conversation, Topaz had left us her fortune. If Tansy could be believed, it looked as if the brother would have a strong case in court. I wondered if he'd been in touch with Tansy already.

'What happened after that?'

'She finished her breakfast and opened her letters.'

'Was there anything unusual?'

For once, Tansy hesitated. 'Not really.'

'But there was something?'

'Nothing special. One of them was a big envelope with a little box inside it, and a card. She smiled to herself at what was on the card, then showed me what was in the box.'

'What was it?'

'Nothing special, as I said. Just a big fire

17

opal in a pendant. It looked a bit old-fashioned to me and it was nothing to the things some of them gave her.'

'But she seemed pleased with it?'

'Quite pleased, yes. But it was nothing to get excited about.'

'What then?'

'Well, we got ready for her bath. I laid out her stockings and the ivory silk chemise with the apricot ribbons and Chantilly lace. One of the ribbons was hanging by a few threads so I had to see to it, and she said that just showed we needed Rose over to help. She was always very fastidious about her lingerie. That was one of the things that shocked me when I found her.'

Her voice went cold and bleak. I think, while she'd been talking about Topaz, Tansy had almost forgotten that she was dead. Now she sat there, staring across her tea cup at the window. From the road below us the sound of hooters and carriage wheels reminded me that the town was going about its normal business of amusing itself.

I said, as gently as I could, 'From what you say, it was all very happy and normal that last morning, but that night, she killed herself. Can you . . . ?'

She crashed her cup down and stood up. At five foot two she could hardly tower over me even when I was sitting down, but she did her best.

'You're as bad as the rest of them. Haven't you been listening to a word I've been telling you?'

'Of course I have. But if she killed herself...'

'She didn't kill herself. Topaz didn't kill herself. She had no reason to kill herself. She was murdered.'

Alarmed at the course her grief was taking, I stood up and put my arm round her stiff but unresisting shoulders.

'Miss Mills, I know you're upset, I know it must have been a shock for you, but...'

She glared at me from close quarters, dry eyed.

'She was murdered,' she repeated.

From outside in the hallway a bell rang.

'That will be Mr Jules. I'll have to go down and let him in.'

Efficient again, as if the word 'murdered' had never been spoken, she took a key from her pocket and hurried out. I heard a lift going down, then coming up again. Who Mr Jules was, beyond the man who was helping Tansy sort out Topaz's papers, I had no idea. I stood there with the luxurious detritus of Topaz Brown's career around me, wondering how much, if any, of this I should report to Emmeline.

CHAPTER TWO

When Jules Estevan walked in and found me there, his look was unmistakably one of relief. I don't know what, if anything, Tansy had told him in the lift, but I think he was glad to see anybody who might share the burden of looking after Tansy. As for me, my impression was of a tall young man, in his early thirties, almost painfully thin, with the kind of face you see carved in marble on mediaeval tombs. To say he was well dressed would be like calling Leonardo da Vinci a man who sketched. His suit, hat and waistcoat were a harmony of greys and silvers. He wore pale lilac-coloured gloves and carried a black ebony cane, topped with silver.

'May I introduce myself? My name is Jules Estevan. I was a friend of Miss Brown.'

His voice was low and pleasant, with just a trace of accent to show that English was not his first language.

'He's the one who wrote the poem I told you about,' Tansy said.

I told him my name. 'You are a poet, Mr Estevan?'

He shrugged: 'I am a *flâneur*, Miss Bray.'

He said it as one would say lawyer or doctor. It struck me that I was probably meeting the first of Topaz's clients. He seemed to read my mind.

'You may be wondering about my relationship with Miss Brown. I can claim to be nothing other than a friend. We met here last season. I found her one of the least tedious people in the resort and she was good enough to return the compliment. Shall we sit down?'

Tansy didn't seem to resent Jules acting as host. She remained standing while I resumed my seat and Jules settled himself on a *chaise-longue*, moving aside a pile of lacy things.

I said, 'I represent the Women's Social and Political Union. I've been asking Miss Mills about the events leading up to Miss Brown's death.'

I didn't say suicide. I didn't want another outburst from Tansy. He nodded slightly. I had the impression that he already knew about the brother's challenge to the legacy. I don't know why, except Jules always contrived to give the impression of knowing about everything and being bored by most of it.

'I've told her she was murdered,' Tansy said.

'I'm sure you have. What exactly did you want to know, Miss Bray?'

'I want to understand more about her state of mind when she made her will.'

21

He smiled a little. 'I think we can help with that, can't we Tansy?'

She'd left the room for a minute and returned with a glass and an opened half bottle on a tray.

'Today,' he said, 'you'll only find this vintage in three places: the Royal cellars in Budapest, the Vatican—and Topaz's little store here in Biarritz. She and I usually shared a half bottle at this time of day. Will you join me in drinking to her memory now?'

It would have been ill-mannered to refuse. Tansy, her face impassive, went to fetch another glass and Jules poured for both of us.

'To Topaz.'

'To Topaz.'

We drank. I said, 'You came to see her every day?'

'At noon, every day except Saturday and Sunday. It was a ritual. She always liked to know what everybody had been doing the night before. I was usually able to tell her a little. She laughed a lot. She enjoyed laughing.'

He said it like a man who rarely laughed himself.

'And that last day, the Wednesday, you came as usual?'

'Oh yes.'

'And what did you talk about?'

'People. About Lord Beverley and his father. About La Pucelle. About a dozen

22

things that probably wouldn't mean much to you. She'd always tell me what invitations had come in the morning post, and we'd discuss which would be amusing and which wouldn't.'

'Was there anything else about the post?'

'She showed me a pendant that had been sent to her and wanted me to guess who it was from. I made a guess or two, but she said none of them was right.'

'A valuable pendant?'

He shook his head. 'Only opal.'

I could feel Tansy's eyes on me. She must have guessed I was testing the truth of what she'd told me.

'Did you talk about her work?'

I expected a cooling of the atmosphere. So far both Tansy and Jules Estevan had been talking as if Topaz Brown were any lady of leisure. I was almost falling into the trap of it, and thought it time to introduce a little reality. Jules seemed quite unconcerned.

'Well, Miss Bray, I suppose you'd have to class poor Lord Beverley as work.'

'You mean he was one of her clients? And why poor Lord Beverley?'

'Client. What a terrible word. It makes Topaz sound like a dentist. As for "poor", he's spent all his money and his father the Duke's arrived to take him home to England. That's what Topaz and I were talking about.'

'Was she disappointed at losing him?'

23

'Not in the least. I remember saying at the time that she seemed in no hurry to choose a replacement. I can see why now, of course.'

He sipped his wine, looking at me over the glass.

'And who is La Pucelle?'

'Oh dear, hasn't Tansy told you about La Pucelle yet? It's her favourite topic of conversation.'

From behind me, Tansy made a derisive noise. It struck me that the relationship between her and Jules was a strange one, demanding none of the respect usual between a rich man and a lady's maid.

'Well, since she hasn't, I should tell you that as far as Topaz Brown had a rival in Biarritz it was Marie de la Tourelle, known amongst the vulgar as La Pucelle. I'm sure Tansy could tell you why.'

Tansy said, explosively, 'He says it's French for a girl who's still a virgin. Goodness knows why, because she's no girl and she certainly isn't the other thing either.'

Jules smiled. 'It was something of a tribute to her constant martyrdoms. One of the most interesting things to an onlooker about the rivalry between Topaz and Marie was the contrast between them. Topaz made no secret of enjoying her work, and liking men. Marie lets it be known that she is of the nobility, fallen into her profession through hard times. She, I think, prefers the company of women,

24

except in the line of business, and often claims to regret the life she's forced to lead.'

Tansy said: 'There's always talk that she's going to join a convent and repent, but nothing seems to come of it.'

'Is she as beautiful as Topaz was?'

I couldn't help asking it. I was looking at Topaz's picture at the time.

'Yes,' said Jules.

'Not a bit of it,' said Tansy.

She glared at him, while he went on talking to me.

'Marie is tall and very slender, with the profile of a goddess and long, long hair as dark as the road to perdition. Put her next to Topaz—not that you'd often see them together—it was like the goddess of dawn next to the goddess of the shades.'

'But you said she was a rival to Topaz.'

'Some people, Miss Bray, prefer the shades. Two men have committed suicide over Marie, and two others are in prison for fighting a duel. For some men, that's part of the attraction. It's like taking death itself to bed and surviving.'

Tansy said: 'Nobody was ever the worse for taking up with Topaz.'

'That's probably quite true. I don't know quite how to describe it, Miss Bray, but there was always an abundance of life about Topaz. I think that was part of her success. Men thought, so to speak, that some of that vitality

25

would rub off on them.'

He looked at me closely. I don't know if he expected to see me blush, but if so, he was disappointed.

Tansy said: 'Lord Beverley soon found out which one of them he preferred.'

'Yes indeed. One of Topaz's little triumphs. In fact, I suppose one has to say her last triumph. She took Lord Beverley away from La Pucelle, apparently without even trying.'

'She wouldn't have to try. She could get more than Lord Beverley without trying.'

Tansy was blushing again, hot with indignation. Jules caught my eye and smiled. I thought he enjoyed teasing her, and it wasn't kind.

Tansy stalked over to the window, and stared out.

'I'll bet she's in there, watching us.'

'In where?'

'Marie lives in the other tower, the south one, just like this. She owns a villa just outside the town, but as soon as word got round that Topaz had rented this tower suite for the season, Marie had to have the other one at any price.'

There was an angry exclamation from Tansy.

'Just look at it.'

Then, as Jules and I crossed to the window, 'No, don't look. That's just what

26

she wants.'

Too late, Jules and I were already beside her at the window, looking across to the opposite tower. All the blinds except one were down, but at that window I had a glimpse of a pale profile and a white hand.

'What's she looking at?'

Jules opened a door and stepped out on to the balcony. In spite of Tansy's protests, I followed. We looked down and there in front of the main doors was a florist's gig, drawn by two white ponies. You could only just see the gig and the ponies because it was packed from front to back with white lilies. Behind it two more gigs were drawn up, just as packed, and we could see lines of page boys staggering into reception with armfuls of lilies almost as large as themselves.

'Look at it,' said Jules. 'It's a positive wantonness of purity.'

'Are they all for Marie de la Tourelle?'

'Who else? It's probably the Archduke, apologising for laying lustful hands upon her.'

'He must have bought up every lily in Biarritz.'

Even high up on our balcony, you could smell them above the scent of the sea. The figure had gone from the window opposite, but as we watched lines of boys bearing lilies passed across it.

Jules said sadly, 'How Topaz would have laughed.'

We went back into the salon, where Tansy was busying herself ostentatiously with piles of clothes.

'I don't know how you can stand there and look at her, Mr Jules. If there were any rights in this country . . .'

He picked up his glass and said sharply: 'Tansy, please don't start that again.'

'Well, what am I supposed to do? Stand there and watch her queening it day after day and not say anything, after what she's done?'

She thumped a shawl into a small square, dropped it, had to pick it up and start again. From her voice, I think she was near to tears.

Jules said, sounding weary: 'Tansy thinks Marie murdered Topaz.'

'What!'

'Well, who else did if she didn't? That one hated her, grudged her every breath she took. Then in the end, when she couldn't get at her any other way, she just came and poisoned her.'

She picked up another shawl, took a corner of it in each hand then another corner of it in her teeth, pulled so hard that the delicate fabric tore.

'Now look what you made me do. All her nice things . . .'

She was really crying now. Jules put his arm round her, crouched down beside her.

'Tansy, you mustn't go round saying things

28

like that. You could get yourself into serious trouble.'

'Why won't anyone believe me?'

Between us we managed to get her to sit down on the chaise longue, drink a little of the wine. She became calmer, but still insistent.

'They're all trying to make out she killed herself. She'd never kill herself, not Topaz.'

I looked at Jules.

'Do you believe Topaz killed herself?'

'What else can I think? I certainly don't believe that Marie crept in unobserved and tipped half a bottle of laudanum into her wine.'

'It was laudanum that killed her?'

'Yes.'

'Did she take it habitually?'

Tansy said indignantly: 'She did not. She didn't have it in the place.'

Jules nodded. 'Topaz never had any trouble sleeping.'

'And yet on your evidence, up to and beyond midday on the Wednesday, Topaz was behaving quite normally. When did you leave her?'

'Just before one o'clock. I'd hoped to lunch with her, but she said no, there was something she wanted to discuss with Tansy. I said I'd meet her for a drive that afternoon, if she wasn't otherwise occupied, and left them to it.'

Tansy was calmer, staring at me.

29

'So Topaz had lunch here on her own?'

She shook her head. 'No, Topaz and me had lunch here together.'

I must have looked surprised.

'Don't think that was happening all the time, but we'd do it sometimes. On her birthday and mine, providing there weren't any other engagements, we'd sit down together and talk. Topaz wasn't ashamed of where she came from, not like that one over there. Anyway, that Wednesday, she said she had something to tell me and I should order lunch from the kitchens for both of us. Those little orange-coloured melons, a bit of lobster salad, raspberries and a bottle of her special Chablis. I said, a bit cheeky, "Whose birthday is it, then?" and she said I'd soon find out. I thought she probably wanted to tell me when we were going back to England. She liked to be back in good time for Ascot. Anyway, when we were well into the lobster salad, she sprang it on me.'

Jules was watching both of us like a man who'd heard it before.

'Sprang what?'

'She said she wasn't going back to England. "Not for Ascot?" I said.

' "Not for Ascot or anything else. I'm going to retire, Tansy." I didn't know what to say. There wasn't anybody in Europe who'd had more success than she had. So, as usual, I blurted out the wrong thing.

' "You're good for a few years yet. Your looks haven't even started to go."

'She took no offence.

' "Years ago, Tansy, before I knew you, I swore I'd give it up when I found my first grey hair. It's happened."

' "Where is it? I can't see it."

'I looked at her hair, still hanging down loose over her shoulders.

' "You look as if you wanted to swat it, Tansy, like a wasp. Who said it was on my head?"

'Then she laughed more, seeing me go red.

' "It's cruel, isn't it, Tansy? I do enjoy making you blush. That's probably why we get on so well. You do all my blushing for me."

'I said nothing, because it was still sinking in.

' "Oh, I know I could keep at it for another year or two, before my figure starts spreading and my complexion goes. But I'm thirty-one next birthday and I've been at it for thirteen years. I've made all the money I need for what I want to do."

'I asked her what that was, and she said she was going to buy a vineyard. She'd been looking round and she thought she'd found the right one. She said she was going to let herself get fat and her hair could go how it liked. She was going to drive herself around in a pony cart and shout at her workmen

31

when they got lazy. She'd invite some men to visit her, but only the ones like Mr Jules or some of the others that made her laugh. She was excited as a girl about it, and I thought, well why shouldn't she, after all. So I raised a glass to her and her vineyard and wished her the very best of luck.'

I looked across at Jules.

'Did Topaz say anything to you about this?'

'Not at the time. I think she wanted to tell Tansy first.'

'But what other time was there?'

'You'll have to hear the rest of the story. Go on, Tansy.'

I noticed again that the anger seemed to drain away from Tansy when she was remembering Topaz. She was happy to talk about her.

'Well, the next thing she wanted was me to come with her to this vineyard, as housekeeper. I said she wouldn't really need me there and I'd miss England if I was away from it all the time, but I'd come and visit her. She said she'd miss me, and that we'd stay here in Biarritz for another month, to pack up and give Rose a bit of a holiday. Then she'd give me our fares back to London and a hundred pounds on top of my wages. She always was generous.'

Jules said: 'That's true. Topaz liked money, but she was always generous with it.'

'Anyway, I thanked her, and I only wish we'd left it there. But she has to start asking me what I'd do. She said she was getting what she wanted, and she wished I could have the same. "What would you do, Tansy, if you could have anything you wanted?"

'I closed my eyes and saw it developing like a photograph on a plate. It must have been the wine.

' "A cottage by the river. A vegetable garden. A few ducks. Enough for Rose and me to get by on without going out to service or factory work."

'I thought if Rose had somewhere comfortable like that to live, she wouldn't go worrying about votes. Anyway, for some reason, the idea of ducks really tickled Topaz.

' "Have you ever kept ducks, Tansy?"

' "No, it's just something I fancy."

'Then she came out with it, and I wish she hadn't.

' "Tell you what, Tansy, I'll leave you five hundred pounds in my will. Then if I die before you do, you'll get your ducks one day, even if you're an old lady."

' "In that case, I hope I'm as old as Methuselah."

'Then she said she was meeting her lawyer at the British Consulate after lunch to discuss transferring the money to buy her vineyard. She'd make her will at the same time, and I had to go along with her. Of course, by then I

33

wished I'd never opened my mouth, but off we went in her carriage with me sitting beside her in my best navy blue and all the gentlemen bowing and waving to her as we went along the promenade. We picked up Mr Jules on the way, and he can tell you the rest because I can't think about it without getting angry.'

'The making of the will,' said Jules. 'That's what you really want to know about, isn't it, Miss Bray?'

He was smiling, but I realised that I wasn't the only person in the room trying to find the answers to questions.

CHAPTER THREE

Jules leaned forward, smiling a little, keeping his eyes on me.

'Topaz, I found out, had decided that I should be a witness. At first, Tansy and I had to sit there while she arranged the transfer of most of her money from England in a most businesslike way. When that was done she said, "And I want to make a will."

'The lawyer was a little bald fellow. You could tell he was very much taken with Topaz, as most people were. He said if she'd let him know what she wanted, he'd make a note and send her a draft for her comments.

But Topaz would never wait for anything. She said she wanted to do it there and then, and it wasn't complicated, so he had to give in, as people always did. So she just sat there and dictated. I can remember it word for word: "To my loyal maid and friend, Tansy Mills, I bequeath five hundred pounds for her to buy a cottage and some ducks. That's all."

'Of course, that was the first time I'd heard about the ducks, and I couldn't help laughing. The lawyer stared. "But your estate amounts to considerably more than five hundred pounds."

'"That's all right, then."

'"What is to happen to the residue? Normally it would go to your nearest surviving relative. Is that what you wish?"

'Topaz was furious. "No, it most certainly is not. The only relation I have is a brother, and I'm not leaving him or his family anything. Not a penny."'

Tansy interrupted: 'She told me about this brother. He ignored her for years, tried to borrow a lot of money off her when she started doing well, then said she'd burn in hell for her sinful life when she refused him.'

Jules said: 'The lawyer suggested she might leave the rest of her money to some good cause. But by then Topaz had had her joke and I think she was bored with it all. She said orphanages and old horses weren't very amusing. Then the idea seemed to hit her all

35

of a sudden. She said: "I'll leave it to the suffragettes."'

He waited for a comment from me. I said nothing. I was already beginning to realise that Jules Estevan enjoyed experimenting with people.

'I said to her, "I didn't think you believed in them." She said, "I don't, but think how it would annoy my brother." She was insistent that we must get the name right and we had to hunt up an old copy of *The Times* in the lawyer's office to make sure of it. He drew up the will, Topaz signed it, a man from the consulate and I witnessed it. And that, Miss Bray, is how Topaz Brown came to leave her fortune to the Women's Social and Political Union.'

I said nothing. I was wondering what Emmeline would say when she heard, and reflecting that when this came out in court it would hardly help our case. It might be possible to argue that frivolity was no proof of an unsound mind, but it was hardly an attractive course.

Tansy said: 'I knew no good would come from making a mock of wills. I told her so at the time, but she wouldn't listen.'

I think Jules Estevan was disappointed at getting no obvious reaction from me. He asked:

'Is this money so important to your movement, Miss Bray?'

36

'It's vital. For the first time, the electorate is turning towards us. Last year our intervention decisively influenced the result of by-elections in Peckham, Mid Devon and Manchester North-West. The next general election will matter more to us than any in our history and we must have the money to support candidates who will vote for our cause in Parliament.'

'And you'd accept Topaz's money—after what you've heard?'

'I'd accept money from the devil himself, if it would help us.'

Tansy muttered something that I couldn't hear. I pushed my half-empty glass of wine aside. It was so good that I wanted to drink more, but the room was warm, my head was buzzing already and there was still a long way to go.

I asked Jules: 'What time was it when you left the lawyer's office?'

He looked at Tansy, questioningly.

'After four,' she said. 'I know that because by the time we got back here it was time for her tea.'

'What was Topaz's mood on the way back?'

'She kept laughing about the ducks and the suffragettes and her brother!'

'Hysterical laughter?'

'Normal laughter. She was like a child who'd been given some exceptionally amusing toy.'

37

'Did you go back to tea with her?'

'No. I had another engagement, so she dropped me outside one of the other hotels. That was the last I saw of her.'

'What was the last thing she said to you?'

'She waved to me as her carriage went off and said she'd see me at the usual time tomorrow.'

'As normal?'

'Exactly as normal.'

'You had no premonition then?'

'None.'

I turned to Tansy. 'Were there any guests at tea?'

'No. Tea was when she'd plan the serious part of the day. We'd see to it that this room and the bedroom were ready and the flowers arranged, with the bouquet from whoever she was entertaining that night given the best place. If she was going out to dinner or a reception, that was when she'd decide what dress to wear and what jewels to go with it. If she was entertaining here it would be a matter of ordering up supper from the hotel kitchens and choosing the wine from her special store. She might write a note or two, answering invitations. Then, if it suited her, she'd usually let me know who the guest was going to be. I'd guessed Lord Beverley, but she said nothing.'

'Did she write any notes that day?'

'A couple.'

'Who to?'

'I don't know. I just put them on the table outside and a boy comes up to collect them before dinner. I didn't look.'

'Long notes?'

'No. She didn't go in for long notes. Usually just a word or two.'

'What did she do after she'd written the notes?'

'She sat there drinking tea and looking at some more mail that had arrived while we were out.'

'Was there anything in it that disturbed her?'

'No.'

'No change from her usual routine?'

I expected another no, but this time it didn't come. There was a look of distress on Tansy's face and the fingers of her right hand were rubbing and twisting at a fold of her black dress.

'That was when she started acting ... not like she usually did.'

It hurt her to admit it.

'In what way?'

'Well, when she'd been just sitting there for a bit, I thought I should remind her that time was getting on. After all, we hadn't retired just yet. I said, "Which is it tonight, out or at home?" She looked up from a letter. "Oh, at home."

'"His Lordship, is it?"

'I sensed that she was in an odd sort of mood, like the mood children get into when they're ready for more devilment. She said no, his father the Duke had arrived, so he couldn't come and see her, but she still didn't say who she was expecting instead. So I asked her if she'd decided what she wanted ordering for supper. Nothing, she said.

'I made myself busy collecting up the tea things, a bit annoyed with her. You may say I shouldn't have been, on account of the five hundred pounds, but that was hardly in my mind at all. I thought it was one of her jokes, a way of spicing up a boring afternoon at the lawyer's, and that was that. After another few minutes, when she still hadn't said anything, I said: "What dress would you like me to put out then?"

'"The plain brown one, with the cream-coloured shawl and brown straw hat."

'I was flabbergasted. "But that's a day dress."

'It was the plainest one in her whole wardrobe.

'"I know it is. I'm going out to do some shopping."

'Well, that was unheard of. Ladies don't shop at nearly six o'clock in the evening, do they? That's only tradesmen's wives getting things for their supper. I said: "What in the world could you be wanting to buy at this hour?"

'"Oh, just a few things."'

'"Well, tell me what they are, and I'll go out and get them for you." But no, she would insist on going herself. She changed into the brown dress, went out and came back less than an hour later. I was in the bedroom at the time, so I didn't see if she was carrying anything. When I came back into the salon she'd opened a window on to the balcony and was standing there, looking out. She said to me: "Tansy, how would you like this evening free?"'

'"Free ma'am?"'

'She said: "I shan't be needing you this evening. In fact, I don't want you to be here."'

Tansy's flow of words had stopped. She was staring at me as if waiting for me to register something—shock, disbelief, I don't know what. I was puzzled because it seemed to me quite an ordinary thing for a woman to say to her maid, especially a woman of Topaz Brown's kind. When she failed to get the right reaction from me, Tansy started talking again, not far from tears.

'I was cut to the heart. I never gossiped, Mr Jules will tell you. In six years with her, I'd been discretion itself. There wasn't the money in the world that would make me let down Topaz. She must have seen she'd hurt me, because she came over and put her arm round my shoulder.

41

' "Oh Tansy, I don't mean that. If I had all the royal princes in Europe in here at once, and the President of the United States as well, I wouldn't send you away. I trust you more than I trust myself." '

' "I'd thought so, ma'am," I said.'

' "You know so. Now, stop looking so tragic. I've booked you a nice little room for the night on the second floor and you can go and see that friend of yours down by the harbour this evening." '

'She was practically pleading with me, like a mother trying to stop a child turning awkward.

' "Then in the morning you can bring me my breakfast as usual and perhaps I'll tell you all about it. But I want to be on my own tonight." '

'I said, still hard: "You shouldn't have gone to so much trouble." '

' "Tansy, it's nothing against you, I promise. It's only a kind of joke I'm planning." ' '

I couldn't help interrupting.

'She said that—a joke?'

'Yes. It made me feel better at the time. She loved practical jokes, didn't she, Mr Jules? She'd go to endless time and trouble planning them.'

Jules said: 'That's quite true. Topaz would do almost anything for a joke.'

'So you went?' I asked Tansy.

42

'I had no choice. She could hardly get me out of the way quick enough. She let me pour her bath and lay out her dressing gown, and that was it. The last thing I saw of her was her stepping into her bath, the scent of sandalwood all round her, and that smile on her face, like a child up to something.'

'And you did what she said, you didn't come back till morning?'

'No. I feel like choking when I think about it.'

'But if she'd told you not to...'

'I should have taken no notice of her. I should have known she wasn't safe on her own, with that one over there, biding her time.'

I'd already decided that Tansy was scarcely sane on the question of Topaz's rival. To change the subject, I asked her if she'd gone to see her friend.

'Yes. Janet her name is. I met her when we were over here last year. She's Scottish but she went and married a French customs officer. As it happened, I stayed the night with her so I never used that room Topaz had booked for me. Her husband was away and one of the children was poorly, so by the time I'd got the other children to bed, cooked us some supper and had a good long talk with Janet it was after midnight. She didn't want me to walk back to the hotel on my own, and there were no cabs to be had down by the

43

harbour at that hour, so I stayed and shared her bed.'

'What time did you get back in the morning?'

'I didn't hurry back. She never wanted her breakfast before ten. I got to the hotel just after nine and went in at the main entrance, instead of our side door, to see if there was a letter from Rose. When I got up to our suite her bedroom door was still closed, like it usually was, so I went to my room and tidied up a bit. Then the waiter came up with her breakfast tray as usual, and I went and tapped on her bedroom door, as usual.'

'And went in and found her...?'

'I thought she was just asleep at first, but she didn't move, didn't stir. I said, quite loud, "Your breakfast, ma'am," but there was something about my voice when I said it that sent the shivers through me. When she still didn't move I touched her on the shoulder, quite gently, and then of course I knew. Cold. But I still wouldn't let myself believe it. I pulled the sheets down, to feel for a heartbeat. I just couldn't believe what I was seeing.'

Jules was leaning forward intently, I thought almost ghoulishly.

'Now, this bit really is strange. Tell Miss Bray what you couldn't believe.'

I braced myself for some horror, and at first couldn't understand what Tansy was

44

saying. The words tumbled out indignantly. 'You see, I knew how fastidious she was. The Empress of Russia herself couldn't have been more choosy about her lingerie, all hand stitched from the finest silk and satin that money could buy. But what she was wearing—cheap cotton knickers, clean enough, but the kind a shopgirl might wear on honeymoon at Southend, pink bows and a bit of machine-made broderie anglaise. And a petticoat down beside the bed, pink muslin with a net flounce and more scrappy little bows, common as they come. I couldn't help myself. I said: "Oh Topaz, what have you done to yourself? What have you done?"'

CHAPTER FOUR

Two pairs of eyes were on me, Tansy's tragic and resentful, Jules' with that experimenting look. I said slowly, trying not to make the question sound as ridiculous as I knew it would:

'You're saying when you found Topaz Brown dead, she was wearing lingerie she wouldn't usually wear?'

'She wouldn't have been seen d...'

Tansy stopped just before she went over the edge, and went red.

'That's how I knew, you see, right from the

45

start, that she hadn't killed herself. Apart from everything else, I mean. Then there was that wine they took away.'

Jules explained: 'There were an empty glass and a half-full bottle of wine beside her. The police took them away, naturally. The laudanum had been in the glass of wine.'

'But she'd never drink wine like that. Even I knew that. You explain to Miss Bray, Jules.'

Jules sighed and shifted in his seat.

'The first thing to grasp is that Topaz was genuinely knowledgeable about wine and had laid up an excellent small cellar. People said she chose her lovers according to the quality of their vineyards. Like many things said about Topaz, that wasn't entirely true, but it wasn't so wide off the mark either.'

'I see, so I take it she drank the laudanum in a particularly good vintage of wine.'

'Quite the reverse. The bottle found at Topaz's bedside contained a villainously cheap wine, the kind of thing they serve in the worst sort of workmen's cafés. Tansy says Topaz would never wear lingerie like that. I can say that never, in her right mind, would she have drunk a glass of wine from that bottle.'

'In her right mind.' I found that phrase depressing and Jules knew it.

I said: 'Perhaps if she were putting laudanum in it, she wouldn't want to spoil a good wine.'

46

Check Out Receipt

BPL - Codman Square Branch Library
617-436-8214
http://www.bpl.org/branches/codman.htm

Friday, September 16, 2016 11:52:22 AM

Item: 39999061780035
Title: Home
Material: Book
Due: 10/07/2016

Item: 0411/9043
Title: hes
Material: Book
Due: /2016

Title:
Material:
Due: 10/0 /2016

Title: it got to the
Material: Book
Due: 10/0

Total items: 4

Thank You!

Jules nodded. 'That's just possible.'

But would that be evidence for or against sound mind?

'Topaz, from what you both tell me, could be described as a person of expensive tastes.' Tansy and Jules both nodded. 'So why should she want to kill herself wearing cheap underwear and drinking cheap wine?'

A diagnosis of acute self-disgust might have covered it, but that hardly went with their description of Topaz's last day in the world.

Tansy said: 'It was done to shame her.'

Jules obviously knew what was coming. 'Tansy, if that means you think Marie came up here, persuaded Topaz to drink poison in a glass of wine that was practically poisonous anyway, then dressed her in awful underwear just to humiliate her, I can only say you're approaching a state of dangerous insanity.'

Tansy glared.

I said, more gently: 'From what you've told me, Topaz took great care to send you away for the night. Doesn't that look as if she'd made up her mind what she was going to do?'

'But she was happy, as happy as a sandboy, that day especially. You can't tell me somebody behaves like that then goes and poisons herself.'

Jules said: 'Tansy, I'm afraid several of my friends have killed themselves for various reasons. In every case, they were more cheerful just before they did it than for

47

months past. I think it's because they've made up their minds.'

I said: 'Mr Estevan, do you believe Topaz Brown killed herself?'

'What else can I think?'

It must have been well past lunchtime by then. The sun had shifted over to the west and was shining in directly through the big windows. Jules had made no move to go, and neither did I. If, as seemed likely, our claim to Topaz's money hinged on her state of mind that day, we could afford no gaps.

'Miss Mills, you were under the impression that Topaz Brown was expecting a visitor that evening.'

'I supposed she must be. Why else would she stay in?'

'But you had no idea who it was?'

'No.'

'Have you any idea who might have visited her, Mr Estevan?'

'Half a dozen or so people might have. I don't know who did, if anybody.'

'Naturally, I'm wondering if there might have been a visitor who brought news so bad that she decided to kill herself.'

'Naturally.'

'I assume the police will have asked the hotel reception if there were any callers.'

'I doubt it. The police, like most other people, would know that very few of Topaz's visitors went through the hotel reception.'

48

'Why not?'

'Did you notice the small private lift off the hallway in this suite? There's a flight of stairs too. They go down to a little door in a side street. There's a similar arrangement in Marie's tower on the other side.'

'Very convenient.'

'Indeed. The local joke was that the architect was an *homme du monde* designing for *les femmes du demi-monde*. That's one of the reasons why these two tower suites command such very high rents.'

'And were Miss Brown's visitors' (I remembered not to say 'clients') 'issued with keys to this private door?'

'I believe not, though Tansy could tell you.'

She shook her head. 'There were only three keys. She had one, I had one and the other one was always kept locked up in the manager's office.'

'Did you have yours with you on Wednesday evening?'

'Yes. I let myself out of the side door and locked it behind me as usual.'

Jules said: 'When the police called, after Tansy found Topaz's body, they naturally came through the main hotel entrance. But Tansy took it upon herself to check the side door, didn't you, Tansy?'

'It was locked.'

'Just as Tansy had left it?' I couldn't see

49

what Jules was driving at.

'Yes, but there is a little mystery. Tansy can't find Topaz's own key. It seems to worry her for some reason.'

Tansy glared at him. 'She always kept it in the drawer of that little table. It wasn't there or anywhere else. I've looked.'

Jules was watching me, waiting for my reaction. I asked him what he deduced from that.

'Nothing whatsoever. Keys get lost all the time. But that's not the way Tansy sees it.'

Tansy said, as if there were no doubt about it: 'The person who killed her went out of that side door and took the key away with her.'

'Did you tell the police?'

'I tried to. They wouldn't listen.'

Jules shrugged. 'It was evident that Topaz killed herself. Why ask questions that would only embarrass people?'

We sat there for a while, then for no reason I could think of, I asked if I could see Topaz's bedroom. Tansy looked alarmed.

'I haven't been in there since they took her out.'

Jules said: 'You'll have to go in there some time, Tansy. Why not now?'

He stood up and led the way across the thick carpet to white and gold double doors, stretching the full height of the room. I was struck by Tansy's stubbornness and misery,

50

staying there on her own in the luxurious suite, scared to open those doors. I followed Jules, with Tansy behind me.

The first impression when the doors were opened was of dimness and a fusty smell, reminiscent of something I preferred not to think about. Only the faintest sunlight filtered through the thick velvet curtains drawn across all the windows, enough to show a pale tent-like shape and scattered glints of gold. Jules was not, I think, reverent by nature but he moved across the room as slowly as a man in a ritual and drew back curtains to let the light in. It was a more ornate room than the salon, with a painting copied from Versailles on the ceiling and delicate chairs and tables that were either Louis Quatorze or good imitations. The bed was on a dais under a canopy of white damask, looped up with gold cords. The bedsheets, of dusky gold satin, were still disordered and Tansy's face crumpled when she looked at them.

I asked where the wine bottle had been. I couldn't help speaking in a whisper. Jules pointed to a small round table beside the dais, and the marks on it where a bottle and glass had stood. On the floor near the table was a pink petticoat, presumably the one that had offended Tansy. When I picked it up I smelt sandalwood, but I was still conscious of that other unidentified smell in the room.

I tried to disregard Tansy's disapproving eyes and went up the shallow steps of the dais to the bed. One of the gold pillows was still dented from her head. Thinking to spare Tansy that, at least, I lifted it to plump it up.

'Mr Estevan.'

My urgent whisper brought him across the room and up the step in two strides, Tansy jealously behind him.

'Didn't anybody see this?'

Where the pillow had been there was a sheet of white notepaper, folded double.

'Oh God. I thought it was strange that she hadn't left a note.'

He sounded shaken. I noticed that his right fist was tightly clenched. I think we neither of us wanted to pick it up.

'What is it?' Tansy's voice was sharp.

I picked up the paper and unfolded it. It was good quality notepaper with the name and crest of the Hôtel des Empereurs on the top of it. The note on it was a short one, oddly set out.

Too late.
8 p.m. Return of I.O.U. for one career.
Vin Poison.

Then a scrawled signature—Topaz Brown.

I showed it to Tansy.

'Is that her writing?'

'Yes. But what's it supposed to mean?' She

was pale and her mouth was trembling.

I said, as gently as I could: 'I think it means she didn't want to go on any more with the life she was living ... with her career as she saw it.'

'But she wasn't. I told you, she was going to retire.'

'She says "Too late."'

'And I.O.U.—that's when you owe people money.'

'Perhaps she felt she owed the world some kind of debt.'

'Topaz didn't owe anybody anything,' said Tansy flatly.

Jules read the note again, looking over her shoulder.

'I don't understand why she wrote that line about the wine and poison. She must have known the police would discover that in any case.'

'And took the trouble to write it in French. Did she know much French?'

'She could speak it a little, in fact she was picking it up quite quickly. But as for reading and writing it, no more than she needed to find her way round a menu or a couturier's bill.'

Tansy handed the note back to me, as if she wanted nothing to do with it.

I said: 'I suppose the police should see it.'

Jules seemed unconcerned. 'They know it's suicide anyway.'

I suggested that since I was going to see Topaz's solicitor again I should give the note to him. It seemed to me more likely to advance our case than otherwise. Tansy, after a last look at the disordered bed, went back to the salon and we followed.

She walked round fidgeting at piles of notes and papers, those stiff square envelopes with the foreign gentlemen's smells.

'I'll have to do something with all this.'

Jules said: 'Leave it for the solicitors, Tansy.'

'She wouldn't want that. Do you know, that solicitor had the nerve to send a man up on the Friday, just the day after she died, wanting to take her papers away. I sent him packing. Her not even in her grave, and they want to come poking round, disturbing all her things. I wasn't having that.'

She turned away from us, sounding near to tears. Jules and I exchanged looks. At some time, presumably, somebody would have to prise Tansy away from her guardianship of Topaz's treasures, but it wasn't our responsibility. Jules apparently guessed what I was thinking.

'I suppose, Miss Bray, all this may legally belong to you, or rather to your organisation.'

His smile seemed malicious, to have in it that taint of male superiority that says 'enemy'.

I looked round at the pictures and

ornaments, the piles of gauzy scarves and stoles.

'I can't think what we should do with it.'

'Indeed, it's the money that matters, isn't it? It's a pity that wasn't what she wanted. I expect you'd like to believe that she entertained her visitors with your colours pinned secretly over her heart—or elsewhere.'

I glared at him, but was saved the trouble of replying when somebody knocked on the door into the salon from the landing. Tansy went to open it.

'Oh, it's you, is it?'

The words were practically hissed, but she opened the door and one of the most beautiful women I've ever seen swept in. She was as slim as a foxglove and tall, with pale creamy skin and enormous dark eyes. She wore an afternoon gown of light coffee-coloured silk with real white rosebuds tucked into the belt, and an expression of pure tragedy. Jules went to meet her, still with that malicious smile on his face.

'Miss Bray, may I introduce you to Mademoiselle Marie de la Tourelle. Marie, Miss Bray of the Women's Social and Political Union.'

A hand as light as a bird's wing fluttered briefly against mine, then she stepped wordlessly past me and collapsed on to a chaise longue like a shot swan.

'How dreadful . . . such despair . . . I blame myself.'

Tansy stood staring down at her with a look of total disgust, and it was left to Jules to fetch another glass and pour the last of the Tokay. Marie sipped weakly then put a hand to her forehead, palm outwards, in a pose I'd never seen before except in Royal Academy paintings. There was a great bracelet of pearls and diamonds on her fragile wrist.

'Why do you blame yourself?' I asked.

'It is a very dreadful thing—jealousy.'

Her English was good, but with a drawling accent.

'Jealousy of whom?' asked Jules.

At least his urge to experiment was consistent, rather than just directed against me. I'd noticed that when he'd brought the wine glass he'd caught Tansy's eye and given her a look that practically dared her to make trouble. So far she'd stood mute but mutinous, watching Marie's every move.

Marie looked at Jules, hurt. 'Of me, of course. Who else?'

'Why?'

She sighed. 'Because of Lord Beverley.'

Tansy burst out: 'He'd left you and come to her. It was you who was jealous.'

The contrast between the angry little woman in her serviceable black and Marie, long and silky on the couch, was almost laughable. If looks could have killed, Tansy would have been beside her mistress in the morgue, but after that one look Marie ignored her and spoke to Jules.

'Lord Beverley found Topaz *vulgaire*. He told me so, poor boy, when he was begging me to take him back.'

'Sez you,' said Tansy. Marie ignored her.

'He is so very repentant. All those lilies. You saw them.'

Tansy said: 'Those lilies came from the old goat of an Archduke. Everybody knows about him.'

'Then on Wednesday afternoon, I was with Lord Beverley in his motor-car when Topaz went past in her carriage. I think it must have been then she decided to do this terrible thing.'

Tansy said: 'Didn't you see him giving her a wink? If you want to know what she thought about it, she was laughing herself sick.'

'Hiding her heartache,' Marie said to Jules, placing her hand over her heart with another flash of diamonds. 'So you see, I blame myself for bringing this terrible despair on her, that drove her to do this thing.'

She closed her eyes and lay back. Tansy advanced and stood over her.

'She didn't care a fiddlestick for you or Lord Beverley or any of the rest of it. She'd decided to give it up.'

Jules repeated what Topaz had said to Tansy about the first grey hair. I could see

57

Tansy wished he hadn't. Marie opened her tragic eyes.

'You see, she knew she was growing old and it was all over for her. It will come to all of us in time, even to me, and if you have no faith to support you, what is there but to despair?'

'You'll never see thirty again either,' Tansy said.

I had the impression she was beginning to enjoy herself. It must have been difficult for Marie to go on ignoring her, but she managed it.

'I have come because I think it is my duty to see she is buried in holy ground, in spite of her sin.'

'Any sins she committed you've done too, only not as well.'

Jules cut in: 'I think Marie is talking about the sin of suicide.'

'But of course. The only sin for which there is no time to repent.'

Tansy said: 'It wasn't suicide,' but saw Jules' eye on her and turned away with an expression of disgust.

Later, when Marie and Jules were discussing arrangements for the funeral, he asked Tansy if there were any relatives who should be involved.

'The man from the consulate says the brother won't do anything. Anyway, she hated him like...'

She went red again and hurried away, probably to her bedroom. I think she couldn't trust herself to stay in the same room as Marie.

I left Marie and Jules in the process of deciding that Topaz, for all anyone knew to the contrary, might once have been a Roman Catholic and Marie saying she would speak to Father Benedict. When he saw I was going, Jules came to the door with me.

'I wonder whether I might call on you tomorrow, Mr Estevan. There are still some things I'd like to ask you.'

He bowed ironically and gave me his card.

I went back to my pension and spent most of the afternoon making notes of what I'd been told by the lawyer, Tansy and Jules Estevan. Then, drowsy from sitting up all night in the train, I decided I'd catnap for half an hour before going out to find dinner. I must have been more tired than I realised because I missed dinner altogether and slept the evening and night through on the pension's narrow white bed.

CHAPTER FIVE

Most of the next morning was taken up with composing a telegraph message for Emmeline Pankhurst, more remarkable for what it left out than what it told her. She'd been reluctant enough to take Topaz's bequest in the first place, and I didn't want to discourage her any further. I walked to the post office in the Rue Gambetta to send it, then decided to stroll back along the parade beside the sea in front of the grand hotels. It was just after lunch by then and I watched the visitors spilling decorously out for their afternoon of sea air, children bound for the beach under the care of starched white nursemaids, invalids in bath chairs drawn by donkeys, men's top hats and women's parasols turning unruly in the breeze from the sea. For some reason I stopped opposite the Hôtel d'Angleterre, rather less ornate than the one where Topaz had lived, slightly old fashioned. With my mind more than half on other things I watched a carriage with a plump woman sitting in it under a grey sunshade, with two little girls of about eight and six years old, smartly dressed but with faces dull as muffins. As I watched they were joined by a tall man in a grey suit and top hat. He was in his early forties, brown hair just flecked with grey, a square, lined forehead and a jutting chin ending in a sharp ledge of beard, like a cow-catcher on the front of an American railway engine. His eyes were grey and hard. Of course I couldn't see his eyes from the other side of the parade, but I didn't need to. I remembered them all too well from

60

when he was making the speech for the prosecution that sent me to Holloway. Mr David Chester MP, barrister at law, on holiday with his family.

He didn't notice me, which was just as well, seeing that he'd described me as a vengeful virago and managed to convert my half brick into an assault on the fabric of society. That was quite mild by his standards. He was, you may remember, the man who said in the Commons that Christabel Pankhurst was 'a woman barren of everything except bitterness and anarchy' and that he'd as soon see his daughters scrubbing floors as going into a polling booth. As I watched him settling into the carriage I found my throwing arm twitching and had to remind myself that on my present mission I was supposed to be unobtrusive. I looked away from the family group and found myself staring, over a distance of a few feet, into a pair of eyes that mirrored so exactly what I was feeling that I thought at first I'd conjured them up.

They were brown eyes and they belonged to a young woman in her twenties with an oval face, serious and pale as if she spent too much time indoors. She was small and quite thin, but there was a determined set to her neck and shoulders, a forcefulness about the curve of the eyebrows and lips, that said the world wouldn't elbow her aside. She was wearing a skirt and jacket of brown serge, too

61

heavy for Biarritz in the spring, and a plain straw boater with a brown ribbon round it.

She said, and it sounded like an accusation: 'You're Nell Bray.'

'I am. I see you recognise David Chester.'

'I recognise him.'

She stood there looking at me, making no move.

I said: 'Would I be wrong in thinking you're one of us?'

She nodded. 'That's how I knew you. I heard you speaking in Trafalgar Square.'

I was puzzled. From her voice, she wasn't the kind of girl who could afford holidays in Biarritz or, from her manner, one who'd enjoy them. But she didn't look or sound like a servant.

'Does Bobbie know you're here?'

That, at least, answered one of my questions. I knew that Bobbie was there and obviously she'd brought a friend with her. There was an obvious gulf in social class between them, but a movement like ours breaks down barriers.

'Bobbie Fieldfare doesn't know I'm here. I was sent by Mrs Pankhurst.'

That seemed to alarm her. She was on the point of saying something, but stopped herself.

I said: 'It's a coincidence, isn't it, that David Chester should be here too?'

'Yes.' Then, abruptly: 'Can I talk to you?'

I'd been instructed to keep clear of Bobbie and all her works, but I couldn't walk away from this girl. There was something like panic in those few words.

'Of course. Let's walk on the beach, shall we?'

I made for a stretch of open sand, well away from the family parties. Now that she had my company, the urge to talk seemed to have gone. I asked her how she'd met Bobbie.

'She pulled me out from under the hooves of a police horse in Parliament Square. She could have been killed.'

'And you've been friends ever since?'

'Well, we met a couple of times after that when she came down to meetings in the East End.'

'And she suggested you should come to Biarritz with her?'

'I think that was because of my sister.'

'Your sister?'

'She worked as a maid to a rich woman who was living here. Bobbie said it would be useful...'

Light dawned. 'Good heavens, you're Rose Mills, Tansy's sister.'

She stopped and stared at me, eyes furious. 'Has Bobbie been telling you about that?'

'I've had nothing to do with Bobbie. Tansy's been talking about you. I hadn't realised you were here.'

'Tansy doesn't know I'm here.'

'But she wrote, asking you to come. Topaz Brown wanted you to come.'

'That . . . that woman wanted me to come here?'

'Yes. Tansy had told her that you were in the WSPU. Topaz suggested she should invite you over here.'

'But . . . but she was a woman who . . . who sold herself.'

Her eyes were both defiant and miserable, blaming me, blaming anybody.

'Didn't you get Tansy's letters?'

She shook her head. 'I moved lodgings.'

Several things had fallen into place. It had seemed to me strange from the start that a firebrand like Bobbie had chosen to go on a seaside holiday, too much of a coincidence that two pairs of hostile eyes should be observing David Chester.

I said: 'How did Bobbie know that David Chester was coming here?'

'It was in one of the society papers. One of his children has been ill.'

'Why Mr Chester, particularly? Aren't there enough people to demonstrate against back in England?'

'He sent Bobbie's mother to prison, and her aunt.'

That would have been motive enough for Bobbie. The Fieldfares tend to take their politics personally.

'And you're keeping him under observation

64

to pick the best time to act. I hope you've considered that the French police may be even rougher than the English.'

'Yes.'

We started walking again, slowly because our boots sank into the dry sand. I believed at that point that what Bobbie had in mind was the kind of demonstration we staged against politicians in Britain, throwing paint or dung, perhaps, among the more militant members, attempting a public horse-whipping. It seemed to me to be squandering energy and money to go all the way to France to do it, but then Bobbie Fieldfare had plenty of both.

Rose said: 'You seem to take it very lightly.'

I started to say that I was hardly likely to get excited about a little dung-spreading on foreign soil, then I saw her face.

'What exactly is Bobbie planning to do?'

'I don't know. I thought you did.'

'I've got nothing to do with whatever she's planning.'

'But I thought Mrs Pankhurst sent you.'

'She sent me because of Topaz Brown's money. I've orders to keep well clear of Bobbie.'

Rose stopped again and groaned like a child, weary and in deep trouble.

'You shouldn't have let me think that . . . I shouldn't have told you . . . what am I going to do?'

She was a strong-minded girl, but very near the end of her tether. I put my arm round her shoulders and made her sit down on the sand beside me.

'Rose, you can't betray Bobbie by talking to me. If you're worried about what's going to happen, then you must tell me.'

She took her time to think about it. I could practically feel the wrenching of loyalties in her head, like a tree branch before it gives way. Then she started to talk, quietly, looking out to sea.

'On the way out we stayed overnight in Paris. We wanted to save money so we found a cheap hotel near the station, only it turned out to be a rough area and there were two men banging on our door, trying to get in. We pushed the chest of drawers up against the door, but Bobbie thought I was still nervous...'

'You had a right to be.'

'...and she said I shouldn't be because she had her father's pistol with her and if the worst...'

'Bobbie Fieldfare brought a pistol with her?'

'In her carpet bag, wrapped in a scarf. She said she'd been practising with it.'

I'd always known that Bobbie was one of our wilder sisters, but this was beyond everything.

Rose said: 'She hasn't taken it out of the

bag since we've been here. She leaves it in our
room when she goes out.'

'Does she go out a lot?'

'Yes, especially in the evenings. She knows
a lot of people here, her sort, from society.
She's trying to find out what he does, where
he goes.'

'And you take your turn in the day.'

'Sometimes.'

'Why haven't you been to see your sister?
She's worried about you.'

'I don't want to bring her into it.'

'But Bobbie does. Isn't that why you're
here?'

I thought I could guess why. When there'd
been an assassination attempt, successful or
bungled, Tansy's part would have been to
hide or disguise them, for love of her sister,
until they could get across the border into
Spain.

'I don't know. She asked a lot about Tansy
at first, not so much after we heard about that
woman killing herself.'

That made sense. Once the attention of the
police had been drawn to Topaz's household,
for whatever reason, Bobbie would have to
look elsewhere for her refuge. Which left
Rose high, dry and in danger.

'You should go to your sister. She's alone.
She needs somebody with her.'

She shook her head.

67

'I'm staying with Bobbie, whatever happens.'

'At least come and see Tansy. You owe her that much.'

I hoped that once I'd got them together, Rose would agree to stay.

'Where is she?'

'At Topaz Brown's hotel. I'll come with you.'

On the way Rose asked: 'Why did she leave us her money?'

'It's an odd story. I'll tell you later.'

I didn't want to tell her at all.

No sooner had Rose walked through the door of the suite than Tansy was clasped round her, hugging her ferociously.

'Rose. At last.'

She stood back and checked her sister's appearance like a cat with a newly-recovered kitten. Then:

'But it's too late, Rose. She's dead. Topaz is dead.'

I was angry with myself for not going ahead to prepare the way. Tansy naturally thought her sister had only just arrived in Biarritz.

'Look at you, you must have been travelling for days. You can't have got the letter telling you to come until . . .'

'I didn't get the letter.'

'The one telling you to hurry up and come out here because she wanted you. After I sent the one with her ten pounds in . . .'

Rose said slowly: 'Why did Topaz Brown want me?'

'I'd told her all about you and what you were up to, and nothing would satisfy her but I should write and tell you to come.'

Rose looked at me. I'd expected confusion, but there was something like triumph in her eyes. I saw what was coming, but too late. Again, I blamed myself for not being more explicit, but really, how could I have known?

Rose said: 'You mean because of what I told you in my letters, Topaz Brown wanted me to come and tell her about our fight for the vote?'

'Talk to Topaz about votes? Why in the world would she want you to do that? No, she wanted you to mend the ribbons on her underthings.'

If Rose had suddenly been dropped five floors in the lift, she could not have looked more astounded. Tansy had no idea that she was being cruel but, although unintentional, it brought cruelty back on her.

After a moment's humming silence Rose said: 'You were going to bring me here to sew ribbons on a harlot's knickers?'

Tansy darted at her and slapped her face, hard and sharp. Rose stared at her, then went out without another word. The door slammed, and Tansy and I looked at each other as we heard feet running along the corridor.

'Oh,' said Tansy, 'I could kill that Mrs Pankhurst.'

I'd have laughed, if I hadn't been aching with regret for both of them. In her grief, Tansy had forgotten who I was, or didn't care. She went on for minutes on end, as fluent as any speaker I've ever heard, about the wickedness of the suffragettes in breaking up families and making girls discontented. The most bitter of our male opponents couldn't have equalled Tansy in full flight. All the time half my mind was with Rose, but I knew it would have been no help trying to follow her, even if I had been quicker off the mark. With some justice she might blame me for her humiliation, although it had been the last thing I wanted.

After some considerable time Tansy simply ran out of breath, although not of aggression, and stood there glaring at me. I said the first thing that had come into my mind.

'Don't you think that you and I should go shopping?'

CHAPTER SIX

Once Tansy had grasped what I meant to do—and it didn't take her long—her anger faded to a grim satisfaction.

'We're going to do what she did?'

'If we can.'

70

I arranged to call back at the hotel for her just before six, about the time that Topaz had left on her shopping trip the week before. When I arrived, she was ready with her hat and coat on.

'That means you believe me. You don't think she killed herself either.'

'Don't take it that I agree with you. I'm puzzled, that's all. I like to be clear about things.'

At the very least, it was a missing piece of jigsaw.

We hesitated in front of the hotel.

I said: 'That evening, did Topaz go down by your private lift, or out at the front?'

'She used our lift.'

That meant she'd have come out by the side door. Tansy led me round the side of the hotel to that private entrance, an unobtrusive door with a small porch and its own bell button. I tried to imagine Topaz standing there.

'Which way would you go to get to the shops from here?'

'If it was the posh shops, back to the terrace, then turn right.'

'But it wasn't the posh shops, was it? She was wearing her plainest dress.'

'The other ones are back this way.'

We walked away from the hotel, along a side street at right angles to the sea. There were children playing in gutters and

71

open-fronted shops with counters of bright vegetables and fruit. We went round a corner with a café on it and men playing cards on a table outside, into a square with more small shops. We'd been walking for twelve minutes. Topaz, I remembered, had been away for under an hour on her shopping trip, say twenty-four minutes there and back, with only half an hour for purchases.

'What about this one, Tansy?' I'd given up calling her Miss Mills.

Next to the pork butcher's shop was a lighted window full of dispirited-looking hats and bonnets, the sort women would buy for necessity rather than frivolity.

'I go there for my sewing things,' Tansy said.

'Does it sell underclothes?'

'Yes.'

'Tansy, did you think of doing this yourself?'

'I can't speak the language. When I go shopping, I just point.'

I hastily reviewed my own vocabulary, hoping it was adequate.

'Tansy, tell me again, what did the knickers look like?'

She told me. I took a deep breath, walked into the narrow shop with Tansy close behind and told my needs to the rock-faced woman behind the counter.

The apparition of a middle-aged English

woman demanding white knickers with pink bows and a pink muslin petticoat produced from her an indrawn hissing sound, between teeth clenched so tightly that you'd have thought we were infecting the air. She regretted—in a tone implying relief rather than regret—that she dealt in nothing of that kind. When I persisted, asking what kind of underwear she could show me, she produced boxes from beneath the counter and began thumping out the kind of garments that might have been useful to Florence Nightingale in the Crimea, corsets as severe as strait-jackets, bloomers that would have enveloped me from rib to knee.

'Not those,' said Tansy scornfully, from behind me.

Cowed by the woman's expression, I bought a plain camisole and several metres of elastic strong enough to moor ships with. Tansy picked up the parcel and we retreated in more or less good order.

'What did you want to go and buy that for?'

I said something apologetically about not wasting people's time and looked at my watch. The transaction had taken ten minutes.

'There's the other one,' Tansy said.

She led the way across the square into a side street, and I had to stride out to keep up with her.

'There it is.'

This shop too had hats in its window, but of a more frivolous design, running to artificial roses and violets and the occasional feather. I glanced inside and saw that the woman at the counter looked reassuringly young and good natured. We marched in and again I opened negotiations. The assistant hardly blinked. But of course. The counter became a froth of white and pastel as she rifled box after box, spilling their contents in front of us. I caught a glimpse of pink and intercepted it.

'Tansy?'

She caught her breath. 'Just like it.'

I told the assistant I'd take the petticoat and began looking through piles of knickers. When I found a likely pair I'd show it to Tansy, and I could see the assistant was beginning to look puzzled, wondering why I should consult my maid on such an intimate matter.

'What about these?'

'No, they had broderie anglaise round the legs, not lace.'

'These?'

'That's more like it, only the ribbons are the wrong colour. They were pink.'

I asked the assistant if they had the same style with pink ribbons, to match the petticoat. She replied that they had stocked

74

some with pink, but sold the last of them a week ago.

I asked, trying to sound casual, if those had been sold to an Englishwoman too. She seemed surprised at the question, but not suspicious. Certainly they were sold to a foreign lady who spoke very little French. They'd laughed a lot, she and the lady, trying to convey in sign language what was wanted, but she'd been in a hurry and made up her mind quickly. A beautiful foreign lady, I asked? The direction of the question, though not its details, must have been clear to Tansy. I felt her tugging at my elbow and drew it away, annoyed. What was this foreign lady wearing? Could it have been a plain brown dress with a cream-coloured shawl? Yes. Tansy pulled at my elbow again.

'Show her this.'

It was a postcard-sized photograph of Topaz Brown, *en fête* with shoulders bare and a diamond choker round her neck, diamond bracelets, more jewels with a feather plume in her hair. The assistant took it and gave me a surprised glance.

'*Oui, c'etait madame. Mais c'est Topaz Brown.*'

I hadn't realised until then quite what a celebrity Topaz had been. To this girl, dreaming over her flowered hats and cheap underwear, she seemed to be as well known as royalty and, judging by her expression, every bit as enviable. Her first reaction was simple pride that the likes of Topaz should have patronised her shop. Then puzzlement.

'*Mais on m'a dit qu'ell est morte.*'

She looked from me to Tansy and back again, face full of questions. I said that, unhappily, that was true. I had the impression of having stepped too hastily, of things moving too fast. To avoid more questions, I said I'd take the knickers with the blue ribbons too and made a performance of finding the right money. After all that, I'd have left the parcel on the counter if Tansy hadn't remembered to snatch it up.

When we were back in the square, Tansy said: 'So she bought them herself.'

'Evidently.' I hoped that would put paid to any absurd ideas about Marie.

'Well, that proves it, doesn't it?'

'Proves what?'

'That she didn't kill herself.'

'I'm sorry, Tansy, but it proves nothing of the kind. All that this proves is that whatever happened, Topaz planned it herself.'

I knew too that I'd just spent some pounds of the organisation's money damaging our case. If a court heard that a woman as rich as Topaz had spent some of the last hours of her life buying cheap underwear, it would come near to proving an unbalanced state of mind.

'But it must have been for a joke, don't you see that? She wouldn't have gone to all this trouble if she was just going to kill herself.'

76

I tried hard to think myself into Topaz's state of mind, suddenly disgusted with herself to the point of suicide, planning a bitter farewell to the world. But if that had been the case, wouldn't she have gone to one extreme or the other, either dressed herself up in all her dearly-bought finery or worn the simplest thing in her wardrobe as a gesture of contempt for it all? Instead, she'd taken pains to fall between the two extremes. She'd died in glamour of a kind, but cheap glamour. Even allowing for the fact that Topaz's mind was not mine, I couldn't see the point of it.

A joke, on the other hand, made more sense. Somebody pays for a night with one of the most expensive women in Europe and arrives to find her dressed like—well, like the kind of woman you could probably buy for a sovereign back in London. That might appeal to a sense of humour of a certain kind. Then if the joke went horribly wrong and the client, instead of being amused . . . No, that made no sense either. They kept no laudanum in the suite, or so Tansy had said. That meant that the murderer . . . I caught myself up. It was the first time I'd used the word, even in my head.

We were standing outside the café, with Tansy looking up at me as if to ask what we did next.

'The wine, I suppose,' I said. 'Can you remember what the bottle looked like?'

77

'An old fat man and bunches of grapes.'

We'd passed a small provision shop on the other side of the square. I led the way back there, following the smell of cheese and garlic. It was scarcely more than a dimly lit cave, hung about with swathes of dried herbs and stalactites of sausages. We squeezed in behind a fat woman who was taking her time about buying a few grammes of anchovies. I touched Tansy's arm and pointed to a row of bottles on a shelf. Even in the dim light, Bacchus and his bunches of grapes looked as garish as a bank holiday fairground.

'Yes. That was it.'

The sharp face of the woman behind the counter showed no expression when I paid my few francs for a bottle of wine, or when I produced Tansy's picture of Topaz. She mumbled that she had so many customers she could hardly be expected to remember all of them. It was patently untrue. Topaz, even in her plain brown dress, would have stood out in that cave like a lyre bird among sparrows. From the way she looked at me, I knew she was lying by custom and instinct. The world outside her cave was hostile and she wanted nothing to do with it.

'What does she say?' Tansy asked from behind me.

'She says she can't remember, but I think she's lying.'

'Of course she is, silly old cow.'

Tansy gave the woman a withering look, took the bottle of wine from me and marched out of the shop.

'That's what I don't like about living in foreign places. You never know what they're saying about you, and you can bet ... oops, sorry, *pardon, mademoiselle.*'

Loaded with parcels, her attention distracted, she'd almost bumped into a depressed looking woman clustered with young children. The woman was carrying a baby in a shawl and an untidy parcel wrapped in newspaper. The impact of Tansy rocked both of them and I went to help, holding the parcel while the woman settled the baby. It left grease traces on my gloves and an oddly familiar smell. The woman thanked me and murmured something about going out to get their dinner. In Biarritz it seemed, just as in London, there were families so poor that they had no stoves of their own, and must fetch cooked food from the shops. I said I hoped her family would enjoy their fish. As I spoke the word *poisson* something fell into place so fast that it felt like a physical blow. I asked the woman where she'd bought it. She was incredulous at first, then pointed up a side street. I went like a dog on the scent, Tansy with her parcels protesting behind me.

'You don't want that. You know what their kitchens are like.'

The smell of fish led me on to an

open-fronted shop consisting of no more than a wooden counter with a great stove and a man in a white apron behind it.

I ordered fish, and he slapped a large fillet into a pan on the top of the stove. His eyes were bright and amused.

'Madame is English?'

'Yes.'

'I work in London for two years at the Bayswater Caprice Hotel. You know it?'

I regretted that I didn't.

He grinned. 'I think you English ladies like my fish.'

'Why? Have there been other English ladies?'

'Just last week, last Wednesday evening. She knew the Bayswater Caprice Hotel, that lady. She said my fish reminded her of London.'

Again I produced Tansy's postcard.

'That lady?'

'Yes, that same lady. She was very, very beautiful. She is your friend?'

I nodded. If he'd recognised her as Topaz Brown, he gave no sign of it.

'Did she buy a lot of fish?'

'Enough for two. I lent her a little dish to take it away. Will you please give your friend my regards and say it doesn't matter about the little dish until next time she comes. Tell her, when she comes to see me again, I give her fish free.'

80

He flipped my portion of fish out of the pan, wrapped it in newspaper and handed it to Tansy. She propped it under her chin, on top of the wine bottle and the two parcels of underwear.

We got back to the side entrance of the hotel an hour and twenty minutes after we'd left it. Topaz had been quicker, but then she'd known exactly where to go for what she wanted. In the salon, Tansy put the wine and underwear on a chair, but handed me the parcel of fish.

'Are you eating it here or taking it out with you?'

She went towards a window with the intention, I think, of opening it to get rid of the smell, then found it was open already.

'That's funny, I could have sworn I shut the windows before we went out. I hope that maid hasn't been in again.'

She seemed put out by it, but I didn't pay much attention. She'd given me another idea.

'Tansy, you remember how you described seeing Topaz when she got back from the shopping trip. She had the window to the balcony open and was standing by it.'

'Yes.'

'Why?'

'How should I know why?'

'Could she have been putting something out on the balcony, like a parcel of fish, so that you wouldn't smell it and ask questions?'

81

'Why should she want to do that?'

'Why would she want to buy fish in the first place?'

'That's what I can't understand. She could have any fish she wanted sent up from the kitchens here.'

'Yes, but that would be expensive fish. Cheap underwear, cheap wine—and now, cheap fish.'

Tansy was looking as if I were out of my mind. I walked up and down the room, trying to think.

'It was on a plate, but she'd need to heat it up again. There's the spirit lamp...'

Tansy said, grudgingly: 'That was left out, after the police had been, but I was in such a taking then, I didn't think anything about it.'

'Then she took it to the bedroom, that was where the smell was, with the wine. What happened to it?'

Would anybody have thought about a plate of cooked fish, when there was a bottle of poisoned wine to analyse? The police might have cleared it away when they took the wine.

Tansy said: 'I can't see why you're making such a fuss about a piece of fish.'

I had to tell somebody my theory. Rightly or wrongly, I told Tansy.

'If I'm right, that plate of fish may prove that Topaz didn't kill herself after all.'

She was unimpressed. 'That's what I've been saying all along. But it wasn't the fish that had the poison in it, it was the wine.'

'It all hinges on that note she left.' I took it out of my bag and unfolded it.

Too late.
8 p.m. Return of I.O.U. for one career.
Vin Poison

'We took it for a suicide note. It wasn't that at all. It's an invitation. She's inviting somebody to come at 8 p.m. and offering him wine and fish. But she got one letter wrong and put "poison" instead of *"poisson"*.'

Tansy still refused to be excited. 'But what's all that about I.O.U.?'

'I don't know. It must have been part of the joke.'

'You didn't believe me when I said it was a joke.'

'Tansy, I thought you wanted to prove she didn't kill herself.'

'What I want to see is whoever did it pays for it.'

I was still pacing up and down, full of triumph and excitement. At the time, I wasn't even thinking that a verdict of murder rather than suicide would help our case. I was not even concerned about justice. It was the excitement of the hunt, pure and primitive, and I'm afraid I started giving orders to poor Tansy as if she were a hunt servant.

'Tansy, I want you to sit down and write

83

me a list of all Topaz's clients—or visitors, if you prefer—that you can remember. Start with this year in Biarritz, then last year, then all of them you can remember over the time you've been with her. Then if . . .' I paused in mid-flow. I'd caught sight of her face.

'No.'

'No what?'

'I've never gossiped about that while she was alive and I'm not going to do it after she's dead. She could trust me. She knew that.'

'Tansy, it isn't gossip. It's investigation.'

'It doesn't matter what you call it.'

I've sometimes been called stubborn, but my stubbornness was no match for Tansy's. She just stood there with her arms folded, as unmoved by my arguments as a granite rock in a whirlpool. She'd never talked about Topaz's business affairs, never would, and that was that.

'Not even to catch her murderer?'

'It wasn't one of them that killed her.'

'Tansy, you can't know that.'

'I know.'

In the end, I had to admit defeat.

'Very well then, I shall just have to find out from other sources.'

'That's up to you.'

Once I'd conceded defeat, a kind of peace was restored and she made tea for us. When we were sitting down drinking it she suddenly started chuckling to herself.

84

'What's funny?'

'I was thinking, it was a caution you going off after that fish. Took Mr Shadow by surprise too.'

'Mr Shadow? What are you talking about, Tansy?'

She grinned, enjoying her triumph in being more observant than I was.

'Didn't you notice him? I picked him out almost as soon as we started. Then when we came out of the second place where you bought the underthings, there he was on the other side of the road. He was the man from the solicitor's.'

'What man from what solicitor's?'

'The one I told you about who came round on Friday wanting to go through her papers.'

'Why didn't you say something?'

'I didn't want anything to do with him.'

'What does he look like?'

She considered. 'Quite tall, a bit on the plump side. Red-faced and clean-shaven. Forty or older, I'd say. Black coat and hat, respectable enough but not what you'd call a gentleman.'

'French or English?'

'English.'

'And you think he was following us?'

'I don't think, I know.'

I didn't suspect Tansy of making it up entirely, but I thought she might have exaggerated a chance reappearance of the man into the belief that she was being followed. I was beginning to recognise, under her no-nonsense manners, a strong taste for the dramatic. I told her to let me know if she saw the man again, finished my tea and got up to go.

'Mr Jules said he'll come tomorrow to let me know about her funeral. Will you be going?'

I said I would, and that I'd call on Jules Estevan in the morning. Tansy came down in the lift to the side door to let me out. She insisted I took the fish away with me, so I donated it to a deserving cat beside the hotel dustbins. In itself, it hardly counted as evidence.

CHAPTER SEVEN

I walked round to the front of the hotel, intending to find my way back from there to my own part of the town and buy myself dinner. It was just after eight o'clock and there was a long line of carriages by the steps, bringing people to dine at the hotel. I stood watching idly, watching beaded dresses and jewels flashing in the electric light from the foyer, feather fans waving in the sea air. The simplest of those gowns would amount to six months' wages for the likes of Rose and Tansy.

No sooner had I let myself be lulled into this reflective state of mind than two things happened to throw me out of it. The first was seeing David Chester for the second time that day. He and his plump wife, unwisely dressed in green satin, were in an open carriage with another couple in evening dress, waiting until the press of traffic allowed them to drive the extra few yards to the hotel entrance. Finding my throwing arm twitching again, I was about to walk out of the way of temptation until something, I don't know what, made me look up at the front of the hotel.

There were lights among the garlands and nymphs, and the first thing I was aware of was a shadow moving near the head of the caryatid on the right. I thought at first it had been made by a roosting pigeon, but the thing that cast it was too large for that. Then it moved again and revealed itself as a young man in tweed jacket and breeches. If he lost his footing from the ledge beside the caryatid's head, he'd fall forty feet or so on to the flagstones below, yet he moved lightly. He took a step towards one of the lights and I had a better view of him. He was hatless, his dark hair curly and artistically long. He'd been looking down at the carriages by the steps then, just for a second, he raised his head and stared straight out to sea. In that second I recognised him. It wasn't a man at all. I'd have bet all the money in Biarritz that I was looking at Bobbie Fieldfare. And, forty feet below her, about to be drawn into pistol range, David Chester said something to his friend and turned to face the hotel, his white shirt front presenting as prominent a target as an inexperienced assassin could wish.

I had a second to think, and for half of that second my hatred of David Chester said yes, let her do it. Then I thought of the certainty that it would set our cause back for years, perhaps for ever. I shouted: 'Look. *Regardez*,' and pointed at the caryatid. There were shouts and gasps as other people saw what I was pointing at. The doormen ran down the steps to look, and people in open carriages stood up for a better view. Then the horror turned to laughter.

'A drop too much of the bubbly,' an English voice said.

Apparently young men swarming round the outside of hotels were part of the natural fauna of Biarritz. As for the tweed-jacketed figure, when the laughter broke out it stood there quite still, looking down. I wanted to shout to Bobbie to run for it, but was afraid of making her lose her balance. Already a doorman had said something to a porter and I was sure staff were rushing to the first floor to deal with the nuisance. I thought, if they arrest Bobbie I must introduce myself at once as a friend of the family and try to pass it off as a harmless prank.

The figure stood, toes on the narrow ledge, one arm hooked around the head-dress of the statue. Then, to gasps, it let go and stood unsupported, advancing even closer to the edge. I thought, 'Oh, God, she's going to jump.' I was biting my knuckles, trying not to scream. Bobbie—by then I was sure of it—stared down at us. Then, very slowly, she bent forwards like a person about to dive. More gasps, a woman's scream. It seemed an eternity that the figure stayed there, bent in the light. Then, just as slowly, it straightened up, stepped back and waved its hand to the crowd, having accomplished the slowest and most courtly of bows. There was a gust of relieved laughter, even a scattering of applause.

'Drunk as an archbishop,' said the English voice that did not sound notably sober itself. 'Positively pie-eyed.'

By now several members of the hotel staff were on first floor balconies, yelling at the figure to come in. Bobbie looked at them, shook her head solemnly, then, with a speed that seemed all the greater for her previous deliberate slowness, walked along the ledge to a drainpipe at the corner of the building and began shinning down. She jumped the last ten feet or so, fell, picked herself up and sprinted off across the road and along the parade. Picking up my skirts, envying her the advantage of breeches, I followed. Behind us came the cries of the hotel staff, shouting to her to stop.

We must have been one of the oddest sights of the season as we scudded along the parade, Bobbie in sporting costume and hatless, me with the turn of speed you learn if you are trying to evade the close attentions of the Metropolitan Police. A few people called to us, asking what was going on. Some citizen tried to stand in Bobbie's path, but she dodged aside, and I saw the surprised expression on the man's face as I flew past in my turn. We'd gone about half a mile, easily outdistancing the hotel people, past the fashionable hotels and towards the fishing harbour. Bobbie was gaining ground all the time. I count myself a reasonable athlete, but I am ten years older than Bobbie, and I suppose prison takes its toll. I should never have caught her if she hadn't made the mistake of dashing into the path of a rag and bone cart on its evening duties as she rounded the corner of the home straight.

Bobbie was up at once and I could see she wasn't much hurt, but the cart owner's language was forceful. He grabbed her by the arm and wouldn't let go. She made a desperate effort to pull away as she saw me running up, then, as I got within a few steps of her, shouted out with relief.

'Nell Bray, always there when you're

needed. What's this man yelling about?'

'He seems to think you've damaged his horse.'

Bobbie snorted, much like a horse herself.

'Of course I haven't. With the legs on that animal it would take a charging elephant to damage it. Look.'

The man had released her arm. She bent down and ran an expert hand over the horse's knees and thick fetlocks. 'Sound as a bell.'

I pushed a handful of coins into the man's fist and dragged her into a shop doorway. She was panting as I was, but grinning like a schoolgirl playing truant.

'Was it you chasing me all the time? I thought it was the gendarmerie.'

I said: 'You'd better give me the pistol in case the gendarmerie catch up with you after all.'

Her eyes opened wide. 'But I haven't got it with me. It's back in my room.'

She didn't seem in the least bothered that I knew about it.

'What were you doing up there?'

A wry look, as if I were a tiresome school prefect.

'Waiting.'

'For David Chester?'

'Yes.'

'I want to talk to you about that. Over here.'

She came with me, unprotesting, towards a

line of black fishing boats moored against the harbour wall and we sat on two coils of rope among tar-smelling lobster pots.

'Nobody authorised this,' I said.

She shrugged.

'You think that doesn't matter? If you're part of a movement, you have to accept its discipline.'

'Discipline is a useful excuse for moral cowardice.'

'Are all the rest of us cowards, then?'

'I didn't mean you, Nell.'

'But it affects me. It affects all of us if what you do destroys everything we've worked for. Our cause depends on winning public opinion to our side. Desperate measures like yours...'

She interrupted: 'Don't they use desperate measures? Their prisons, their brutal police, corrupt lawyers, ignorant judges, lying newspapers. And we're supposed to sit there saying, "Please, kind gentlemen, give us the vote."'

'You don't have to make speeches at me. Even if you were successful, what difference would the absence of one man make?'

'It would be a warning to all the rest of the smug hypocrites.'

'Bobbie, I appeal to you not to go on with this.'

As a member of the committee of the Women's Social and Political Union, I

92

suppose I could have ordered her, but orders don't go far with the Fieldfares, mother or daughter.

'And if I refuse, will you betray me to the French police?'

'Don't be ridiculous.'

'Well then.'

The implied question was what was I going to do about it.

'I shall have to make sure I'm always there to prevent it, as I was tonight.'

'It was you who shouted, was it?'

That at least seemed to disturb her. I didn't spoil the effect by telling her I was only on the scene by accident.

'Don't you think you should at least have been honest with Rose Mills about what you were dragging her into?'

'You've seen Rose?'

'This afternoon. And if you're wondering how much she told me, I guessed more than she told. She's a loyal girl.'

'If there's any risk, I'm taking it, not Rose. Besides, it wasn't a case of dragging. She's as convinced as any of us.'

'What about Rose's sister? She isn't one of us, yet you were quite prepared to involve her in it too.'

Bobbie was silent for a while, feeling guilty, I hoped. When she spoke, her voice was less certain.

'I'm not going to involve Rose's sister. Not now.'

'Yes, not now that it doesn't suit your plans. But you'd have used her if you could, wouldn't you?'

'Yes. Yes, I would.'

I let her think about it for a while.

'Bobbie, whatever you do, please send Rose back to England. It's not fair on her.'

'Shouldn't she decide that for herself?'

But the tone was thoughtful rather than aggressive. I thought I'd scored a few points and would get nowhere by pushing her any further. I couldn't see how, though, with my other duty in Biarritz, I could watch Bobbie every minute of the day.

It was late by then, and the cold and damp were settling round us. I offered to walk with Bobbie back to her lodgings, but she said she'd be all right. She still didn't move. She asked suddenly:

'Did you know Topaz Brown's being buried tomorrow evening?'

'No. How did you hear?'

'Everybody seems to know.'

I said: 'Did you ever meet her?'

'No, never. I heard about her.'

It was too dark to see her expression but I could detect no strain in her voice.

'And yet you heard about her legacy to us. You must have telegraphed Emmeline soon after she died.'

'Everybody knew about that too.'

94

Even allowing for society's specialised use of 'everybody', meaning, in my experience, a few dozen, this surprised me.

'Nell, why did she kill herself?'

'I don't know.'

We both of us stood up together. I put my hand on her arm and could feel the tension humming through it.

'Bobbie, go home. There's plenty of work to do there. Forget this.'

She shook her head slowly and turned away. Once we reached the main road we went our separate ways.

CHAPTER EIGHT

I'd told Tansy that I'd find my list of Topaz's lovers from sources other than her, but it was something of an empty boast. I've become reasonably thick-skinned and resourceful, but even I could hardly tour Europe's capitals and watering places asking men if they'd ever paid for the services of Topaz Brown. So at ten o'clock the next morning I was on the doorstep of Jules Estevan. He lived in a tall white-painted house to the south of the town, with a vine putting out its shoots around a wrought-iron verandah. The door was opened by an elderly woman in black, presumably

95

the housekeeper, who said Mr Estevan was at breakfast.

'Please tell him Nell Bray would like to speak to him.'

She gave me a resentful look, but returned a few minutes later to show me upstairs.

'I was wondering when you'd call, Miss Bray.'

He was wearing a dressing gown of black silk with purple facings, drinking chocolate from a white porcelain cup. The room was so large that it must have run the length and width of the house, and was unlike anything I'd seen before. Apart from a huge square couch upholstered in white and a pair of carved and gilded pews it contained none of the things that most people find necessary for living, no small tables, no ornaments, no comfortable chairs. A huge mural of a rising sun with various horned and antlered creatures stretching out to it covered the wall opposite the windows. An ivory pillar carved for the whole of its length with skulls supported an opera cape and a top hat. A tailor's dummy stood in the middle of the room swathed in an oriental ballet costume, topped with a life-sized china head. The floor was of plain polished wood with islands of Bokhara carpets. Jules invited me to sit down, and I chose one of the pews.

'Have you heard, Topaz is being buried at six o'clock tonight in the cemetery outside the town? It was the best Marie and Father

96

Benedict could do.'

I said I'd be there. 'There was something else too, Mr Estevan.'

'I hope I can be of service, Miss Bray.'

He sat on the edge of the white couch, quite unembarrassed by his state of undress or his calves and bare feet showing beneath the dressing gown. I'd never seen a man's feet so well-shaped.

I said: 'I want a list of Topaz Brown's lovers.'

He whistled and almost slopped his chocolate. I think it was a defeat for him to show surprise at anything, because after that first reaction he reverted to his usual attitude of amused cynicism, but sharper than before.

'Are you writing her biography, Miss Bray, or should I say hagiography? Is she to be numbered among the patron saints of your movement?'

'I'll leave that to the poets like you, Mr Estevan. I have a practical reason for asking.'

He looked at me, smiling but eyes shrewd. I knew he was longing to ask what my reason was, but wouldn't condescend to simple curiosity.

'I'm not sure that I'm your best authority. Wouldn't the maid help?'

'I tried. Apparently it offended her sense of professional discretion.'

He laughed. 'Poor Tansy. She is so desperately respectable.'

I waited.

'So you had to come to me. You realise that I'd only known Topaz for fourteen months or so, and that mostly here in Biarritz. We were together briefly in Paris last autumn, then met again when she came back here in February.

'But you talked to her every day. She must have said something about her...'

'Clients? Yes indeed. She was very candid.'

'Well, let's start with the men you know about in Biarritz this season.'

He put his cup down on the floor and sat up straight. 'I think you've gathered that the Englishman, Lord Beverley, was the current favourite, but that was only for the past week or so. There was a German baron for most of February, but his health broke down a couple of weeks ago, so he took himself off to Baden Baden. There was a man from the circus the baron didn't know about, but he doesn't count because he wasn't paying. Between you and me and the rest of Biarritz, the baron wanted her more for show than for anything, so naturally Topaz took her entertainment elsewhere.'

'What would have happened if the baron found out?'

'I don't know, because he never did. The latest news from Baden Baden is that the poor old devil is just about able to totter to the pump house.'

'Who else?'

'In between the baron and Lord Beverley there was an Italian, ugly as sin, but owned half Piedmont, who whisked her off to Paris for a few days, mainly to annoy his wife who was having a blatant affair with a Russian violinist.'

'And that's all?'

'You're implying that Topaz was hardly over-working? I defer to your knowledge of these matters. To be honest, the same thought had struck me. In the light of what we know now, I can understand why.'

'Do you mean her retirement or her suicide?'

He shrugged. I'd been wondering all the way there whether I should tell him about the underwear and the fish and admit that I didn't now believe it was suicide. I still wondered.

'If any of Topaz's former clients knew she was going to retire, would they have been worried that she might become indiscreet?'

He laughed. 'That's Tansy's influence showing. What do you mean by indiscreet?'

'Well, that she might do damage by talking about who her lovers had been...'

'My dear Miss Bray, if Topaz published advertisements in the newspapers, she could hardly tell the world anything it didn't know already. What you don't understand is that a man who becomes the lover of a woman as well known as Topaz is virtually taking up a public position. Isn't that the whole purpose of it?'

'Purpose?'

'To show he can afford her, to show he has the confidence to live at her level. It's not like some father of a family, good bourgeois church-goer in Paris or London, giving a handful of silver to a slut for ten minutes he hopes nobody will ever know about. What would be the point of paying a small fortune to women like Topaz or Marie if nobody knew about it?'

'I see.' I sat there, watching the sun bringing out the colours of the carpets, trying to adjust to this scheme of things. 'But didn't Lord Beverley have to stop seeing her when his father arrived?'

'His father, yes—although I'm sure the old boy's heard about it by now. But you may be sure young Beverley will be the hero of his clubs when he gets back. Worth losing a fortune for.'

'Has he lost a fortune?'

'So they say.'

'What about last year? Who were her lovers then?'

He put his hands to his temples, feigning weariness.

'Oh my dear Miss Bray, you are a hard taskmistress. Last year is a world away, further than the fall of Rome. If you insist, I shall try to make you out a list, but it will take some time.'

I left it at that for a while, and began to work my way round to another question, that had been worrying me since my conversation with Bobbie Fieldfare.

'You were there last Wednesday afternoon when Topaz made her will. In fact, you witnessed it. I don't want to imply that you would betray a confidence, but I wonder if it's possible that you mentioned it to anybody at all afterwards.'

I tried to be tactful, because I expected him to be mortally offended. All I got was another of his twisted smiles, as if he was amused against his will.

'Mentioned it? Only to about half of Biarritz by dinner time.'

I must have looked disapproving.

'You are about to tell me, Miss Bray, that a will is confidential. If I'd thought she intended it as her real will, I don't suppose I should have told a soul.'

'You didn't think it was meant as a real will?'

'Of course not. It was simply a good story, and Topaz would have been highly disappointed in me if I hadn't passed it on to as many people as possible.'

Again, my expression must have spoken for me.

'You see, some of us write poems or paint

pictures. Topaz delighted in doing unexpected or amusing things and having them talked about. If every dinner table that mattered that evening had not been talking about Topaz Brown leaving all her money to the suffragettes, I should have been failing in my duty.'

'I see.'

We were silent for a while. I think he was interested to see that the idea hurt me. After a while I said I'd taken up enough of his time, and should see him at the funeral. He told me that he'd promised to escort Tansy Mills. I wondered whether that was because he thought it amusing to be seen in the company of the maid, or whether there was a touch of kindness in him.

'Marie will be there?'

'Of course. It will be a chance for her to practise her attitudes.'

'Attitudes?'

'Didn't you know she's to embark on a stage career? There's an American impresario who thinks she'll be the new Bernhardt—as long as she's not required to speak.'

I stood up. I'd still said nothing to him about my investigations.

'One thing I haven't asked, you've told me you and Topaz liked jokes. Were you planning a joke that last night?'

'No.'

'Is it possible that she was?'

He gave me a quick look: 'The underwear and the wine, you mean?'

'Can you think of any explanation for them?'

'No. Can you?'

'Topaz was ... expensive, wasn't she? If somebody paid a good deal for a night with her and arrived to find her looking like, well...'

'Like any cheap tart?'

'Thank you. And the kind of food and wine that would cost a few francs in a back street café. Would that be Topaz's idea of a joke?'

He shook his head.

'Women don't make as much money as Topaz did without being serious about their work.'

'But did it matter to her any more? Suppose she decided to finish her career by making some kind of derisive gesture at the life she'd been living.'

'She wouldn't do that. It would be like a painter deliberately choosing the wrong colour, or a musician playing a wrong note.'

It seemed to matter to him that I should understand. I wasn't sure that I did.

'Suppose it had been somebody she'd hated for a long time, but had to tolerate because he was paying her.'

'Topaz didn't hate people. Besides, she could pick and choose. She once turned down two thousand pounds to spend a night with a man because she didn't like the shape of his beard.'

'I thought you said she took her work seriously.'

'She did. He went straight off to the barber's and sent her the beard in a parcel, along with a bank draft for three thousand pounds. He told everybody it was worth every whisker.'

As he showed me downstairs, I said I hoped Tansy would not make trouble with Marie at the funeral. His shrug was not reassuring. I think he saw life as a theatre-goer, a connoisseur of scenes. Perhaps that was why he'd decided to go to the funeral with Tansy. Perhaps that too was the reason for his sudden invitation to me, for a very different event.

'I wonder if you happen to be free tomorrow evening. Marie is giving a *Soirée Ancienne*.'

'What's that?'

'It's by way of being a preview of her stage performance, for an invited audience. Great ladies of the ancient world. All the guests are to wear classical costumes too. There's hardly a sandal or a laurel leaf left in Biarritz.'

'Alas, I've left my toga at home.'

'You could go as a Maenad. I'm sure they were continually throwing bricks.'

'I'm sorry to disappoint you, but I don't make a social habit of it. Is that why you wanted to take me there?'

He opened the front door, winced away from the rush of sunlight and sea air, recovered quickly.

'No. I thought you might appreciate the chance to keep at least one of your suspects under observation. I'll see you at the funeral, Miss Bray.'

I was angry with myself for under-estimating Jules. It occurred to me too late that Tansy might have told him every detail of our shopping trip, including my guess about the suicide note. I couldn't trust either of them, and yet they were my two main sources of information. It was this annoyance at being trapped within Topaz's circle that led to my next move. I wanted some scientific facts instead of this web of personalities and values only partly understood.

I went to the consulate and asked them to recommend a good doctor. They assured me that everybody—meaning everybody from English society—went to Dr Campbell. They spoke highly of his friendliness and good manners and, as an afterthought, his professional skills. He lived and practised at a house in the Avenue de Bayonne, in the new quarter of the town north of the Grande Plage. There are medicinal baths there, fed by warm saline springs, and the numbers of fine new mansions and doctors' plates prove

105

their popularity among fashionable invalids. I took the tramline—paying ten sous and saving on the cab fare—and found Dr Campbell's plate outside one of the most attractive of the mansions. After a short wait, a woman in an elegant grey dress showed me into a consulting room that looked more like a salon.

The man facing me was younger than I expected, but with a touch of grey in his square-cut beard, setting off an aquiline nose and intelligent, assessing eyes. There was an air of self-satisfaction about him as he invited me to take a seat, so I decided to waste no time tip-toeing around the point.

'Dr Campbell,' I said, 'how long would a fatal dose of laudanum take to work?'

'Why do you ask, Miss Bray?'

'Because I've become involved in the legal affairs of somebody who died from an overdose of laudanum.'

'Are we by any chance talking about the late Miss Topaz Brown?'

'We are.'

The fashionable doctor to the English community would naturally hear all the gossip. It was part of his work. He leaned back in his chair, gazing over my shoulder at a picture on the wall. It was a nocturne by Whistler, evidence of both fashionable taste and fashionable fees.

'It would depend on many things—the

general health of the subject, body weight, whether the subject had taken alcohol...'

'There's evidence that she drank it in wine.'

'That might delay the onset of symptoms. But you could take it that the person would be overcome by a feeling of intense sleepiness within an hour. Soon after that she would lapse into sleep, then unconsciousness, then a state of deep coma. If no preventive action were taken, one would expect her to be dead within twelve hours of taking the dose.'

Topaz had invited her visitor to call at eight. She was dead and cold when Tansy found her at about ten o'clock the following morning. That would suggest the poison had been taken soon after her visitor's arrival.

Dr Campbell got up and moved over to the window. Yellow curtains framed a garden of daphnes and mimosa trees, the scent drifting in. He was proud of his position and his possessions.

'Was Miss Brown a patient of yours?'

'She never consulted me.'

He sounded disappointed. There were invitation cards and calling cards arranged along his mantelpiece, apparently casually but giving no doubt of his social success. Lord something would welcome his company at dinner. Sir John so and so requested the pleasure of calling at four.

'You said, doctor, "if no preventive action

were taken". Do you mean her life might have been saved?'

'Indeed. Poisoning by laudanum, or other opium derivatives, is a comparatively gradual process. It's not like strychnine or cyanide. If the patient is reached in time, the prognosis may be hopeful.'

'There's an antidote?'

'The antidote is, in layman's terms, simply keeping the patient awake. Copious quantities of black coffee, walking her up and down, fighting off by any means the onset of unconsciousness may be effective.'

'What if somebody had found Miss Brown unconscious? Could she have been revived?'

'There would be a point when the coma became irreversible, but within limits, yes.'

'What limits? An hour after she'd taken it? Two hours? More?'

'It's almost impossible to answer that with any accuracy.'

'An informed guess, then. Suppose somebody had found Miss Brown three hours after she'd drunk the laudanum.'

'I should not wish to give this as evidence in a court of law, and it would depend on the dosage. But I should hazard a guess that if Miss Brown had been found up to three hours after losing consciousness, her life might have been saved.'

'And beyond that?'

'Beyond that, I should refuse even to guess.'

He picked up an invitation card from the display on his mantelpiece and turned it over and back, letting the sun glint off its gilt edge. I tried to adjust my view of Topaz's death to what he'd just told me. I'd assumed that the poisoning would be a quick process, that the murderer—if there had been a murderer—could kill her and go. But that wasn't the case at all. He, or she, couldn't be sure that nobody would find Topaz in those three hours, and if Topaz had been revived, surely her first words would accuse whoever had given her the wine. He, or she, would have to sit beside the sleeping woman for three hours or perhaps longer, until sleep became irreversible. I looked up and found the doctor's eyes on me.

'How much would it take to kill her?'

'That would depend on many things. If the person had been accustomed to using laudanum, then it would take quite a large amount. Laudanum contains only one per cent morphine. I've even heard of some nurse-maids giving a drop of it to children on a sugar lump to send them to sleep, not that that's a practice I'd recommend. An addict might drink it by the glassful and survive. Another person—a child or an adult in poor health—might be killed by a coffeespoonful.'

'So two or three teaspoons in a glass of wine . . . ?'

109

'Might kill a person unaccustomed to laudanum, yes.'

'And yet I could walk out of here and buy as many bottles as I liked at any chemist's.'

'Indeed. But then I daresay you've taken Dover's Powders from time to time.'

'Occasionally for a stomach upset, when travelling.'

'And yet those powders, too, contain opium, Miss Bray. Should they be locked in a poison cabinet?'

I thanked Dr Campbell and said he must send me his bill.

'I believe you know my aunt, Lady Fieldfare,' he said.

'Indeed I do. We spent a lot of time together quite recently.'

He looked gratified, but a little embarrassed. 'Or my aunt by marriage, I should say. My mother's brother married her younger sister.'

He'd been helpful, and if he chose to take out some of his fee in harmless snobbery, I didn't resent it.

'Did you know that Lady Fieldfare's daughter Roberta is here in Biarritz? A charming young lady. I hope she is sleeping better.'

'Bobbie came to you with sleeping problems?'

'I hope you don't think I would betray my patients' confidence, Miss Bray. It was

110

nothing at all serious, I assure you. As I told Miss Fieldfare, travelling often causes some disruption in ladies' sleeping habits.'

I'd got up to go, but this struck me stock-still, on the way to the door. Travelling might disrupt some women's sleep, but I was prepared to bet that Bobbie would not be one of them. The doctor was staring at me, and I did my best to sound unconcerned.

'I'm sure you were able to prescribe something helpful for her, doctor.'

But professional discretion had reasserted itself. He smiled, held the door for me and hoped I'd call on him again if he could do anything to help. His receptionist was standing at her desk, fiddling with a pot of mimosa.

'Mrs David Chester and her little girl will be here in five minutes,' he said to her. 'Show them in straightaway.'

He said it, I'm sure, only for the pleasure of using the MP's name, but it was an uncomfortable moment. I thought I'd rather not meet her and hurried down the path, hoping to be well out of the way by the time she arrived.

But Mrs Chester was early. I'd only just closed the gate behind me when a cab drew up, and the plump woman I'd last seen beside David Chester climbed out clumsily, her face full of worries. Everything about her was rounded, her calves exposed in clambering

111

down, her eyes, her flushed cheeks, but it was a heavy rather than a comfortable roundness, as if her own body were one of her many burdens.

She didn't see me at first and turned back inside the cab, making plaintive noises. The driver showed no signs of helping her and sat there flicking at the reins, so that just as a child was stepping down the horse lurched forward and she came tumbling down the step, missed her mother's arms and landed on her knee in the gutter. It would have taken a harder woman than I am to resist the child's bawling and the mother's distress. I picked up the girl, no light weight, and set her down on the path.

'There, let's have a look at you.'

The child went on yelling. A smudge of red was appearing on the knee of her white stocking.

'Oh dear, oh dear,' said Mrs Chester. 'I knew something was going to happen.'

'It's all right,' I told her. 'It's only grazed.'

In an attempt to stop the bawling, I tried on the child a formula that worked very well with my nephews.

'Come along, dry your tears and be a brave little soldier.'

The child stopped bawling just long enough to give me a look that reminded me disconcertingly of her father in court.

'Girls can't be soldiers,' she said. Then she

started yelling again.

I suggested to Mrs Chester that we should get the child into the house and let the doctor have a look at her.

'Don't like the doctor. Don't want to see the doctor.'

Her mother gave me a despairing look.

'She won't go in, not when she's in that mood, and Louisa must see him.'

'Mummy, what's happening, Mummy?'

Another child's voice, older but plaintive, came from inside the cab. A pale round face looked out.

'Wait a minute, Louisa. Your sister's ... Oh Naomi, please stop crying ... oh dear ...'

The sight of the woman's complete helplessness gave me my idea. She was, in spite of her plumpness, a feather for any wind. Fate had shown me, in this yelling infant, a means of spoiling Bobbie's plans, and I was not going to neglect it.

I said to Mrs Chester: 'Would you like me to look after little Naomi in the garden, while you go in and see the doctor?'

'Oh dear ... oh would you ...? I'm sorry to be such a nuisance, only ...'

I led Naomi firmly to a little gazebo in front of the house, sat her on the bench and tied up the knee with my handkerchief.

'You see, we're quite all right here, aren't we, Naomi?'

With many backward glances and nervous
113

waves, Mrs Chester made for the doctor's front door, the older pale child trailing behind her. Naomi went on snivelling for a while after the door had closed behind them, until she realised that I was not a sympathetic audience.

'It hurts.'

'Try counting up to fifty and see if it still hurts.'

She got as far as fifteen then: 'Are you a governess?'

'Why do you ask?'

'You sound like a governess.'

I didn't contradict her. It was as good an identity as any.

'Do you like being here at the seaside?'

'No. I hate the seaside. We're here because of Louisa's lungs.' She said it as if she disliked her sister's lungs intensely.

'What's wrong with Louisa's lungs?'

'She coughs a lot, especially at nights.'

'That's a pity.'

'Yes, it is, because it wakes me up. Anyway, it used to wake me up, only now I sleep in the same room as Mummy, and the nurse sleeps with Louisa. Well, she did, until Mummy gave her notice.'

'Oh dear. What for?'

'Mummy said she'd been disrespectful to Daddy. Mummy says foreigners are disrespectful and dirty most of the time, especially the women.'

'Doesn't your mummy like foreign countries?'

'No, Mummy wants to go home to London. Daddy will have to go home soon anyway. Mummy says he's a very important man and the King can't do without him.'

Can't do without him, I thought, for sending my friends to Holloway. Still, what the horrible child was telling me was good news. It sounded as if it would take very little to detach the family from Biarritz.

'My daddy's in Parliament.'

'Is he? Are you going to be in Parliament when you grow up?' I thought I'd try a seed or two, even in this unlikely ground.

Again, that look of her father's. 'Ladies can't be in Parliament. I'm going to marry the Prime Minister and have lots of dresses with long trains and go to tea with the Queen.'

Gradually, she forgot about the graze on her knee and chattered on as if she'd known me for years. They had a parrot at home in Knightsbridge that she was anxious to see again, and a little dog belonging to her mother. Louisa had to take nasty medicines, but always got the second helping at meals because of building her up. Daddy liked Louisa best because she was the eldest, but her hair was nowhere near as long as Naomi's. Most of this passed me by like the buzzing of the early bees in the garden, then the door opened and Mrs Chester came out, holding Louisa by the hand and looking a little less worried.

Now that she'd had time to collect her wits she seemed to notice me properly for the first time, but to my relief there was no sign of recognition. She would leave anything to do with politics or the law courts to her husband.

'Have you been good, Naomi? I'm so grateful to you, Miss...'

'Miss Jones,' I said. 'Jane Jones.'

'She's a governess,' Naomi piped up. I didn't contradict her. We walked together to the cab, Naomi holding my hand in her hot, plump paw.

'May we drop you anywhere, Miss Jones?'

'That's very kind.'

I named a hotel at some distance from my own and asked how the consultation with the doctor had gone.

'He was quite pleased with her, wasn't he, Louisa. He says she's got to keep on taking the medicine, and make sure she gets her sleep in the afternoons.'

Louisa made a face. I was sure there was nothing seriously wrong with her that looser clothes and a run along the sands wouldn't cure, but Dr Campbell couldn't buy Whistler paintings on that kind of prescription.

I said earnestly: 'And I'm sure she'll be a lot better when you can get her away from Biarritz.'

'What?'

Mrs Chester's jaw dropped, and her mouth went as wide as her eyes.

I chattered on: 'Such an unhealthy spot for children, but of course there's no help for it if your husband has to be here and I'm sure Louisa will pick up wonderfully when you go home.'

'But ... but ... everybody said it was such a healthy place.'

I dropped my voice. 'Well, it would just suit the French to say that, wouldn't it?'

'But the King comes here.'

It was a wail of appeal to the highest authority.

'Yes, but he's not looking very well either, is he, poor man? And I happen to know ...' I dropped my voice even lower, as if imparting state secrets. 'I happen to know that he almost didn't come here last year because of a cholera scare. Of course, they pretended that they'd done something to improve the drains and it was all hushed up, but...'

'The drains. Oh dear, oh dear.'

She stared at me, then, to my alarm, large tears ran slowly down her cheeks.

'Oh dear, what will my husband say?'

'Your husband can hardly blame you for the state of the municipal drains.'

I'm afraid I spoke more sharply than a governess should, but luckily she didn't notice.

'He didn't want to come here at all. He's

such a busy man. Only he'd do anything for Louisa so when the doctor in London recommended here, I persuaded him and ... oh dear.'

Both the girls were quite impassive, as if it was normal to see their mother in tears. I'd have accused myself of cruelty, except that I was trying to avoid a worse cause for tears. Although, when I saw what the man had done to his wife and daughters, I was half inclined to let Bobbie shoot him after all.

I persevered. 'And then there are the other things.'

'Other things?'

Her eyes darted round the cab, as if expecting to see plague germs made visible.

'The things we mustn't talk about in front of the little ones.' Naomi began to pay attention, face avid. 'Some of the people who come here, walking up and down the parade as bold as brass. You simply wouldn't believe...'

I saw from her face that she had caught my meaning, would have been half eager for me to go on, if the children hadn't been there.

'Altogether,' I said, 'if the choice were mine, I'd be on my way back to England tomorrow.'

Short of throwing train timetables at her, I thought I could hardly do more. With luck, the Chester family would be on its way home within days. Even if Bobbie followed them, her opportunities would be fewer in London and the rest of the organisation would be there to restrain her.

I got down from the cab at the hotel I'd named with the sense of a piece of work well done. For the while at least I'd done what I could about one of my problems, and could turn my mind to the other. As a small experiment, I found a chemist's shop and asked for a bottle of laudanum. The apothecary took my money, wrapped up a bottle in blue paper and handed it over, hardly looking at me. It was as simple as that.

CHAPTER NINE

Topaz Brown was buried that evening in a churchyard on a cliff top. I arrived early, while two labourers were still digging the grave, and took my stand among the tombs. I watched as the hearse rumbled up the steep road drawn by two black horses with nodding plumes, two carriages behind it. A trim little priest got out of the first one, followed by a woman in a black cloak and a very elegant hat, heavily veiled, carrying sprays of mauve and white lilac. As they came nearer, I realised it must be Marie de la Tourelle.

The second carriage contained Tansy, Jules Estevan and the bald solicitor. Tansy and

Jules made an odd pair as they stepped carefully among the graves, he tall and well-tailored, she clinging to his arm in her thick black coat, looking smaller than ever. Then, some way behind, there was a motor-car. I saw the first five arrivals looking at it and was near enough to hear a gasp from Marie when a man got out. He was dressed strangely for a funeral in full evening dress with cloak and top hat. But it was, all things considered, very civil of Lord Beverley to find time to pay his last respects to Topaz. They arranged themselves round the open grave after the hired pall-bearers had manoeuvred the coffin into place, the priest at one side, Marie close to him, Tansy as far away from Marie as she could get, with Jules beside her and the solicitor hovering in between. Lord Beverley, after looking around with a lost air as if wondering when the next race was due to start, stood beside Tansy.

I'd begun to hope that the occasion would pass off without the official presence of the Women's Social and Political Union when the churchyard gate creaked open and the largest wreath I'd ever seen walked in. That, at least, was the first impression because I couldn't see Bobbie and Rose behind it. The outside of the wreath was laurel, the inner part a mass of white flowers with a bullseye of purple violets in the centre. A ribbon lashed across it read 'Votes for Women'. The assemblage halted not far from Tansy. She gave one glance towards Rose, then looked away. Caught between the wreath and Marie with her lilacs she looked red with anger, and I was relieved when the priest began reading.

During the service I had the unmistakable feeling of being watched. It was not by any of the group at the graveside. They were too intent on the priest or each other. Eventually I let my eyes follow the feeling. Not twenty yards away from me was a plump, clean-shaven man in a black coat and hat, standing very still, looking very carefully. He seemed to be doing as I was, attending the funeral but keeping far enough away from it to avoid contact with the other mourners. In fact, from the way he had tucked himself in beside a stone angel, you might almost have said that he was hiding. Tansy's Mr Shadow, beyond a doubt. The man who'd followed us on our shopping trip. The man from the solicitor's who said he wanted to see Topaz's papers. Well, Tansy might have believed that, but I didn't. To my eyes, the man had plain-clothes police officer written all over him. It was typical, I thought, of police tactics against us that they should find out about Topaz's legacy even before we did and send somebody to snoop round and do his best to discredit us.

I was so annoyed at first that I intended, as soon as the funeral was over, to go and have it out with him. I'd come to France with no dangerous intent, and it was bitter to find myself trailed like a criminal. Then I saw Bobbie glance at him from behind her wreath and knew what a waste it would be to drive him away. Nothing would be more likely to cramp the style of a prospective assassin than finding Scotland Yard or its French equivalent dogging her steps. The only problem would be to get him to transfer his attentions from myself to Bobbie, but unless I was greatly mistaken, she was likely to attend to that herself soon enough.

At the graveside, Jules and Marie were joining the priest in prayer. Tansy was crying into a large white handkerchief provided by Jules. The priest finished his prayer and rained down a handful of earth. As it pattered on the coffin lid, Marie stepped forward like an actress on cue.

'Farewell,' she said, flung the lilacs on top of the coffin, crossed herself then stood with head bent, as still as a statue. But the effect was spoiled by Bobbie, who could also recognise a cue. She left Rose staggering under the weight of the giant wreath, took a step back from the graveside and let fly.

'We have come here to pay tribute to our sister, Topaz Brown.' Her beautiful voice, deep but clear, rang out over the darkening graveyard. I heard a gasp of protest from somebody.

'Yes, our sister. However degraded a life she may have led, however tarnished in the eyes of the world, our sister Topaz Brown kept alive in her heart and in her mind one great hope, the hope that one day women would rise up and claim...'

There was a babble. Marie the statue had come alive and uttered cries of protest when Bobbie talked about Topaz's degraded life. Jules Estevan moved towards her, taking his attention away from Tansy. So when Bobbie got to women rising up, Tansy called out:

'That's rubbish.'

Jules lunged away from Marie back towards Tansy, without being able to stop either of them shouting. The priest was making shushing sounds at Marie and the solicitor at Bobbie, without any effect on either. Bobbie, who was used to worse interruptions than this, pressed on.

'...would rise up and claim their rights. Topaz Brown, alas, did not live to see that new dawn. She died a victim of the world that men have imposed upon women. Although her death may have been, in one sense, by her own hand...'

Marie shouted out something in French. The priest raised his voice in protest. The solicitor laid a hand on Bobbie's arm and was shaken off. But all these things were nothing in comparison with what Tansy did. She took a step towards Bobbie and yelled at the very

123

top of her voice:

'It wasn't by her own hand. She was murdered, and the person who did it is standing here.'

And that was almost the end of Topaz Brown's funeral. Bobbie went on with her speech, but most of the audience faded away. Jules got his arm round Tansy, half support and half restraint, and led her off sobbing towards the gate, the solicitor following. The priest nudged Marie, who had reverted to her mourning statue pose, and led her in the same direction, but with more dignity, and only after we had heard Jules' carriage driving away. That left just three of them at the graveside: Bobbie still talking about the wrongs of women to the flying clouds, Rose staring after her sister and Lord Beverley with the air of somebody who was finding events more interesting than he'd expected.

'Topaz Brown, we honour you,' Bobbie concluded.

She and Rose laid down the wreath.

'Jolly well done,' said Lord Beverley.

Bobbie glared at him, took Rose's arm and they moved off together. I looked towards the stone angel where the plump man had been standing, but there was no sign of him. He could easily have slipped away while everybody was arguing.

That left only Lord Beverley. He jumped when I walked over and introduced myself.

124

'I've heard about you. You're the woman who throws bricks and things.'

'Only in a good cause.'

'Quite,' he said. 'Oh quite.'

He was perhaps twenty-seven or twenty-eight, tall and fair haired, with an aquiline nose and well-shaped lips.

'Got a lot of sympathy for you myself,' he said. 'Very plucky women.'

'I'd like to talk to you.'

He shied away. 'Not very political, I'm afraid.'

'It's not about politics. It's about Topaz Brown.'

I'd half expected him to walk away, but he looked mildly interested.

'That's it, is it? What about coming back to town with me in my motor?'

As we walked away, the labourers moved in and began shovelling the banked earth into the grave. Lord Beverley helped me up into the passenger seat and began the long business of starting the motor. Then, suddenly:

'Well I'll be ... What's going on there?'

He was looking back towards the site of the grave. Perched up as we were, we could see it well, and the two labourers leaning on their shovels. But there was something else, and when I saw it I couldn't help gasping, hit by the superstition that will never leave even the most rational of us in graveyards. Topaz

125

Brown's grave had suddenly acquired its own statue, an equestrian statue, of marble so white that it seemed to generate a light of its own in the dusk, with the black form of a rider just visible on its back. Lord Beverley let the engine die and we stared, transfixed. Then, as we watched, the marble horse moved, extended a foreleg, bowed down its head in a long gesture of respect and grief. It held the pose for what seemed like minutes but were probably only seconds, then raised its head and moved away quite collectedly, like any horse of flesh and blood, away from the grave, picking its way through the tombs, out of our sight.

'Well,' Lord Beverley said. 'Well.'

He started the motor again, and talk was impossible on the journey back to town because of the noise. When we got back to the promenade he stopped the car and a merciful silence fell. It was dark by now, except for strings of coloured lights, with the sea thumping at the beach a few yards away.

'Who was the chap on the horse?'

'I don't know. Do you?'

'Whoever he was, I wouldn't mind his stable. She knew a lot of people, of course, foreign royalty and so on.'

He sounded almost cheerful again. I think the horse incident had shaken him as it had shaken me, but he was not a man who pondered things for long. If anything, the idea of some exotic prince riding up to pay a last farewell to Topaz seemed to please him. There was still, ten years after Eton or Harrow, something of the schoolboy about Lord Beverley.

I said: 'You know Topaz Brown left our movement a great deal of money?'

'Bit of a surprise, what?'

'Indeed. Is it true you'd left Topaz and gone back to the woman they called La Pucelle?'

He gave a little 'phew' of surprise, but I saw no reason for beating about the bush.

'It was the other way about. I, um, started with Marie, so to speak, and moved on to Topaz.'

Once he'd got over his surprise he seemed quite happy to talk about it, but then a man might be complacent to have two of the best-known courtesans in Europe competing for his custom.

'Marie seemed to think you'd changed your mind again. She said you found Topaz *vulgaire*.'

'Did she indeed? Well, if it means she liked to enjoy herself and didn't mind who knew it, then I suppose Topaz was vulgar. But in the best possible way, if you see what I mean. After La Pucelle, she came as rather a relief.'

'Marie was temperamental?'

'Marie likes to play the goddess.'

'And since you were footing the bill, you

127

didn't see why you should provide the worship as well?'

He whistled. 'You're remarkably straight talking, Miss Bray.'

It was just as well I hadn't bruised his aristocratic ears with some of the things I heard in Holloway.

'Anyway,' he said, 'I have the impression that Marie, um, prefers women. When she's not on duty, so to speak.'

It was too dark to see, but I believe he was blushing.

'Lord Beverley, would I be right in thinking that this kind of thing is all rather new to you?'

'Oh dash it. Come off it. I mean naturally a fellow's been around a bit...'

'I mean the likes of Marie and Topaz.'

'You're wondering how a chap like me can compete, you mean? You haven't heard about my stroke of luck?'

I said I'd only recently arrived in Biarritz.

'But it was all over London as well. I won ten thousand pounds in one afternoon at the Cheltenham spring meeting and I thought well, I'll jolly well spend it. I mean, I'm getting married next month so I shan't have many other chances, shall I? Nearly all gone now, worse luck, and the guv'nor's arrived to read the riot act. *Les jeux sont faits*, so to speak. And now Topaz is dead as well.'

He sounded quite sad about it. We listened

128

to the waves for a while, then he said: 'I was probably the last man, um, with her, so to speak.'

'When?'

'The night before she killed herself. Tuesday night.'

'Did she seem unhappy?'

'No, merry as a grig. One of the best times I ever had.'

'And you had no appointment to see her on the Wednesday evening?'

'We'd planned a motor trip along the coast but I had to call it off. I heard the guv'nor was on his way, prodigal son's presence required in sackcloth and ashes.'

'When did you call it off?'

'I sent a note round to her hotel early on the Wednesday morning.'

So Topaz had been left with Wednesday evening unexpectedly free. Whatever she had planned for it must have been decided at short notice.

'Miss Bray, may I ask you something? Her maid, that outburst about Topaz being, um, murdered. Was there anything in that?'

'Tansy is upset. She thinks Marie poisoned Topaz.'

'But why, for goodness' sake?'

'Jealousy. Over you.'

He groaned. 'I hope that one doesn't get to the guv'nor. Wild oats is one thing, but being mixed up in this sort of thing—well, that

129

would be a bit over the odds.'

'You don't believe it?'

'It's insane. You must stop the woman saying things like that.'

I said I'd do what I could. I still needed his co-operation.

'Lord Beverley, I'd be grateful if you could tell me something about the procedure when you visited Topaz.'

'Ye gods, Miss Bray . . .'

I think he was on the point of jumping out of his motor-car and bolting.

'For instance, I suppose you used her private door at the side of the hotel. Did she give you a key to it?'

'Oh no. You rang a bell and the maid came down and let you in. Then you went up in the lift while the maid waited downstairs. I suppose she came back up later.'

'Did you ever go through the main hotel entrance instead?'

'No, you didn't do that.'

He was beginning to relax again, although he was obviously puzzled.

'One more thing, when you sent Topaz a note to say you wouldn't be seeing her on Wednesday, did you send anything else with it?'

'No.'

'Did you ever send her a fire opal pendant?'

'No, nothing in the way of jewellery. A flower or two, but apart from that she made it pretty clear she preferred the money direct. Saved a great deal of messing about.'

'When you were with Topaz on Tuesday, did she say anything about a practical joke she was planning?'

'No, no particular joke that I can think of. We laughed a lot, though. You did, with Topaz.'

He sighed. I said I must let him go to his dinner.

'Can't say I'm looking forward to it very much. Lecture from the guv'nor, probably, on being a good husband and father. By George, Miss Bray, you women keep on about not having opportunities, but we men lead a dog's life too sometimes, you know.'

I said he must tell the House of Lords about it in due course.

'You will stop that maid of hers going around talking nonsense, won't you? Apart from anything else, Marie couldn't have killed her on Wednesday night. She has a whatjumacallit . . . an alibi.'

'Has she?'

'She was in the hotel dining room having supper until after midnight. I noticed because I was afraid she'd come across and say something while I was with the guv'nor, but luckily she didn't.'

'Who was with her?'

'Plump little Yankee fellow. Seems he's a theatre producer and he's going to put her on the stage as Mary Stuart or Cleopatra or somebody like that. Anyway, there they were with their heads together, so it's all nonsense about her and Topaz.'

He helped me out then roared off along the promenade, steering with one hand, raising his top hat to me with the other.

I walked until I'd found what I wanted. It didn't take long. The posters were all over the town and I'd noticed them with half an eye, not thinking there was anything significant about them because one circus poster looks much like another. Until, that is, you look at one of them closely in the light from a hotel foyer and see a white horse standing on its hind legs and a masked rider, cloak billowing out, plumed hat flourished in his left hand. El Cid and his wonderful white horses, said the poster. There were performances daily at 5 p.m. and 8 p.m. When I'd told Lord Beverley that I didn't know who the rider of the white horse could be, I'd spoken the truth. But I'd had my suspicions and didn't share his romantic notion of a farewell from anonymous royalty.

El Cid, though, would have to wait till morning. I spent the next few hours in a shop doorway, watching the rooms above a grocer's in an unfashionable street where, as Rose had told me, she and Bobbie were lodging. Rose returned alone soon after I took up my position. Her shoulders were slumped and

132

she was walking slowly, looking depressed. More than an hour later Bobbie arrived, also alone, striding along as purposefully as usual. I waited, alert for a young man in sporting dress, but by midnight neither of them had reappeared. By then I judged that David Chester should be safe in his bed and I could go to mine. I wondered whether Lord Beverley had enjoyed his evening with his father, and whether anybody could possibly be as innocent as that young man appeared to be.

CHAPTER TEN

Next morning I walked to the Champ de Pioche, an open space about a mile outside the town where the circus had its camp. I arrived, judging by the noise and the smells, just as they were mucking out the animals. Nobody seemed to notice me as I wandered past the big top into the village of caravans, huts and cages that made up the living quarters. Eventually I stopped a red-haired lad in an overcoat several sizes too large for him and asked him in French where I could find El Cid. He replied, in fluent Liverpudlian, that I'd find him at the stables. Straight on past the llamas and turn left at the camels. The stables turned out to be remarkably solid structures for a travelling circus, made mostly of wood with canvas roofs. A row of shining, shifting haunches was visible over the half doors, there was a smell of good hay and the sound of champing from inside the boxes. I saw a man shovelling dung into a basket and again asked for El Cid. He grinned, dumped a shovelful and yelled cheerfully:

'Sid, lady wants you.'

The face that appeared from the end box was as brown and creased as a sailor's, with bright dark eyes under a helmet of black hair. The man called Sid looked at me then walked out to meet me, taking his time, wiping his hands on his breeches. He was smaller than I am, jockey-sized, but with shoulders as broad as a prize-fighter's under a grey jersey. His legs were bowed from much riding, and he must have been forty or more, but he walked as if he were pleased with himself. A cock on a dung-heap, if ever there was one. I thought of Lord Beverley and his European royalty, and couldn't help smiling. The little man smiled back, like a child letting another child in on a joke.

'What can I do for you, lady?'

The voice could have come from any street market in London.

I said: 'I believe you knew Topaz Brown.'

He nodded, quite at ease.

'My name's Nell Bray. I wonder if I could

134

have a word with you.'

'Sidney Greenbow at your service, otherwise known as El Cid. I'm giving Grandee his grooming. If you'd like to step in with me we could have our chat while I'm getting on with it.'

The other man had stopped shovelling dung and was grinning at me, curious, I think, to see if I'd accept the invitation. Sid Greenbow swung back the half door and I followed him into the dim light of the box. Clean golden straw came almost up to my knees. A gleaming white horse stopped eating from the manger and swung his head towards me, whickering a little. I stroked his muzzle and found it as soft as a cat's fur.

'Was it Grandee you took to Topaz Brown's funeral last night?'

'Of course. Nothing but the best for Topaz.'

The horse turned back to his feed and Sidney picked up a body brush and curry comb and began smoothing his flank in long, arching strokes. At every third stroke he ran the brush over the teeth of the curry comb with a shimmering, rasping sound, hissing gently through his teeth all the time. He showed no curiosity at all about why I was there and for the first few minutes I just watched him at work, lulled by the dim light and the soft regular sounds.

At last I said: 'Had you known her long?'

He was brushing the horse's belly by then, and didn't look up or break the rhythm of his brushing.

'Twelve years or more. When I first met her, she was on the halls. I had an act myself, "Cuthbert the Calculating Horse", pot-bellied skewbald with a liking for mint pastilles, so naturally we'd find ourselves on the same bill from time to time.'

'I didn't know Topaz was on the halls. What did she do?'

'Precious little. She was part of a novelty singing act called the Chanson Sisters, though they weren't any more sisters than I am. The other one did most of the singing and Topaz did the good looks, only she wasn't called Topaz then. She took that up after she went into her present line of work—or her past line of work I should say.'

He sounded regretful, but not grief stricken, though perhaps it's hard to sound grief stricken when you're gently brushing round a horse's most intimate parts. The animal fidgeted, but calmed down at once when he murmured a few words to it.

'How long ago was that?'

'About ten years. For a while she kept up both lines and went on doing a bit on the halls, then she was doing so well on the other thing she gave it up.'

'But you kept on seeing her?'

I knew, from a sociological study I'd read

on the subject, that most prostitutes had a man as a kind of manager and guardian who took much of their profits. I thought that might have been Sidney Greenbow's rôle in Topaz's life.

'No, not kept on. I'd just see her from time to time, and we'd have a drink together and tell each other how we were doing. The thing about Topaz, however famous she was, she never went standoffish. I remember one night I saw her coming out of the Empire on the arm of some toff and I'd just come straight from doing my act so was in my diddicoy gear. I yelled out "How'y doing, Topaz?" not thinking. And she turned round and smiled at me and called out, "Not so bad, Sid. Are you going to tell my fortune for me?" You should have seen the toff's face, but the crowd loved it. She'd do anything for a laugh, would Topaz.'

'What about when she started travelling? Did you go with her?'

'Of course not. I had my act, didn't I? By then I'd got together with an Irishman and we'd worked up a comic cossack turn and were doing the circuses. But now and then it would happen that I'd be somewhere and she'd be somewhere, and we'd meet each other again, and so it would go.'

He moved sideways and started working on the horse's near hind quarter. I was relieved to find him so willing to talk, but worried

137

about what would happen when we came to his more recent relationship with Topaz. From what Jules had said, there was considerably more to it than meeting for an occasional drink.

'Did you know she was going to be here in Biarritz?'

'Oh yes. I tried to work it so I'd be here at the same time as she would. I wanted her to see the Dons working; after all she was a shareholder, wasn't she?'

'Shareholder? In what?'

'In this.' He tapped the body brush gently on the horse's haunch. 'Grandee and the rest of the Dons. She gave me the money for them.'

'The Dons.'

'The horses. That's my name for them, on account of them being high bred Spaniards. I told Topaz, "You and I might have come out of the gutter, but we own six horses with better pedigrees than half the royalty in Europe." She liked that.'

'Were they very expensive?'

He whistled. 'You can say they were. A thousand for Grandee here, he's the stallion, five hundred for the two geldings, then another two thousand for the three mares. I'll show you them later. We have to keep them over the other side of the ground because of Grandee.'

That made, according to my calculations,

three thousand five hundred pounds worth of horseflesh.

'And she paid for all that?'

'All but a few hundred I'd managed to save. What happened, I met her in Paris three years ago, a bit down on my luck because the circus I'd been with had gone bankrupt. Anyway, we had a drink as usual, and I told her about these horses I'd heard of for sale in Barcelona. The owner had died and the whole circus world knew these were class horses. Anyway, not thinking anything, I talked about it to Topaz and said what an act I could get up with horses like that. I knew there was no more chance of me having them than getting the Archangel Gabriel to come down and sit in a canary cage. And she said, cool as you please: "Well, why don't we buy them?"

'Of course, I didn't believe her at first, but she said she had a bit of money to spare, and nothing would content her but we should both go off to Barcelona as soon as she was free and buy them. Which was just what we did.'

'You said she was a shareholder?'

'That's right. We had a regular business proposition. I had the right to work them for three years, building up the act. After that I'd start paying back the money, until in the end I'd paid her back the original capital, plus five hundred interest, and the Dons would be mine outright.'

'It would take you a long time to pay back that sort of money, wouldn't it?'

'Not as long as you might think. We're doing very nicely now, me and the Dons. After Biarritz it's Nice, then the summer in Paris, then back to London for Christmas. Anyway, it wouldn't have mattered with Topaz. She'd never have pressed me for money I hadn't got.'

'And what happens now she's dead?'

For the first time he stopped his brushing and looked at me directly.

'What do you mean, what happens?'

'About the horses?'

'Well, they're my horses. That's what she wanted.'

He went on brushing, carefully moving the thick tail aside from the horse's hocks. I wondered if he was as blind as he seemed to be to the legal complexities, and whether there'd been anything in writing. I already knew enough about Topaz to doubt that. I moved on to equally sensitive ground.

'You'd been seeing quite a lot of Topaz while you were here in Biarritz, hadn't you?'

'Who told you that? Tansy, I suppose.' He sounded amused rather than annoyed.

'No, not Tansy.'

'I know who it is then.' Again, no annoyance. He'd moved over to the offside leg, so now I could see his face as he worked. 'If you're asking were Topaz and I keeping company, well, yes we were for a while.'

I was struck by that 'keeping company', the homely old-fashioned phrase that might go with a country courtship and sounded so oddly here.

'While she was earning her money from the baron?'

He laughed. 'Yes, I do know who you've been talking to.'

He glanced up at me, as if it had struck him for the first time that I was there for some reason other than idle curiosity. But his tone didn't change.

'Yes, it would happen from time to time. Topaz was a girl who needed her exercise, and not every man who paid through the nose for her company knew what to do with it when he got it. Topaz said the baron was a nice enough old gent and of course she did what she could for him, which with Topaz would be something like his money's worth, but there wasn't much steam left in the boiler. So I'd go round to see her now and then and we'd...'

He whistled two chirpy notes.

'At her hotel?'

'Yes. That's why I thought you'd heard about me from Tansy. Tansy didn't approve of me one little bit, what with being from the circus and not paying for it. She'd come down to let me in with a face on her that said if it was left to her she'd kick me straight out again.'

'You didn't have a key to that side door?'

'Of course not. Topaz didn't give people keys. You can see why not. I mean, supposing I was to walk in while the baron was there doing his best?'

I said, feeling thankful that I didn't blush easily: 'Would Topaz wear anything special for you?'

I had in mind, of course, the shop-girl's honeymoon underwear and whether it would appeal to Sid. I stared straight down into his face, expecting anger or ridicule. What I did not expect was the expression on it of sudden tenderness, an expression reminding me that this little man had ridden a valuable horse a long way in the dusk, to make one sorrowing gesture at Topaz's grave.

'It was always special with her. Silk so fine you could see her skin through it. Satin you'd think would purr when you stroked it. Nothing flashy though, never flashy. Taste she had, better than a lot of women who were born to it. I'd open the bedroom door and she'd be lying there: "What do you think of this then, Sid?" And I'd tell her what I thought of it. In my own way I'd tell her.'

He'd put the body brush down, and while he was talking he'd been stroking the horse's gleaming haunch with his hand, long, lingering strokes. He went on stroking when he finished talking, staring at nothing.

142

I said: 'You'd have a glass of wine?'

'Oh yes.' He smiled, but it was a sad smile. 'She was trying to educate me, you see. She'd get them to send up a bottle from her stock along with a little something from the kitchens, and I had to guess what it was and when it was grown. She said we owed it to ourselves and where we'd come from to get the best there was and know when we'd got it.'

If Sid was speaking the truth, nothing in all this went with cheap underwear and cheap wine. And yet they sounded so much like a parody of what Sid had described that I was sure there must be a connection.

'Did she ever play jokes on you? Dress up as somebody else, for instance?'

'No, not with me. I'd be in, sometimes, on jokes she played on other people.'

'What sort of jokes?'

He picked up the body brush and started work again.

'Well, last year there was that time she pretended to be a Red Indian princess. I found her the ponies, of course, and two or three of the lads done up in grease paint and feathers. You should have seen the faces when they all turned up outside the hotel just at lunch time and asked for buffalo steaks.'

'Was she planning any sort of joke last week?'

He shook his head. 'Not that I'd heard of.

143

She'd usually be in touch with me when she was planning something elaborate. But I hadn't seen her for a week or ten days because she was spending a lot of time with that young toff who won the fortune at Cheltenham.'

He sounded bitter about Lord Beverley, but perhaps that wasn't surprising. As for the joke, Topaz wouldn't have needed circus ponies or grease paint for what she'd been planning on Wednesday night.

'How did she get in touch with you when she wanted to see you?'

'She'd send somebody down with a note.'

'Did she send a note asking to see you at eight o'clock on Wednesday night?'

'No, she didn't. She didn't send for me at all, but if she had it wouldn't have been for eight o'clock. She knew I'd be in the ring at eight o'clock. It was always later when I went to her, after the second show.' He was beginning to sound annoyed, and I could hardly blame him. He went on with his grooming for a few minutes, then: 'So they think she was killed at eight o'clock, do they?'

'Killed?'

'Yes. Isn't that what it's all about?'

'You know the verdict was suicide?'

The sound he made brought the horse's head swinging round to know what the trouble was.

144

'Topaz would never kill herself.' He said it with total certainty.

'But if you thought she'd been murdered, why didn't you do something about it?'

He shrugged. 'It wouldn't have brought her back, would it? Anyway, if you go making trouble for the authorities, they don't forget it, no matter what the reason might be.'

'Who do you think killed her?'

Another shrug. 'It could have been anybody. She was in a dangerous trade. She knew that.'

I'd been so well-schooled by Jules and Tansy in the gulf between Topaz and the street corner prostitute that this almost shocked me.

'You're talking as if she was operating up alleyways in Whitechapel.'

'It doesn't matter if the trapeze bar's solid gold. Make a mistake on it, and you're just as dead.'

'You think Topaz was killed by a client?'

He, at least, didn't object to that word.

'Yes, I do think that. What else is there to think?'

'And you haven't told anybody, haven't tried to get the police to investigate?'

'What would be the use? The kind of clients she had, they'd only hush it up.'

'Did she have any enemies you knew of?'

'Topaz didn't go in for enemies.'

145

He'd worked his way round to the stallion's head and was brushing, with great gentleness, between the wide brown eyes. When he'd finished he ran the brush down the curry comb for one last time, took something out of his pocket and fed it to the animal.

'There, that'll do him for now. Come and look at the mares.'

Various eyes followed us as we walked across the field, but without much curiosity. A woman was exercising a troupe of jet black greyhounds. A girl was hanging coloured tights to dry outside a brightly painted caravan. The three white mares shared their stable block with a group of Shetland ponies. We leaned over the half doors, looking in.

Sid said: 'I haven't asked you what your interest is.'

It was fair enough.

'I'm a member of the Women's Social and Political Union. Suffragettes, if you like. Topaz left all her money to us. You'd heard about that, I suppose.'

He nodded.

'Were you surprised?'

'It's her money.'

He didn't sound resentful.

'Did you think she might have left some to you?'

'Why should she? We didn't think about dying, either of us. If it happens, it happens.'

'Did she tell you she was going to retire this

year and buy a vineyard?'

'Not this year, no. But I knew she was thinking of it. Does it make any difference to getting the money, finding out who murdered her?'

'It shouldn't.'

I didn't want to go into the legal implications.

'Well then?'

'I suppose ... I suppose it seems unfair to take Topaz's money without trying to get ... justice for her.'

It surprised me as I said it, but I realised I meant it. Sid gave me one of his twisted smiles. His hand was stroking a rug flung over the stable door. It seemed that he always needed to be stroking something.

'Will it do her any good?'

We stood leaning on the door for a while, so close together that I could feel the steady rhythm of his breathing. After a while I said I must go and he said he'd walk back with me to the gate. When we were almost there he said:

'Did you ever meet her?'

'No.'

'You're like her in some ways. No, I don't mean in looks. It was the way that when she wanted something, she'd go all out for it, no matter what.'

I took it as a compliment. But on the way back to town that phrase from Topaz's last

147

note was going round and round in my mind. *I.O.U. for one career.* I'd taken it that she meant her own career, but supposing the I.O.U. was in the other direction? By Sid's own account, when Topaz had helped him he'd been half a comic cossack act, down on his luck. Now he was El Cid, proprietor of six of the finest horses I was ever likely to see. Everybody talked about Topaz's generosity, but surely it had its limits. Perhaps, needing money for her vineyard, she'd decided to call in an I.O.U. I thought of Sid stroking the stallion's white haunch and talking about satin underwear. I stopped beside one of the circus posters and there was El Cid, masked and cloaked on his rearing white horse. Performances 5 p.m. and 8 p.m. 'She knew I'd be in the ring at eight o'clock.' But one man, masked and cloaked on horseback, looks very much like another and Sidney Greenbow would hardly be the only rider in the circus. *I.O.U. for one career.*

CHAPTER ELEVEN

It was nearly midday when I found myself back at Topaz's hotel, outside her private door. The sun was warm, and I stood there in a daze, trying to calculate. Her note had said 8 p.m. If her guest were punctual, and if

Topaz drank the poisoned wine almost at once, she would be deeply asleep by nine, or say nine thirty at the latest. But if the doctor's guess was right, her coma would not have become irreversible until well after midnight. I assumed that the murderer would have done some research into the effects of laudanum and would know that it would be unsafe to leave until, say, one o'clock in the morning. Alternatively, if the guest left as soon as Topaz became unconscious, he or she would have to return at some time after one, to make sure that everything had gone as intended. It would be safer, from every point of view, to stay. Then I thought of the steady ruthlessness it would take to sit for four hours or so, watching over the sleep of a woman you were killing, and felt cold in spite of the sun. Either way, stay or return, the murderer would surely have to leave Topaz's suite at some time between one o'clock and daylight.

I stared at the door. There was no light over it, and the nearest street lamp was a good thirty yards away on the corner. Even at midday there were few people coming and going in the street. As safe an escape route as any murderer could expect. As I stood there thinking, I'd been half conscious of a voice near me, piping away in French. I'd assumed it was a child's and it came as a shock when I turned round and saw a figure with an adult's lined face and a stocky body no more than four and a half feet tall. He was dressed in grey flannel trousers and a tweed sporting jacket that came down to his knees. The piping words were a request, insistent but civil, for a few sous. I found some coins and gave them to him, surprised by the formality of his thanks. I expected him to go away when he had the money, but he didn't. I asked him what his name was.

'Demi-tasse. Demi to my friends.'

He spoke French with a strong Basque accent.

'Where do you live, Demi?'

He smiled and pointed towards the back of the hotel, where the kitchen doors and the dustbins were.

'I saw you giving fish to the cats. You keep it for me next time?'

I began to wonder how many people had been watching me on that shopping trip; first Mr Shadow, now Demi-tasse. Still, he was something of a godsend.

'Do you spend all your time in this street?'

'I used to.'

'Used to?'

He glanced up towards Topaz's tower.

'Yes, because of her.'

'The English lady?'

'Yes, the one who is dead.'

I'm afraid my first idea was that this little man had cherished a hopeless passion for

150

Topaz Brown. I should have known France better.

'Men were always pleased with themselves after her. I'd ask for sous, and they'd give me more, sometimes much more.'

'But you're still waiting here?'

'Perhaps I must move to the other side. I am sorry about that.'

'Demi-tasse, would you like to have lunch?'

His eyes went bright. I took him to the café on the corner of the square that I'd noticed when shopping with Tansy. The pair of us got some odd looks as I ordered *boeuf en daube* for two.

'The wine here is also very good,' he mentioned.

His self possession was almost complete, but the looks he was giving other people's food had them edging their plates away. With some misgiving, I ordered a half carafe of red wine. It would not suit my purpose to get him drunk. But in all humanity I waited until he finished his casserole before I started questioning him.

'You used to watch for men coming out of Topaz's special door?'

He nodded.

'Do you remember that last night, the night before she was found dead?'

'Yes, I do.'

'Where were you?'

'In the street outside her door.'

'When?'

151

'As usual, from when I finish helping with the potatoes in the kitchen. That is, about seven.'

'You have a watch?'

'No. I hear the church clock striking.'

'So you were watching Topaz's door from soon after seven o'clock. Did you see anybody go in?'

'No. I saw somebody coming out.'

'Who?'

'The other English woman, her maid I think.'

'Did you speak to her?'

'No. She never gives me anything. She is always angry.'

'When did she come out?'

'After seven, before eight.'

'Did you see anybody go in before eight?'

'Nobody.'

'You're quite sure about that?'

'Nobody.'

'What did you do then?'

'I waited, as usual. Then I needed a *pipi*. I went round the corner. That's how I came to miss the gentleman.'

My hand jerked so that I almost spilled my wine.

'What gentleman?'

'I came back round the corner, and there was a gentleman at the door.'

'Going in?'

'No, coming out. He was locking the door

152

behind him. I heard the key turning in the lock.'

Both Tansy and Sid had said that Topaz would never give a key to anybody.

'You're quite certain that nobody went in that door between the time that the maid left and when you saw this gentleman coming out?'

'Certain.'

'What time was it when you saw him?'

'After nine. About halfway between nine and ten.'

'Did you recognise him?'

'No. It was dark.'

'Didn't you follow him to ask him for money?'

'I do not run after people in the streets. That is only for children.'

It was a dignified rebuke. I apologised.

'But this is very important, Demi. Where did the gentleman go?'

'Towards the sea.'

'How was he dressed? Was he tall, short, fat, thin?'

'As far as I could tell he was dressed like any gentleman, black coat, black top hat. I do not know if he was fat or thin because of the coat. Tall?' He shrugged. 'Like anybody.'

To Demi, almost anybody would look tall.

I felt both gratified and scared, like somebody who rubs a lamp and meets a genie. I'd deduced a visitor leaving Topaz at

153

some time after nine, but hardly expected
him to become real. True, it was a shadowy
reality, this gentleman who might have been
fat or thin, tall or short, but for all that I had
the feeling of cold again. I refilled our glasses,
ordered another half carafe and Camembert
for us both.

'What did you do then?'

'Waited.'

'But the gentleman had left.'

'I waited. What else should I do?'

'Did you see anybody else?'

'Yes. After ten o'clock there was the other
gentleman. The nervous gentleman.'

'Did he go in?'

'No. That was why I called him the
nervous gentleman to myself. He kept
walking up and down, up and down, on the
pavement opposite her door. I thought, He's
wondering whether he dare ring her bell.'

'Did you go over and speak to him?'

'No, I kept in the shadows on my side. If
he'd seen me, he might have gone away.'

He probably knew from experience that
nervous suitors brought no sous.

'Was it the same gentleman you saw
coming out?'

He shook his head, concentrating on an
advancing wedge of Camembert.

'Why are you so sure of that? You didn't
know what the other man looked like.'

'The second one wasn't in evening dress

154

and he walked differently. The first gentleman walked like that.' His fingers on either side of the plate tapped out a deliberate, heavy beat. 'The other one walked like this.' The beat was lighter and quicker. 'He'd walk up and down, then he'd stop for a while, then walk again. He was there for a long time.'

'How long?'

'It was after midnight when he went.'

'Went where?'

'Just walked away towards the parade, like the other one.'

'Without going in?'

'Without going in. I felt sorry for him.'

I was reluctant to ask the next question, but there was no avoiding it.

'What did the second one look like? You were watching him for more than an hour and a half. You must have some idea.'

He cut a small piece of Camembert and ate it, savouring, considering.

'There's a gas lamp on the corner with the promenade. It's a long way from her door.'

'Yes, I noticed.'

'When he was walking up and down, he'd sometimes come near the lamp. I could see a little more clearly, but not very clearly because he was some way away then.'

'Yes, so what did he look like?'

I don't think Demi was making me wait deliberately, but the effect was the same. He swallowed his cheese and spoke slowly, screwing up his eyes to think.

'He was not fat. Quite young. He was wearing jacket and breeches and a cap. Once he took his cap off. His hair was dark.'

'Straight or curly?'

'I think not very straight. I'm not sure.'

I waited, but there was no more. The footsteps though, beaten out by Demi's short fingers, were enough to trouble me.

'And this young man was walking up and down opposite Topaz's door from some time after ten until after midnight?'

'Yes.'

'Did he come back?'

'No. Nobody came.'

'You were watching all night?'

'No. A man must sleep.'

He said it as if he had a four-poster bed and a valet waiting to turn back the covers.

'When did you leave?'

'When the clock struck two, as usual. By that time, the staff in the kitchen have finished clearing up the supper things. A sous-chef is my friend. If there is a slice of meat left on a plate, a glass of wine in a bottle, he keeps them for me. Afterwards, I sleep on the steps near the boilers. In the mornings, I help them unload the vegetables and they give me a bowl of coffee and bread.'

'I suppose the boilers are round at the back near the dustbins.'

156

'Yes.'

So after two o'clock he would have heard and seen nothing. He was staring at me, not defensively and yet not quite trusting. He hadn't asked me why I wanted to know all this. He survived in the world simply by being there, not by questioning it. We finished the cheese and wine and walked back to the hotel together, Demi thanking me for his lunch with fine formality. Opposite Topaz's door he wished me good afternoon.

'If you need to speak to me again, you know where to find me. Either here or on the other side.'

I walked on towards the parade, so deep in thought that I almost bumped into Jules Estevan, by the very lamppost Demi and I had been talking about.

'Good afternoon, Miss Bray. Have you been having a pleasant conversation with Demi?'

I was beginning to think I couldn't move without somebody watching me.

'You know him?'

'Everybody knows Demi. He's an institution.'

I should have liked to ask him how far anyone could rely on Demi, but then I wanted to ask the same question about Jules Estevan. I sensed that he knew a lot more than he admitted about what I was doing.

'I've been looking for you all morning,

Miss Bray. Where have you been?'

'At the circus.'

I watched to see how he reacted, but his expression didn't change.

'Did you find it entertaining?'

'Instructive, at any rate. I had a long conversation with El Cid.'

He raised his hat half an inch, mockingly. 'Your hunting instincts are infallible.'

'Far from it. I wonder why you didn't tell me who Topaz's circus lover was in the first place.'

'I'd no idea it was important to your investigations. Did El Cid cast any light on Topaz's ... suicide?'

There was the faintest of pauses before the last word.

'He's convinced she didn't kill herself.'

Almost without realising it, we'd strolled round the corner and joined the fashionable throng taking its afternoon stroll by the sea. Jules said, 'Really', as if I'd told him that it looked like rain. I wondered if anything would shake his affectation of calm.

'Why were you looking for me this morning?'

'To make arrangements to take you to Marie's *Soirée Ancienne*. You remember you accepted yesterday.'

'I did nothing of the kind.'

My evening would be spent like the

previous one, trying to keep an eye on Bobbie.

'I think you'd find it interesting.'

'Frankly, I doubt it. I've had a fair sample of Marie's histrionic talents already.'

'There'll be at least one other friend of yours there.'

'Who?'

'Miss Fieldfare.'

I stopped walking, and the couple behind almost cannoned into us.

'Bobbie's going to Marie's soirée?'

'She told me so herself this morning.'

The idea of Bobbie doing anything half so frivolous amazed me. Unless...

'Excuse me, Mr Estevan, I've just seen somebody I simply must talk to.'

We'd drawn level with the hotel where David Chester and his family were staying and I could see three unmistakable figures crossing the road to the beach, a plump woman with a sunshade and two small girls in shiny boots and pink frills. A maid, loaded with bags, trailed behind them. Jules looked from them to me and, for once, registered mild surprise.

'Your circle of acquaintances amazes me. I shall call for you at your hotel at seven thirty this evening.'

I caught up with Mrs Chester as she was trying to choose the least germ-laden patch of the beach. Her pleasure at seeing me was touching and might have made me guilty about my duplicity, except that it was in a good cause—if preserving the life of David Chester could be described as that.

'Miss ... Oh, I am glad to see you. I've been feeling guilty all day for not thanking you properly for looking after Naomi yesterday.'

Her manner, from MP's wife to supposed governess, would have been almost too friendly. But I was English among foreigners, had shown kindness to one of her daughters and that was enough for her. I chose a defensible patch of territory for them and helped the maid with cushions, lemonade bottles and the sunshade. Mrs Chester settled herself and I stood and watched the two girls as they began, dutifully, to scrape at the sand with wooden spades.

'Be careful, Louisa. Don't do too much.'

The child had hardly moved a muscle. I restrained myself from saying that half an hour of solid digging would do her all the good in the world.

'Doesn't your husband come to the beach?'

'Oh no. He's brought so much work with him.'

That was a relief. If he saw a vengeful virago like me in his wife's company he'd probably have called the gendarmes out. His wife clearly had no suspicions, and for the first time in my life I was grateful for political ignorance in a woman.

160

'Still, I expect you get out in the evenings together.'

In her place, I'd have regarded that as impertinent, but I couldn't waste time.

'Oh no, there's Louisa to think of. We shall have company tonight though. Mr and Mrs Prendergast are coming to dine with us. Do you know them?'

Relieved, I said I didn't.

'His brother's a bishop. We're going to play bridge in our suite after dinner. Mrs Prendergast was ladies' bridge champion of Somerset last year.'

She said it with timid gloom. I could imagine Mrs Prendergast's cold eyes, poor Mrs Chester's apologetic fumblings, her husband's relentless post mortem. And, in the next room, the over-protected child coughing and fretful. All the pleasures of matrimony and motherhood.

'That will be nice,' I said.

'Yes, very nice.' She sighed. 'I suppose you're engaged.'

'What?'

For a moment I'd forgotten my rôle of governess.

'Engaged for the season, I mean. You're with a family?'

'Oh, yes.'

Another sigh. 'I'd been hoping ... My husband won't have another foreign girl, and since the last one left we've had so much to do

161

looking after Louisa, and with all his work as well it's not fair on him ...'

She'd been on the point of offering me a post.

'But you'll be going back to England soon, won't you?'

'On Tuesday. My husband and I had a talk after I saw you yesterday and we agreed it wasn't doing Louisa as much good as we hoped. We've paid till the end of the week, and he won't travel on a Sunday, and ...'

I let her run on about travel arrangements, working out that there were four days left in which I'd have to keep Bobbie away from David Chester. That was longer than I'd hoped, but at least there was no need to worry about that evening, if Jules was right.

I wished Mrs Chester good luck with the bridge and took my leave. There were two things I had to do before keeping my appointment with Jules, and the first of them was something I wasn't looking forward to in the least. But with shifting sands all round me I needed to know that at least one person had been telling me the truth. I went towards the harbour and, in a world drowsy with siesta, asked among officials until I found one who could give me the address of a Scottish girl called Janet who'd married a French customs officer.

It turned out to be a white-painted house clinging to the harbour edge like a house

162

martin's nest. I heard a child's laughter through the open window and a Scots voice chanting 'This little piggy went to market'. There was some delay when I knocked at the door, then a dark-haired young woman appeared, rather harassed, with a baby in her arms.

'My name's Nell Bray. I'm a friend of Tansy Mills.'

She looked surprised, a little suspicious, but was too polite to shut the door on me.

'Tansy knew I was coming down to the harbour. I said I'd look in and see if your child was better.'

'Danielle. Yes, much better, thank you. Will you come in?'

Her accent was from the Highlands, her face square and likeable, with determined eyebrows and direct eyes. She showed me into the sunny living room, where two more children were playing with toys on the floor, and invited me to sit down.

'Will you have some coffee? How is Tansy? I thought when I heard about it I should go to her, then I didn't know whether she'd want it or not.'

It was clear from her blushing that she knew how Tansy's employer had made her living.

'I didn't want her to think I was keeping away, only with the bairns . . .'

'I'm sure she doesn't think that. You know

163

it was when she went back from you that she found her?'

She glanced at the children, but they were absorbed in their game.

'Yes . . . yes, I thought it must have been.' Her voice was a whisper. 'When I heard, I wondered perhaps, if Tansy had got back earlier, if I hadn't persuaded her to stay the night . . .'

'It would have made no difference. She'd have been away for the night in any case. Topaz Brown had booked her a room in another part of the hotel.'

'Yes, she said that. She was grieved about it.'

I tried a wild chance. 'Did she say anything about any visitors Topaz Brown was expecting that night?'

'No, no she wouldn't. We never talked about that.'

What did they talk about, I wondered? Husbands and babies, sisters and cottages with ducks? I already had what I needed from Janet. Without prompting, she'd confirmed Tansy's story of staying the night with her, and Janet did not strike me as a skilled liar. I exchanged a few civilities, talked about the children and her husband's work, then said I must go because I had an appointment. As she opened the door for me, she said: 'Please tell Tansy that she's always welcome here, and she's to send me a note if there's anything I can do.'

I promised. As I walked away from the harbour I looked at my watch. Just in time for the first performance of the circus, if I hurried.

I arrived at the ground to find the big top already alive with noise and expectation and paid for one of the expensive seats, insisting that I wanted to be as close to the ring as possible. I'd just settled in my place when the trumpets blew and the march struck up for the grand parade. The performers came out from the arch facing me, under the orchestra stand, first the ringmaster, then a masked man in a gold-embroidered doublet, flowing cloak and black-plumed hat in the cavalier style, riding a white horse so fine that even this matinée audience of parents and children caught its collective breath. The rider made the horse rear up a little as they came through the arch and hold the position for a second, swept off his hat and bowed low over the horse's shoulder, acknowledging the applause. I found it hard to believe that the dung-hill cock of the morning had been transformed into this magnificence. Even the horse looked larger, gleaming with a silvery whiteness. The other five Dons followed more sedately, their riders also masked and cloaked, but with less in the way of plumes and embroidery.

Their appearance in the grand parade was

only by way of an introduction. I had to sit through dogs, clowns, camels and trapeze artists until they galloped on again as the climax of the entire circus. They had the crowd roaring with enthusiasm at a mock battle with much flashing of swords and flying of banners, designed to show off the paces of the six horses, of Grandee and El Cid above all. It was, as far as I could tell, a fast variation on *haute école* movements, done with enough panache to please the crowd, and yet with a respect for the dignity of the six white horses. As I watched El Cid and Grandee leap off a ramp through the window of a mock fort, white mane flying, plumed hat waving, it struck me that Topaz had been wise in her investment.

The act ended with a hand gallop round the ring, band playing triumphant music, to acknowledge the applause. As they came towards me I stared at the leading rider. Would I know one rider from another under that mask, if I had no reason to be suspicious? El Cid was bowing to the crowd and as he came towards me, for a moment our eyes met. I was instantly certain that he'd recognised me and that was confirmed when, as he passed, he made Grandee turn sideways a little and perform that arrested movement of pawing the air, as he'd done at their first entrance. It took so short a time that I doubt the rest of the audience were even conscious of it, though they may have noticed the bow, a little deeper than the rest, towards where I was sitting. Almost before it had happened, Grandee and the others had galloped out of the ring and the clowns were tumbling in for the piece of slapstick that would send the audience away laughing.

A courteous gesture from El Cid? A mocking gesture from Sidney Greenbow? Or something more than that? There had been a combination of the powerful and the sinister about the white horse and the black-masked figure that might, equally well, have been a warning. As I went out with the rest of the audience I wondered about that, and the question that had brought me there and still wasn't entirely answered. The man who played El Cid would have to be a very good rider, but I wasn't sure that only one man could do it. After all, there were at least five competent riders in Sidney's team and any of them in the appropriate costume would have looked much like his leader. It was the horses rather than the riders that the audience noticed. As I walked back to town, I decided that my experiment had not been conclusive. I'd only learned one thing for the price of my ticket—that a man who loved horses would surely rather do anything than be parted from six such as those.

I got back to my hotel rushed and sticky, with hardly enough time to wash and change before Jules arrived. So I'm afraid that when the proprietor came bustling out of her room as I was halfway upstairs, I didn't give her my whole attention.

'The Englishwoman has gone. She waited for you, but you didn't come so she went.'

'What was she like?'

'Small and not well-mannered.'

Tansy.

My immediate thought, a guilty one, was that while I'd been at the circus Tansy had somehow found out about my visit to Janet and resented it, but I had no time to worry about it then. I added Tansy's anger to the list of things I'd have to deal with in the morning and hurried on upstairs.

CHAPTER TWELVE

My hasty packing in London had included a dictionary of French legal terms and quantities of note books, but no costume suitable for an evening with the demi-monde. The best I could manage was my Liberty silk dress with the fern print, a new pair of white silk stockings unearthed from the bottom of my case and my straw sun hat with a green ribbon. When I came down the proprietor gave me an odd look and said the gentleman was waiting for me outside. Jules was in the driving seat of a smart gig drawn by a fidgety bay mare. He was wearing a white tunic with a purple cloak thrown over it and had a wreath of bay leaves in his hair.

'I am determined to resist the motor-car. A chariot would have been better, but this must serve.'

We turned into the Avenue du Bois de Boulogne which runs southwards from the town, parallel to the long line of cliffs above the second bathing beach, the Plage des Basques. Jules, entering into the charioteer spirit, drove standing up and the mare went along at a spanking trot. It was a magnificent evening, with the sun setting over the Atlantic in scarlet rags of cloud and the scent of thyme blowing off the land.

I enjoyed the drive more than I had any right to and couldn't help thinking about what Emmeline would say if she could see her emissary racing along with one of the most handsome men in Biarritz, his purple cloak flying out in the warm wind like Lord Byron's in a painting, my hair past praying for. Jules took my laughter for encouragement to go faster. There were other carriages on the road and some motor-cars and we went spinning past them, their drivers shouting insults at Jules in a variety of languages. One open brougham contained a Roman legionnaire complete with plumed helmet and three girls in what looked like ballet costume, possibly dryads. A motor-car had come to a halt at the side of the road, with a chauffeur peering into its entrails and an enormously fat woman in a red wig and golden robes shouting at him in French from the passenger's seat to hurry up. After about a mile we turned off into a side road and a series of bends forced even Jules to go at a more considered pace. Somewhere along our journey I'd made up my mind.

'Mr Estevan, did you know a man left Topaz's rooms between nine and ten o'clock on the night she died?'

He was concentrating on the reins and didn't turn round.

'No, I didn't know. Is that what Demi told you?'

'And others.'

I didn't want to put the little man in danger.

'Do you know who the man was?'

'No. All I know is that she'd invited somebody to visit her at eight o'clock.'

He turned round briefly, frowning.

'Eight o'clock. But that was the time on her note.'

'The ... suicide note, you mean?'

I paused before 'suicide', as he'd paused earlier.

'Meaning that you believe Topaz was murdered?'

This time he didn't even turn round. He

might have been talking to the mare.

'You must have suspected it yourself.'

He negotiated another bend. By this time we'd slowed down so much that a queue of other vehicles was forming behind us. He didn't speak until we'd joined the tail end of another queue, waiting to turn in at the gates of Marie's villa. Then he turned round to me, holding the reins in the crook of his elbow.

'Well, Miss Bray?'

'Well what, Mr Estevan?'

'Aren't you going to ask me what I was doing between eight and ten o'clock last Wednesday night?'

'I'd like to ask a lot of people that.'

'Who, for instance?'

Sidney Greenbow, I thought. Also Lord Beverley. Marie de la Tourelle. Bobbie Fieldfare and Rose Mills. And, yes, Jules Estevan.

'Very well, you for instance.'

'This is a new experience. I have never been asked to supply an alibi before. I must admit that I find it banal.'

'Banal?'

'To have so little that's interesting to offer.' He raised his right hand. 'I, Jules Estevan, do solemnly swear that I spent the hours between seven o'clock and midnight last Wednesday insulting a friend about his poetry and drinking too much absinthe.'

'That's a very long insult, Mr Estevan.'

171

'They were very bad poems, Miss Bray.'

Since we'd begun on this, I was determined to go through with it, although Jules had made no attempt to lower his voice and we were attracting curious looks from carriages in front and behind.

'I suppose your friend could confirm that?'

'I very much doubt it. His memory is poor at the best of times, and he drank much more than I did. You should have given me some notice and I'd have worked out a much more interesting alibi for you.'

I should, I suppose, have asked for the friend's name and address, but knew it would be pointless. One drunken poet hardly amounted to a convincing alibi, and Jules had not intended that it should. The carriage in front of us moved forward and at last we turned in at the Villa des Lilas.

Up until then, I'd only seen Marie at her working address, the Hôtel des Empereurs, and although that had seemed luxurious to me it was nothing in comparison with the villa. Villa, in any case, was a deceptive word. I'd imagined a modest little place on the shore. This was a three-storey house on the cliff top, with a columned porch and a terrace looking out to sea with rows of statues, orange trees in pots and banks of white lilies that must have been nursed into flower in hothouses, attracting clouds of moths. The whole thing was lit by flaring torches positioned at intervals along the terrace, and by each torch a boy crouched, dressed in turban, loin cloth and bolero, waiting to renew it when it burned down. More torches on either side of the porch lit the wide gravel sweep where the guests were descending from carriages in costumes that suggested fashionable Biarritz took a liberal view of the ancient world. Noise and music from inside the house showed that the party was already in progress. A groom dressed as an ancient Gaul took charge of our gig, and I let Jules guide me towards the steps, wondering more and more what I was doing there. The moment we were inside the hall a Greek slave stepped forward with what turned out to be glasses of excellent champagne and, without reception or introduction, we were part of the throng.

I took a grateful gulp of the champagne and looked round. On my right, a Pharaoh was chatting to a plump man I recognised as a leading French statesman, quite soberly dressed in a toga and laurel wreath. On my left, a vestal virgin who'd taken possession of a whole bottle of champagne was having a violent argument in Spanish with a man who could only be Nero. Around the room I saw at least six other men who could only be Nero, several with violins. I mentioned this to Jules.

'That's the beauty of the classics,' he said.

'There are sufficient rôles for men who are fat and ugly, whereas all the women are beautiful. For Marie's line, nothing could be more suitable.'

The reminder of the source of all this splendour came as a jolt to me. In spite of Topaz's fortune, I hadn't realised how profitable her way of life could be.

'And all this is Marie's?'

He nodded. 'Given to her, so the story goes, in return for one night of her company by a man from Chicago who made his fortune in pork pies.'

I looked at the marble columns, the silk hangings, the pictures on the walls.

'Just one night?'

'So it's said.'

'Would a night with Marie be so very different from a night with any other woman?'

I'd asked in a simple spirit of inquiry, but Jules' rare shout of laughter brought heads turning towards us.

'Really, Miss Bray, blasphemy in the temple. Ask questions like that, and what would become of it all?'

'Vanish, like a castle in a fairy tale?'

'Something like it. Don't you see, every man who goes to bed with Marie is going to bed with that story? If he hears that somebody else has paid so much, then naturally the thing paid for must be desirable,

174

and with every fortune spent on her, the more desirable she becomes.'

'I see that my studies in economics have been sadly lacking.'

'Then I'm glad to be able to contribute to them.'

But his attention had begun to wander round the room. There were other young men there, good-looking and dressed very much like Jules in tunics, rich-coloured cloaks and sandals laced to the knee. One of them caught Jules' eye and smiled.

I said: 'I'm monopolising you. You must want to talk to your friends. Besides, I must find Mademoiselle de la Tourelle and thank her for letting me come.'

I can see now that this was an outbreak of London manners, quite unsuited to the party.

Jules smiled. 'She's over there.'

A little dais had been built in one corner of the room, surrounded by flowers with shallow steps leading up to it. An ivory-coloured divan was set on the dais with huge ivory and gold cushions round it and on the divan Marie was holding court in best classical style, with favoured guests on the cushions around her. As I came nearer I was taken aback, as I'd been at our first meeting, by the sheer beauty of the woman. In the vortex of other people's bright colours, she was dressed very simply in a white, high-waisted gown in the new style, not a jewel about her, long hair coiled up in a simple chignon, her feet bare. She was saying little, listening to the people on the cushions, smiling occasionally. I stopped at the foot of the steps, knowing I'd be quite out of place if I went further. I'd as soon as exchanged social platitudes with the goddess Athene. I had a crazy vision of sitting down on one of the huge cushions, asking her if she'd be kind enough to tell me what she was doing between eight o'clock and one o'clock on Wednesday night. She'd had supper with her impresario, that much I knew from Lord Beverley, but supper doesn't take all night. Then I thought of the knight of the pork pies and reflected that it might after all.

I was glad none of the people sitting respectfully around her could read my mind. There was the designer, Poiret, on one of the cushions, an Italian tenor on another, but to my surprise there were as many women around her as men. One girl, with a bright, malicious face and a tangle of brown curls was telling a story in French, with much gesticulating and laughter. Among the listeners I was caught by one young man in a saffron-coloured tunic with a wreath tilted over his forehead. All the time the story was going on, he didn't take his eyes off Marie, watching for her reaction, laughing when she laughed.

When the story was finished Marie put a

question to him, asking him in French if he thought her performance would be a success in London. He blushed and stumbled in replying and she shrugged apologetically and repeated the question in English. The voice that answered her confirmed the suspicions that had been forming in my mind for the last few minutes.

'The English are a very unoriginal people. They like to know that something is approved of everywhere else, before...'

She couldn't help making a public speech of it. Bobbie Fieldfare.

I'd known she'd be at the party, but the surprise was to find her already one of Marie's inner circle. I remembered what Lord Beverley had said about Marie's personal preferences and felt suddenly angry. Bobbie's extreme views might be an embarrassment to the suffrage movement, but at least I'd given her credit for being totally committed to it. Now I began to suspect that she was a mere sensation seeker who'd take up any cause for the novelty and self-dramatisation of it. It was a disappointment and another worry too, because although Bobbie Fieldfare's private life was no concern of mine, I owed it to her mother to protect her from unnecessary scandal. But in one sense at least it made my work easier. Bobbie occupied with Marie's little circle would have less time and energy

177

for stalking David Chester with the Fieldfare family pistol.

I turned away before Marie or Bobbie noticed me, making for the terrace and fresh air. On my way out I noticed for the first time among the crowd the man I came to think of as the baggy satyr.

In general, there were enough satyrs at the party to equip a fair sized forest, most of them lissom young men in masks and clinging tights with goatskins belted across their chests. My satyr was not at all lissom and his face under the half mask looked hot and heavy, his neck red. His legs were covered in shaggy pantaloons that might have come from the bottom half of a pantomime bear and a kind of Russian blouse enveloped his chest. The first time I noticed him I thought of him only as a curiosity, wondering if one of the guests had had the wit to come as a satyr in middle age.

It was cool on the terrace, and quiet enough to hear the waves thudding on to the Plage des Basques a long way below. I had it to myself except for the boys with the torches and a giggling couple at the far end where it shaded away into darkness. I sat on a stone bench by an orange tree, trying to get my ideas in order.

'Miss Bray. Miss Bray, may I talk to you?'

I nearly jumped out of my skin. The voice had come whispering up at me from the darkness below the terrace.

178

'Who's that?'

'Rose Mills.'

I stretched out a hand to help her climb up. When she came into the torchlight it was a relief to see that Rose at least was conventionally dressed in blouse, jacket and skirt.

'What's happening? Is Bobbie here?'

She was panting from the scramble and from nervousness.

'At present, she's dressed up as Alcibiades, having a cosy talk with La Pucelle.'

It was cruel to take my annoyance out on Rose. I knew that as soon as I saw the look on her face.

'Oh,' she said, as if I'd touched a bruise. Then, hesitantly: 'It's a funny sort of party, isn't it?'

'It is. Come and sit down. You look tired.'

Her skirt was covered in dust and the toes of her boots were scuffed.

'Have you walked up from the town?'

'Yes.'

She plumped down on the bench beside me. Her tiredness and confusion were something else to be charged to Bobbie's account, when I eventually told that young woman what I thought of her.

'Did you want to see Bobbie?'

'Yes. I knew she was coming here, then I thought...'

I waited for her to go on, but she didn't.

179

'You thought she might be having another try at David Chester?' She nodded. 'Well, you needn't worry. He's playing bridge back at his hotel.'

'Then what's Bobbie doing here?'

'I wish I knew. Listen, why don't you let me take you back to your lodgings? You can talk to her in the morning.'

I thought if necessary I'd commandeer Jules' gig. But Rose shook her head.

'Very well then, I'll try to bring her out to you later.'

The idea of Rose in her scuffed boots hunting Bobbie through that butterfly crowd was too pathetic to be borne. We sat there for a while among the moths and the scent of lilies.

'Rose, this matter of Topaz Brown's legacy to us. Bobbie must have telegraphed Emmeline Pankhurst quite soon after she died.'

'Oh yes. Bobbie knew it was important. She said we must do it before the family arrived.'

'That was sensible. But how did Bobbie know about it?'

She stared. 'Didn't everyone know?'

'When did Bobbie first tell you about the legacy?'

'As soon as she heard she was dead.'

'After she was dead? You're quite sure about that?'

'Of course.'

'Did you have the impression that Bobbie might have known about it while Topaz was still alive?'

'How could she?'

Rose had no contact with fashionable society in Biarritz that, by Jules' account, was talking about Topaz's will almost before the ink was dry on it. On the other hand, Lady Fieldfare's daughter could dodge in and out of it as she pleased. I thought Rose was telling me the truth as far as she knew it.

'You share a room with Bobbie, don't you? Has she been sleeping badly?'

I could feel Rose's tension increasing.

'Why?'

'I was speaking to a Dr Campbell. He happened to mention that Bobbie had been to him complaining of sleeplessness.'

'I don't think so.'

'Don't think she has trouble sleeping, you mean?'

'I . . . I don't know. She goes out a lot at nights.'

'Without you?'

'Yes.'

'In men's clothes?'

She said nothing, biting the knuckle of her glove.

'I know she does,' I said. 'I've seen her.'

'She . . . she says men can go into places that women can't.'

181

'I don't doubt it. Does she ever tell you where she's been?'

'I don't ask. She's collecting information.'

'What for?'

No answer. Her lips were pressed hard together.

'Rose, I know what she's planning. I've told her what I think about it.'

'Why do you ask me, then?'

It was a groan of confusion and suppressed anger. I wondered whether I should tell her that I knew Bobbie had been walking up and down outside Topaz's door on the night she died, and decided against it.

'Rose, leave her to it. Stay with Tansy, she needs you. Take her back to England. I'll look after Bobbie.'

One way or the other, I thought.

'No.'

I could recognise determination when I saw it, however misplaced. It was one thing she had in common with her sister.

'Upon your own head be it.'

A torch flared and guttered. A boy moved to replace it.

Rose said, as if most of our conversation hadn't happened: 'So will you tell her I'm here?'

I sighed. 'If I can. We'd better find somewhere else for you to wait. That looks like a summerhouse down there.'

As I walked with her down the steps into

the dark garden she stopped suddenly, like a horse shying.

'What was that?'

'Where?'

'By the bush.'

I looked where she was pointing just in time to see a figure coming out of a bush and into a circle of torchlight. It stood for a moment, masked face questing, saw us and knew that it had been seen, scurried up the steps and away.

'What on earth was that?'

'Only a satyr. You see a lot of them round here.'

But not many with baggy legs and floppy Russian blouses, not many of such stolidity.

Rose said: 'It really is a very strange party.'

I left her on a seat in the summerhouse, went up the steps to the terrace and plunged back into it.

CHAPTER THIRTEEN

The party had moved to a new phase while I'd been away. Marie's dais was untenanted and her guests were drifting through to an inner room, a columned salon with gilt chairs arranged in rows and a gold-curtained platform at the end. Jules appeared and took my arm.

183

'I've kept two seats for us near the front.'

'Where's Bobbie Fieldfare?'

'Gone to change, I suppose.'

'Change?'

'Didn't you know she was taking part?'

I thought with fury of poor Rose waiting outside in the dark, but short of pulling Bobbie out from behind the scenes, there was nothing for it but to wait.

'When will it start?'

'Soon.'

There were sounds of furniture being moved behind the curtains, but the audience was still chatting loudly and more champagne was circulating.

I said: 'What's Marie doing with Bobbie?'

'I thought you might be able to tell me that. Besides, isn't it a case of what Miss Fieldfare's doing with Marie?'

'Is that why you brought me here, to ask that?'

'It did occur to me that she might be trying to convert Marie to your cause. It could become a regular source of income for you. All over Europe *les grandes horizontales* rise up and pay for votes.'

Before I could reply to that, there was a hush in the audience and a grave, portly man stepped out between the curtains. Marie's American impresario.

'Ladies and gentlemen, we are privileged to present Marie de la Tourelle in a series of

184

classical interludes.'

He repeated it in French, there was a scattering of applause and a group of musicians struck up on flutes and Spanish guitars. The curtains swung back to reveal Marie in a glistening silver robe and an expression suggesting the onset of migraine. One of the turbanned boys ran on and crouched at the side of the platform, carrying a placard helpfully inscribed: *Antigone*.

Anybody who has ever been trapped in the kind of country house weekend where charades are performed would have found the next hour or so all too familiar, except you're allowed to laugh at charades. For Marie's classical interludes a silence descended, in spite of the fancy dress and the amount of champagne consumed, that showed we were in the presence of Art. The French, in any case, tend to take mime rather seriously. After Antigone had emoted over her brothers' bodies and taken part in a wordless confrontation with Creon—played by an imported professional actor—she departed decorously to hang herself off-stage, despair denoted by a lowering of silver-painted lids over huge dark eyes and back of wrist pressed to temples, palm outwards. She'd given me a preview of that particular gesture while mourning Topaz's death. The curtains swung together for another bout of furniture carrying, Attic slaves appeared to refill glasses

185

and conversation revived.

'What's your opinion?' Jules asked me.

'Given audiences with a smattering of classical education and absolutely no sense of the ridiculous, she may escape lynching.'

'My dear, it will make her another fortune.'

'I hardly see how.'

'In Paris, they'll go to see her just because she is Marie. They would pay simply to see her walk across the stage. Then she goes on to St Petersburg, where they will naturally worship anything that's been a success in Paris. In New York and Chicago they'll flock to see the scandalous Frenchwoman who captivated the Czar of Russia...'

'Whether she did or not?'

'The Czar will hardly deny it. As for London, if she goes there, she simply needs to start a rumour that her performance is likely to be banned by the Lord Chamberlain, and success is assured.'

The next interlude was the assassination of Julius Caesar which, in this interpretation, seemed to have been inspired and led by Brutus' wife, Portia, played by Marie in a toga of purest white silk that clung to her breasts and swung apart when she moved to reveal a flash of long white thigh and calves laced with gold sandal straps. There was a rustle of a sigh from the audience and I began to revise my opinion of her likely commercial success. The professional mime artist as

Caesar was duly stabbed, after waiting with stoic patience for Portia to finish a series of attitudes with her dagger that showed her bare arms to great advantage. A group of subordinate assassins who'd been loitering in the background surged forwards to join in.

'For heaven's sake.'

Several people looked at me reproachfully, but I couldn't help it. The sight of Bobbie Fieldfare, in toga and laurel wreath as one of the assassins, had been too much. The interlude ended and Jules laughed at the expression on my face.

'Your young friend seems to have a talent for the work. She killed him most convincingly.'

'She's making a fool of herself. I wish I could get her to come away.'

'But there's still Cleopatra to come.'

The next scene was, I think, something to do with Roxane and Alexander the Great, the main historical point being that it gave Marie the chance to appear in bare feet, harem trousers and jewel-studded bolero. I was too worried to notice much more about it, although I was aware of a longer interval than usual between that and the next scene. When Jules told me that Cleopatra would be the finale, I was relieved that the performance at least had an end to it.

A burst of applause, fuelled by goodwill and champagne, greeted the appearance of

Marie on the Nile. She was lying on a golden barge with a backcloth of pyramids and palm trees, two Indian boys wafting peacock feather fans and a white greyhound with a collar of emeralds and rubies at her side. Her costume was mainly gauze and jewels. If audiences would be paying to see Marie de la Tourelle, this was where she'd be giving them value for their money. The actor who'd played Creon, Caesar and Alexander entered as Mark Anthony and departed after a lingering mimed farewell. Marie again performed her mime for despair, signifying presumably the lapse of time and a battle lost, and Bobbie Fieldfare entered in striped robes and a red fez, bearing a snake in a basket.

Although my knowledge of Egyptology is patchy, I'm reasonably certain that Cleopatra did not commit suicide by means of a small reticulated python. Still, even in Biarritz asps are presumably hard to come by and the audience was in no mood to be critical. There were gasps as Marie took the snake from the basket and draped it carefully round her neck, keeping a firm grip behind its head. Even Jules gasped. But his gasp came a second later than the rest. It wasn't the snake that had surprised him.

'That opal on her wrist.'

Either the surprise was genuine, or Jules was a better actor than any I'd seen on stage.

'Which wrist?'

She was smothered in amazing jewels. I couldn't see that one was any more remarkable than the others.

'The one holding the snake's head. That's why I noticed.'

'Noticed what?'

'I'll tell you afterwards.'

He was tense with excitement, sitting forward on the edge of his seat. Anybody watching would have thought he was carried away by Marie's performance. I could see the jewel he meant, a fire opal in a rather heavy setting, but still couldn't understand why it was anything to cause excitement. The audience held its breath. Marie, clasping the python's head to her breast, gave a little shudder and fell elegantly on her couch, body arched, head thrown back, white throat extended. The curtains closed and the audience burst into applause and cheers.

Jules turned to me.

'You saw it?'

'Yes, but...'

'I've seen it before, ten days ago. You know where.'

Marie, *sans* python, was taking a curtain call. Around us, people were shouting and blowing kisses.

'It's the one Topaz showed me.'

I stared at him, trying to make sense of it.

'Surely you're mistaken. It must have been one that looked like it.'

189

'I don't think so. I looked at it quite carefully at the time because Topaz was making mysteries about who sent it.'

I remembered that Tansy had said something about a pendant and Topaz being quite excited about it.

'Is it very valuable?'

'No, that was the puzzle. By Topaz's standards, or Marie's, it's hardly more than a trinket and the setting's old-fashioned.'

'Then perhaps Topaz passed it on to Marie.'

'Topaz wouldn't have given as much as a fingernail clipping to Marie. In any case, Marie would never have taken a present from Topaz.'

The audience was beginning to turn itself back into a party. Marie had stepped off the platform and into the salon and people were clustering round her, offering congratulations. I saw Bobbie's red fez among the crowd.

Jules was looking at me, waiting for me to make the next move. I remembered again how insistent he'd been on bringing me there and wondered if I could trust him at all.

'But why should Marie...?'

Why should Marie, who wore a fortune in jewels, take a trinket from her rival?

Jules said, guessing what I was thinking: 'Unless it mattered very much who sent it.'

'I want a closer look.'

I didn't know what game Jules was playing, but if I memorised exactly what the jewel looked like I could ask Tansy if it was the one she'd told me about. I began to push my way through the crowd towards Marie, Jules at my heels. When I got near her, I had to take my place in a queue for a chance of a few words with her.

'We met in less happy circumstances a few days ago. May I say that your performance tonight was quite unlike anything I've ever seen before.'

I spoke in French, because I find it easier to be hypocritical in a foreign language, also because I was aware of Bobbie's cool eyes on me from behind Marie's shoulder. Marie extended her hand graciously, inclined her head, thanked me. I should have resigned my place to the next person in the queue, but decided that English eccentricity would have to account for my lack of manners. I held her hand for a second longer than politeness allowed, pretending to notice the opal for the first time.

'What a very curious and beautiful stone. So appropriate for Cleopatra.'

This, of course, was quite unpardonable, more like the behaviour of a huckster than a guest. I could see Marie's eyes going round the crowd, wondering who'd invited me. Luckily, she decided to be amused.

'You admire it? Just a small thing.'

191

She uncoiled the chain from her wrist and dropped the pendant into my hand.

'Have a look at it.'

Somebody giggled. Bobbie's eyes were cold but I took my time, turning it round in my hand, trying to remember every detail of the jewel and setting for Tansy. When I handed it back to Marie at last she shook her head and smiled.

'No, you must keep it as a souvenir of this evening.'

Open laughter. It was a magnanimous gesture and by tomorrow would undoubtedly be all round the town, how Marie had given a jewel worth several hundred pounds to an odd Englishwoman, for a souvenir. I was going to insist that she should take it back, then remembered that I couldn't let myself be so scrupulous. As I thanked her, Marie looked over her shoulder at Bobbie and gave a little shrug, sharing the joke with her. But Bobbie didn't seem to find it in the least funny. For heaven's sake, did she think I was setting up as a rival for Marie's attention? I left her glaring and withdrew from the group, to find Jules waiting for me.

We walked back through the hall, now empty except for tired waiters and empty bottles.

'If this really is Topaz's pendant, how does Marie come to be in possession of it?'

'It is not I who am the detective, Miss Bray.'

'And yet you made sure I should know about it.'

'I was surprised.'

'It's surely inconceivable...'

'...that Marie should poison Topaz for that jewel you're holding?'

'Isn't it? And she knows there's some connection between Topaz and myself. She saw me in Topaz's rooms and at Topaz's funeral. Either it makes no sense at all or...'

'Or what?'

'Or Marie is an exceptionally cool and determined woman.'

I thought of that surprisingly capable grip behind the python's head.

'She's that in any case,' Jules said.

When we came out to the porch the baggy satyr was waiting, propped up against a pillar behind a tub of lilies. He straightened up when he saw us, but pretended not to be watching.

I said to Jules: 'Could that be something to do with you?'

Jules apparently noticed him for the first time.

'Good heavens no. Do you suppose it's somebody's pet?'

'Hound more like.'

'You're fond of animals, aren't you? Why don't you wait here and make friends with it while I go and find our gig?'

193

It was only at that point I remembered Rose, presumably still waiting patiently in the summerhouse.

'Mr Estevan, I'm sorry, there's something I must do here before we go. If you'd be kind enough to wait for ten minutes or so, there's somebody who might be grateful for a seat in the gig.'

'Any friend of yours, Miss Bray...'

'But if I'm not back in ten minutes, please go on and don't wait for me. I'll make my own way back.'

My idea was to persuade Rose to come away without waiting to see Bobbie, but she might prove stubborn.

'And if you can do something to distract that satyr while I'm going, I should be very grateful.'

'What a complicated life you lead. I'll do my best to keep the creature in conversation, if it talks, that is.'

'I think you may find it talks English.'

I ran across the terrace and down the steps to the garden. It was a fine night, but moonless, and it took me some time to find the summerhouse again.

'Rose?'

There was a stirring inside and a dark shape came out to meet me. When I put a hand on Rose's arm I could feel her muscles stiff, through cold or anxiety.

'What's happening? Where's Bobbie?'

'Still inside, rather occupied. Why not come back with me? You'll see her tomorrow.'

'No, I want to see her tonight.'

'Can't I take a message to her?'

The friendship between Marie and Bobbie, the matter of the pendant, made me determined to keep Rose away from them if possible.

'No.'

The refusal was flat to the point of rudeness.

'Rose, whatever you're doing, I don't advise doing it here. That man you saw in the bushes in fancy dress—I've reason to think he's a secret policeman.'

She jumped. 'Where is he?'

'A few minutes ago he was waiting by the front door. You won't get in to see Bobbie without passing him and she can't get out.'

She was standing only a few feet away from me, and I could feel her tension and suspicion.

'There must be a back door.'

'With servants all over the place.' I put my hand on her arm again, tried gently to push her towards the terrace. 'Jules will drive us back to town, then we'll both go and see Bobbie in the morning.'

'No!'

She pulled away from me and went running off through the dark towards the side of the house. I was about to follow her until I heard a thud and a cracking of twigs, followed by heavier steps running in the direction that Rose had gone. The silly girl had managed to get the baggy satyr on her track. I'm afraid my reaction was purely instinctive. If one of your colleagues is being pursued by a policeman, in whatever disguise and for whatever reason, then naturally you do all in your power to obstruct him.

I shouted, 'Here,' and began running as noisily as I could in the direction at right angles to the one Rose had taken, away from the house and towards the cliff. My footsteps made a satisfactory crunch on a gravel path and I was aware at once that the satyr's footsteps had halted. I imagined the shaggy beast confused, not knowing which of us to chase. I shouted again to encourage him and the footsteps began again, this time crunching in my direction. I needed to keep the chase going long enough for Rose to get wherever she was going, so I doubled and twisted among the flower beds, falling once in an explosion of scent among lavender bushes, getting up and running on. I was too clever, perhaps, in my twistings and turnings since the pursuer took a slower but straighter line directly over the flower beds. When I could hear his panting breath as well as the heavy feet I knew I'd let him get too close.

Nymphs, when pursued by satyrs, have

saved themselves by turning into trees. I did the next best thing and climbed one, a spreading magnolia in fine white bloom, just before he arrived on the scene. A rustic bench surrounding it gave me the foothold I needed to get up into its branches and I sat there hidden among the blossoms while the baulked beast quested in the flower beds. He was panting heavily by then, and sighing to himself, and I think his heart wasn't in it. After a while he shambled away and, quite comfortable on my branch, I decided to stay there for half an hour or so until he was well away, then find my way back to town by some means and show Tansy the opal pendant. When I climbed the magnolia I'd hung it round my neck for safety. I let it stay there and passed the time composing mentally the letter I'd never have the heart to send to Mrs Pankhurst:

Dear Emmeline,
In pursuance of your instructions to avoid scandal, I should mention that I have just been pursued by a satyr through a garden owned by a wealthy courtesan, who appears to be much attracted towards one of the young enthusiasts of our cause. I have achieved nothing so far towards ensuring the smooth transition to us of Topaz Brown's legacy, but I have acquired a pendant with a large opal, a set of underwear with ribbon and net trims and

*a kilo of cooked fish, since disposed of. This
afternoon I visited the circus. It is now
midnight and I am sitting in a magnolia tree.
Hoping this finds you as it leaves me.*
                    Yours,
                    Nell Bray

CHAPTER FOURTEEN

I'd been in the tree for nearly half an hour
and the night was turning too cold for
comfort when I heard more steps coming
down the gravel path. They weren't heavy
enough for the satyr so I thought it might be
Rose coming back to look for me and was
about to call out. Then I saw a glow of light
and heard a voice I recognised, pitched
quietly but quite clear.

'Won't they wonder where you are?'

I couldn't hear the reply. It was another
woman's voice, but not Rose's. The light
came nearer and I saw it was one of the
torches that had been used to light the
terrace, guttering towards its end now, but
still enough to show Bobbie's face above it
and the other woman walking beside her. It
was Marie, in a cloak of black sable that
glistened in the torchlight, high collar turned
up at the back to frame her white face.
Bobbie too had wrapped herself in a

black cloak, though not of fur, and had at least discarded the fez. They came on down the path, in no hurry.

'Yes, a magnolia. There's a seat round it. Shall we sit down?'

They settled themselves directly underneath me and Bobbie wedged the torch into the ground. If she'd shined it upwards into the branches they could hardly have failed to see me and the explanation would have been complicated. Luckily, they were absorbed in something else.

'You are quite determined on this?' Marie's voice.

'Quite. You too?'

'I've given you my word.'

'Seriously though, not acting? Not a gesture?'

'You think I only make gestures?'

'I think you take decisions impulsively.' That from Bobbie, of all people.

'Why not, if the impulse is the right one?'

'It is.'

'Well then.'

Silence for a while. The torch died down to no more than a glow and I could only see them in outline. I was becoming cramped on my branch but daren't move a muscle. Then Bobbie's voice again:

'It's desperately important that you shouldn't change your mind at the last minute. I've risked more than I should have done in telling you about it.'

'You think you could have done it if I didn't know about it?'

'Without your knowing beforehand, yes. But it's easier this way.'

'And better?'

'I hope so.'

I could have groaned from annoyance and disappointment. I'd hoped at least that Bobbie's sudden interest in Marie would distract her from plotting assassination. It looked as if the reverse had happened and she'd drawn Marie into the plot, though surely even Bobbie could see what a disastrous ally she'd make.

'But it will be difficult for you,' Marie said.

'I've been practising at home.'

She had too. That was what she said to Rose when she first produced the pistol.

'It's surely a job for a professional.'

'Not if you choose your position carefully and your hand is steady. Besides, I could hardly hire a professional, could I?'

'That's true.'

'We must work out the distance in advance, then I shall be relying on you to keep him still when it matters.'

'There are times when a man stays still,' said Marie.

After this pronouncement there was another silence, then Marie, in spite of her sables, said she was cold.

'Do you want to go back to the house?'

'Yes. Most of them will have gone now.'

'And I must go soon.'

They stood up and Bobbie took the stub of the torch. It threw a red glow round their silhouettes as they walked away. I heard Bobbie say:

'Why did you give the pendant to Nell Bray?'

'An impulse. You don't mind?'

'I wish you hadn't, but it's done now.'

'She's an important woman in your cause, isn't she? Does she know what you're planning?'

'She disapproves.'

I couldn't hear if Marie said anything to that, because they were too far away. I had to suppress the urge to jump down, run after them and argue some sense into them. They were beyond rational argument. How and when Bobbie had won Marie to the cause of women's suffrage I'd have liked to discover. Or perhaps Marie simply saw it as an extension of her classical attitudes, heroic assassination followed by consequences no more serious than the lowering of the curtain and roars of applause. She'd probably ask

201

Poiret to design her something to wear to the guillotine. I gave them a quarter of an hour's start, then got down and spent a little time looking for Rose. I wasted no time going towards the cliff top, because there was no reason why she should be there, and kept to the paths between the magnolia tree and the terrace. There was no sign of her or of anybody else, so after a while I decided that she must have despaired of trying to speak to Bobbie and gone back down to Biarritz. It was time for me to do the same, and with all the cars and carriages long gone there was nothing for it but to walk.

The trek down the empty road with nothing but the sound of the sea for company seemed the most peaceful time I'd had for days and should have been a chance to sort out my ideas. I found, though, that they defied sorting. According to Jules, all the people who mattered in Biarritz had known about Topaz's will within hours of her making it. Bobbie, with her connections, would be well placed to hear gossip. Rose, as Tansy's sister, would also have been well placed to find out the details of Topaz's ménage. Since Topaz's death, Bobbie seemed to have distanced herself from Rose, and Rose was half distracted with worry. It began to cohere into a picture that my mind was very reluctant to develop.

But then my hand went to the pendant round my neck, and that started me on another track. Why should such an unimportant jewel be first in Topaz's hands, then on the wrist of her greatest rival? Surely nobody would kill Topaz for the possession of it. But then, that brought me back to the question of who had sent it to Topaz in the first place. As for Marie, I'd just seen her sitting in her furs under her magnolia tree, talking calmly about a man's death as if it were a piece of stage management. Then again, there was the matter of Topaz's wine and fish invitation, and the cheap new underwear. I couldn't see how any plot of Bobbie's or Marie's could have included those. They seemed rather to point towards Topaz's apprentice days, her music hall past, Sidney Greenbow and his horses. Or to Jules Estevan, her ally in practical jokes. Jules had been intent on taking me to Marie's soirée, and I still didn't know why.

By two o'clock in the morning I was back in the town. It was as quiet as a deserted stage setting, too early for even the earliest workers to be about their business, too late for the most determined pleasure-seeker. Only here and there, as I walked past the seafront hotels, I could see the occasional lighted window. There's something about one lighted window in an otherwise dark building that teases the imagination. I pictured nocturnal gamblers crouching over their cards, sleepless lovers writing letters, nurses sitting by the beds of invalids. Behind one of the windows Mrs Chester, her head swimming from the bridge game, was probably watching over the sleep of her daughter.

It was no more than three hours to dawn, and though I was physically tired I knew that my brain wasn't ready for sleep. I found myself walking down the side road by Topaz's hotel, past the lamp on the corner along to her dark private doorway. There was nobody to hear me. At this hour, even Demi would be curled up on the steps of the boiler room, half an ear open for the sound of the early vegetable carts rumbling in from the country. I turned and walked back to the front of the hotel, looking up from force of habit to Topaz's tower. To my surprise I saw a light, glowing through the curtains of the room I thought was her salon. Until then, I'd forgotten Tansy's appearance at my hotel. It struck me that if she was awake too then I might as well go up then and let her rage at me. The doors of the hotel were closed but the night porter appeared as soon as I rang the bell. It took some persuasion and quite a large tip to convince him that my friend Tansy would be glad to see me at that hour in the morning and I felt his eyes on my back as I walked towards the lift. I turned round.

'What time at night do you lock the doors?'

'One o'clock, madam, until six in the morning.'

So if the other night porters were as vigilant as this one, nobody could have gone up to or down from Topaz's room by the hotel foyer between one and six in the morning without being observed.

I got out of the lift into the carpeted, softly lighted corridor that led to Topaz's suite. On the way up it had occurred to me that I might find Rose there, and that was why the lights were still on. Puzzled by Bobbie's behaviour, scared by the satyr, perhaps from old habit she'd run to her elder sister. I hoped so at least. I knocked softly on the door.

'Who's there?'

Tansy's voice, sharp and aggressive.

'Nell Bray. May I come in?'

'You'll have to wait.'

I waited for several minutes. From inside came the swishing sound of furniture being dragged over carpet, then at last the door opened a few inches and Tansy's face appeared, pale and drawn from lack of sleep.

'I'm sorry you've had to wait, but you

can't blame me, not after what's been going on.'

She was fully dressed in her black. A chest of drawers that had evidently been pushed up against the door had been dragged back just enough to let me in and, incongruously, a rolled-up parasol with an ebony handle was propped against the wall.

'What's this for, Tansy?'

'It was the nearest thing I could find to a weapon.'

'Weapon? Is Rose with you?'

She shook her head.

'What did you want a weapon for?'

'After what happened this afternoon. I went to your hotel to try and tell you, but you weren't there and I couldn't make that Frenchwoman understand anything. I didn't know what to do.'

I took her gently by the arm and guided her over to a chair.

'Tansy, get your breath and tell me what happened.'

Her hands were locked together in her lap, her eyes fixed on me in a glare that I was coming to realise had more to do with anxiety than hostility.

'What was it that happened this afternoon?'

'Somebody tried to come up in the lift.'

Her voice was a creaking whisper and her eyes tried to hypnotise me into sharing her fear. At first I didn't understand. It was a hotel after all. People were coming and going all the time. Then the significance of it hit me.

'Topaz's own lift, you mean? The private lift?'

'That's right.' A grim nod from Tansy. She was satisfied now.

'But there's only one way into that lift, isn't there?'

'That's right. The side door. And the side door was locked.'

I wouldn't give in to her fear without a struggle.

'Are you quite sure of that, Tansy? You might have left it unlocked accidentally.'

'No. It was locked and before you ask, my key's been in my pocket the whole time.'

'Then how could anybody get into the lift?'

'The one with the key could.'

'Which one with the key?'

'The one that took her key away after they killed her.'

'That's nonsense, Tansy. Even if some-body killed her and took the key, why should he risk coming back more than a week later?'

'Well, if it's nonsense, you tell me who it was in the lift and how they got there.'

There was a kind of grim triumph about

her. I asked her to tell me exactly what had happened.

'It was just after two o'clock. I was in this room, putting some of her hats away in their boxes.'

'On your own?'

'Of course I was. I was standing just there, near where you're sitting, then I heard it, that grinding noise it makes when it's coming up. Then it stopped on the landing out there as usual and I heard somebody open the gates.'

'What did you do?'

'At first I was too flabbergasted to do anything. Then I thought ... you know what silly ideas you get sometimes, when somebody's ...' She looked away.

I said: 'You mean, you imagined it might be Topaz Brown coming back?'

She nodded, shame-faced. 'Then I thought, still silly-like, well, it wouldn't be her, she'd have let me know. Then I started thinking properly again and knew it wasn't her out there, it was the other one.'

'Other one?'

'The one with the key. The one that killed her.'

I was sure that, as usual, she meant Marie, but wouldn't risk another argument with me by saying the name. I asked her what she did next.

'I knew the door to this room was locked

from the inside. I went over to it and I said, "Who's that?" I could hear somebody breathing on the other side, but there was no answer. I said, "Who's that?" again, quite sharp. Then I heard some steps on the carpet outside, then the lift going down. I went running down the stairs after it, but by the time I got to the bottom whoever it was had gone and the door was locked again. I'd still got my key in my pocket, so I unlocked it and looked out in the street, but there wasn't anybody there.'

I said nothing for a while, thinking of Tansy, all seven stone or so of her, flinging herself downstairs ready to tackle a murderer. That is, if I believed her story. Something had happened, there was no doubt of that. Tansy wouldn't barricade herself in for nothing.

'So I thought I'd tell you about it. I went to your hotel and waited, but of course you didn't come.'

'I'm sorry. Did you tell anybody else, the police, the hotel management?'

She shook her head. 'What good would they do?'

She sat there for a while, staring into space, then asked me if I'd like some tea. I said I would. It seemed a good idea to give her something to do and champagne and tiredness had given me a sour thirst. While she busied herself with kettle and spirit lamp I tried to fit this latest news into the scrappy picture and failed. If there was something so damaging among Topaz's possessions, why hadn't the murderer come for it a week ago, instead of waiting until the rooms had been searched by the police and anybody else interested? The pendant round my neck only complicated things. I didn't believe that even Bobbie would have committed burglary to set the finishing touch to Marie's Cleopatra costume.

But when we'd drunk the first cup of tea I took the pendant out from under my dress and showed it to Tansy.

'Do you recognise this?'

Her mouth fell open, and she looked at me as if I'd hit her.

'It's hers. The one that was lost.'

'Whose?'

'Topaz's, of course. The one I told you about. You remember, that last day. I told you she showed it to me and wouldn't say who it came from.'

I handed it to her. She seemed reluctant to touch it at first.

'You're quite sure it's the same one?'

'Of course I'm sure. I remember that flame-coloured streak through it, and that scratch on the side of the mount. I couldn't understand why she was so fascinated with it. She had better stones on the back of her hairbrush.'

210

'She was fascinated with it?'

'Well, amused more like.'

'But pleased?'

'I'd say so.'

She sat there for a while, staring at the pendant, then looked at me sharply.

'How did you come by it?'

'I can't tell you that, Tansy.'

If I'd admitted it had been round Marie's wrist, Tansy would have rushed straight out to attack her with her bare hands.

'Why not? Why are you keeping things from me?'

'I can't tell you at the moment. In time I hope to be able to, but not now.'

'It's not yours. It's staying here with all her other things.'

It was a questionable point whether it was mine or not.

'It's evidence, Tansy. I'll keep it safe, I promise you.'

'Evidence of what?'

'I'm not sure yet.'

I took it from her gently. When it left her hands, her face crumpled and she started crying.

'All her nice things. They'll take away all her nice things and there's nothing I can do about it.'

I crouched down beside her and put my arm round her rigid shoulders. Tansy was lonely and confused. Somewhere out there

Rose too was lonely and confused, perhaps worse. The two sisters had never needed each other more but weren't even on speaking terms. I told Tansy that she must keep her spirits up, that Rose might be needing her. She shook her head.

'She's got her other friends. She doesn't need me any more.'

'Those friends might not be good for her.'

'Of course they're no good for her. I knew that. It was you that encouraged her.'

'Tansy, don't let's argue about that. Just promise me that if Rose comes to you for help, you won't turn her away.'

'She won't come to me.'

She was as stubborn in her grief as in everything else. I tried to calm her, made more tea. I suggested that if she was nervous about being in Topaz's suite on her own after the latest events she should go and stay with her friend Janet for a few days. She wouldn't consider it. She was the guardian of Topaz's things and was no more to be moved than a dog from its master's grave.

It was getting light outside by the time I left. I walked back to my hotel, where I found the proprietress up and about, inclined to be censorious of my return at daylight, still in my best party dress. I slept for a couple of hours, then revived myself with a cold splash in the hip bath, a pot of piping hot coffee and some croissants and considered what to do next. I decided to give myself one more day. If, by evening, things looked as black against Bobbie as they did at the moment, I had no right to delay any longer.

By nine o'clock I was back in Jules Estevan's living room. I was glad to find him up so early, and told him so.

'I didn't go to bed. Sleep is simply another addiction.'

He looked pale, but then he always did. He was wearing his black dressing gown again. The china head on the tailor's dummy had gained a bay wreath since I last saw it.

'You found your way back safely last night, Miss Bray? I waited for a while, then decided you'd made other arrangements.'

'Mr Estevan, why did you take me to Marie's party?'

'Did you dislike it so very much? I thought you might enjoy it.'

'That's beside the point. You wanted me to see something, didn't you? Was it Bobbie and Marie together, or was it Marie with Topaz's pendant?'

'I assure you, that pendant was as much of a surprise to me as it was to you. Have you shown it to Tansy?'

'Yes. She identifies it. So if it wasn't the

pendant, you wanted to make sure I knew about Bobbie and Marie. Do you know what those two are planning?'

He leaned back on his white couch, blowing out the smoke from a long black cigarette.

'Do you know what they're planning, Miss Bray?'

'I'm afraid so. I knew what Bobbie was trying to do, then I heard her and Marie talking in the garden last night.'

'How careless of them. So what's your opinion of their plan?'

'I'm entirely against it. I dislike the man, but politically it would be quite disastrous for us. I've told Bobbie so. The question is, how can I stop it without getting her arrested?'

'Have you thought of warning the man in question?'

'I'm trying to do something about that, obliquely, but I'm not sure I can manage it in time. Anything more direct would bring Bobbie under suspicion. You know the secret police are following us?'

'Your sylvan friend last night, I suppose.'

He was looking thoughtful. I wondered if he guessed that I had by now even worse fears about Bobbie. I thought he probably did, but hoped that he'd do nothing about it, from indolence if not from discretion.

I said: 'What I can't understand is how Marie can be so suicidally foolish. With Bobbie—well, she comes from a wild family, and at least there's real conviction there, however misdirected, but how in the world can a woman like Marie let herself be involved in this?'

'I suppose it's all good for her legend.'

'Legend!'

'She enjoys grand gestures. You've seen that for yourself.'

I hadn't realised it, but while we'd been talking I'd been walking up and down on the polished floor. I became conscious of it when I saw the quizzical expression on his face.

'Some kind of ceremony, Miss Bray?'

'Ceremony?'

'Ten steps one way, ten steps another.'

'Oh dear. A recent bad habit, I'm afraid.'

'A prison cell habit?'

I nodded.

'Has your mind been on prisons over the last few days? Prisons and law courts?'

I made myself sit down on the pew facing him.

'Why do you say that?'

'It's obvious that something has happened. At first you thought Topaz had killed herself. Then you began wondering if she might have been murdered. Now I

215

think you're sure of it.'

I waited, watching him. When I didn't rise to that bait, he said:

'The question is, do you think you know who killed her? Do you?'

'Know, or think I know?'

I had a feeling that he was closing in, that he, like me, had been piecing together some of Bobbie's activities. That worried me, because I didn't want the initiative to pass to Jules Estevan. I tried to set him off down another trail.

'Topaz had invited somebody that night, I know that. She'd invited him for eight o'clock. An hour before that, she went out on her own for the underwear, the wine and some fish.'

'From which you deduce that the note we found was the invitation itself. I've been thinking about that. I'm sorry, but there are two objections.'

'What?'

'Firstly, what was the note doing under her pillow? Whoever she'd invited wouldn't need to bring it with him.'

'I'd thought of that. He might have regarded it as the I.O.U. that he had to return to her.'

'But which way was the debt? Did she owe somebody for her career, or somebody owe her for his?'

'I'd thought at first that she must be the one in debt. I doubt it now.'

'I doubt it too. But there's a more serious objection than that, you know. Have you got her note here?'

It was still in my bag. I handed it to him.

He read: '*Too late. 8 p.m. Return of I.O.U. for one career.* It's ingenious of you to make out that's an invitation, but why the "Too late"? Is that something one puts on an invitation?'

I hadn't quite forgotten those first two words, but I had pushed them to the back of my mind. Without them, my theory worked so well.

'No, but how do you explain them?'

He shrugged. 'Our first theory. Suicide.'

'But the underwear, the fish?'

'Suicides do strange things.'

He gave the note back to me.

I said: 'I don't believe Topaz killed herself.' I was beginning to sound as stubborn as Tansy.

'In which case, we come back to my question. Who was it, Miss Bray?'

I said I didn't know, that I'd taken up too much of his time. He was as courteous as ever when he showed me out, but since the night's events I'd had the feeling of a threat gathering, and I sensed that Jules might be

217

part of that. He knew as much as I knew, perhaps more.

I wanted very much to believe in the mysterious, probably male, visitor at eight o'clock, so much so that I'd let myself forget one of the facts, and I wasn't grateful to Jules for reminding me of it. 'Too late.' Not too late though to use my brain on it. Assuming that the words didn't mean suicide, taking them at their face value, what had been too late? Then, as I walked along beside the sea, I thought that they might be no more than a reply to another note. Supposing the unknown had tried to fix his own time to see her, but the time had been too late and Topaz had named one more suitable. That would make perfect sense of the note. But if that were the case, then another note must have existed, a first note from the unknown visitor asking to see her at the later time. And if it did exist, then it might still be there among the haphazard piles of correspondence lying around Topaz's hotel suite. When I thought of that, Tansy's story of the person who'd tried to get in took on a new significance. I'd have gone back there and then to search, risking her anger, only there was an engagement I had to keep first. A routine one, I thought. But, as it turned out, what happened there drove the hypothetical note out of my mind. Too late.

CHAPTER FIFTEEN

Several days before, when I'd just arrived and was still giving my mind to the business that had brought me to Biarritz in the first place, I'd made an appointment that morning for another talk with Topaz's solicitor. Although I now had serious doubts that we'd ever be able to claim Topaz's legacy, I kept the appointment and tried to talk as if nothing had changed. I asked if he'd had any response to a telegraph message I'd sent to our office in London.

'Yes, Miss Bray. We heard from your organisation's solicitor this morning. I've already drafted a letter informing him that it may be some time before Miss Brown's estate is settled. Quite informally, I can tell you that the family are contesting her will.'

'The brother?'

'Quite so. He is alleging that Miss Brown could not have been of sound mind when the will was drawn up, in view of the ... um, eccentricity of her bequest to your organisation, and her subsequent suicide.'

He was friendly still but guarded, and I could understand why. If it came to court, as seemed likely, his assessment of Topaz's state of mind would be important evidence.

I said, advancing a cautious foot on to thin ice: 'I suppose the examining magistrate had no doubt that it was suicide.'

'There was no reasonable doubt, was there, even in the absence of a note?'

Topaz's note was still in my bag. Once I'd intended to hand it over to him, but now that seemed a long time ago.

I said: 'Can you tell me if you sent anybody to Topaz Brown's suite the day after she was found dead, asking to go through her papers?'

'No. It will have to be done at some time, of course, but we've taken no steps so far. Why do you ask?'

'A man went to her suite claiming to come from the solicitor's. Middle-aged, thick-set, wearing a black coat and hat.'

He frowned. 'That doesn't sound like anybody we know.'

I think he'd have asked me more about it, but at that point his clerk looked round the door.

'They want you at the consulate, Mr Smith. There's an Englishman drowned and they don't know who it is.'

The solicitor winced at the lack of ceremony.

'I'm in a meeting. I hardly see what I can do that the consul can't. Tell them I'll come down later.'

The youth persisted. 'They want to know if you know whether there were any English visitors holding a fancy dress party last night.'

I felt the air go out of my lungs.

'Fancy dress party?'

Both of them stared at me. I think the clerk hadn't noticed I was there.

The solicitor said: 'Why Miss Bray? Do you know of one?'

I said reluctantly, wishing I'd kept my mouth shut: 'I was a guest at a fancy dress party last night, outside the town. But it wasn't an English party. Anyway, what's that to do with the man who drowned?'

The clerk said: 'Apparently he was wearing some kind of fancy dress.'

The solicitor was giving me a sideways look.

'Where was your party, Miss Bray?'

'At the Villa des Lilas.'

The clerk whistled. 'That's La Pucelle's place.'

He got a withering look from the solicitor, but I could see they were both wondering what I was doing there, and I didn't blame them.

The solicitor said: 'I don't suppose there's any connection, but they might be grateful for a word with you downstairs at the consulate—if you have time, that is.'

I could hardly refuse. The two of us

221

went downstairs and across a hallway into a large room with several desks in it. The consul raised his eyebrows when I was introduced to him, and I braced myself for yet another remark about bricks. He restrained himself and listened to the solicitor explaining why I was there.

'This party of yours, Miss Bray, was it any particular kind of fancy dress?'

'Yes, classical. Mainly togas and Greek tunics and things of that kind.'

He smiled and relaxed, glancing down at a paper on his desk. 'In that case, we seem to be taking up your time unnecessarily. It looks as if the deceased attended a different party.'

'Why?'

'He was found dressed as some kind of animal.'

The relief I'd felt drained away.

'What kind of animal?'

'It's not entirely clear, but he was probably supposed to be a bear.'

'Oh no.'

I heard the consul shouting to somebody to bring brandy. From tiredness and shock I must have staggered where I was standing. I accepted a chair and asked for a glass of water instead of the brandy, trying to gain time.

The consul said, too gently: 'Did you know somebody dressed as a bear?'

Think, I told myself, think. Don't tell them any more than you need. I spoke slowly, hoping they'd put it down to shock.

'There was a man I noticed. I didn't speak to him, so I don't know if he was English or not. I think he was meant to be a satyr, but he was wearing baggy trousers that looked like a bear's legs.'

The consul glanced down again at his paper.

'What did he look like?'

'He was wearing a half mask, so I couldn't see his face. I noticed he was quite thick-set and didn't move like a young man. He had a plump red neck.'

The consul sat with his elbows on his desk, head between the palms of his hands, looking at me.

'Would you be prepared to come with me to the police station? It may help us to identify him.'

Though it was the last thing I wanted, I could hardly refuse. Nor could I refuse when, after an interview at the police station with the consul present, I was politely asked if I would be kind enough to go to the morgue. In the closed vehicle on the way there I asked the consul:

'Why do they think he was English?'

'There was a label inside his vest.'

'A satyr in a vest, poor man.'

The morgue was a square grey building

on the outskirts of the town, a mile and a world away from the grand hotels. I thought that ten days ago Topaz's body would have been driven from the Hôtel des Empereurs to this same building. An *agent de police* led the way along a tiled corridor with the consul on one side of me and the solicitor on the other. It felt horribly like being back in prison. They'd put the corpse in a side room on its own. When the *agent de police* pulled the sheet back I was conscious of a smell of disinfectant and seawater, of a gaping mouth and round open eyes. He'd lost his mask and the plump face was much as I remembered it from when I'd seen him standing beside the stone angel at Topaz's funeral. He was still wearing the Russian tunic, but they kept the sheet over his legs so I couldn't see if they'd taken off the bear-like trousers.

'When I saw him at the party he was wearing a half mask, and I wasn't close to him. But yes, I believe it's the same man.'

Death has its own claims. I could not then, however much I wanted to, walk away from it. I spent more time at the police station, giving a carefully edited account of my dealings with the man. I said simply that I'd seen him a couple of times at the party, and my last sight of him had been in the garden of the Villa des Lilas a little before midnight. I said nothing about the chase through the garden, or of having seen him on any occasion before the party. I told them truthfully that I hadn't exchanged as much as a word with him, and had no idea what his name was or where he came from. It was late afternoon before we'd got through all that, and the consul insisted on delivering me back to my hotel afterwards. He sat on the seat of the fiacre opposite me, staring at me rather apprehensively.

I said: 'I think Scotland Yard may be able to help you identify him.'

'I'm sure the French police will forward a description to them in due course. They'll check the list of missing persons and...'

'I think it's closer to home than that. I think he was working for Scotland Yard.'

'What?'

'I've reason to believe that man was keeping me under observation for most of my time in Biarritz. I have a certain reputation for my political activities, and I believe Scotland Yard arranged to have me followed.'

That, at least, kept us clear of any reference to Bobbie and Rose.

The consul shifted unhappily in his seat. 'Miss Bray, our police don't work like that. They're not spies.'

I said nothing, but he saw the expression on my face.

'If they suspected you or anybody else of illegal activities on foreign soil, they would properly take the precaution of warning the authorities of that country. They would hardly send a man to follow you across Europe. England has no equivalent of the Czar's secret police, Miss Bray.'

It was a waste of breath to argue. It was his duty to say that, but I sensed his uneasiness.

'All the same, I advise you to send your own description of him to Scotland Yard as soon as possible. It's only fair to his family. Wasn't he carrying anything to identify him?'

'No. But then if a man goes out for the evening dressed in half a bear skin, he could hardly carry a wallet of cards with him.'

'He'd have to carry something, wouldn't he? He'd need his cab fare home if nothing else.'

'Perhaps he lost it when he fell in the sea.'

The French police had established that there was a depressed skull fracture at the back of the man's head, suggesting that he'd fallen and knocked himself unconscious on a rock, though death had been due to drowning. He'd been discovered by fishermen on the Plage des Basques about half way between the Villa des Lilas and the town.

Our fiacre jogged slowly along, slowed by the press of horse and motor traffic taking people back to their hotels for the evening.

'Miss Bray...'

He stopped, red in the face.

'Yes?'

'It ... occurs to me that if you believed the man to be following you, however mistakenly, you might have...'

'Might have what?'

I knew very well what was coming.

'You might have indulged in some kind of ... altercation with him.'

'Meaning that I might have hit him on the head with a brick,' (he winced a little at the word), 'and thrown him in the sea? It's possible that I might have, but I can assure you I did nothing of the kind. I was so anxious to avoid any altercation, as you call it, that I actually climbed a tree to avoid him.'

He closed his eyes, looking pained.

'I'm not sure that we shouldn't have told the French police about this.'

'I should wait until you've consulted Scotland Yard. After all, you don't want a diplomatic incident on your hands, do you?'

I could tell, from the way he looked at me, that I'd won my point. He dropped me

227

at my hotel with undisguised relief.

The moment I arrived the proprietress handed me a note with Bobbie's decisive writing on the envelope. The message said simply: *I must speak to you. Can you meet me at 8 p.m. where we talked the other night?*

I was on the quay by the lobster pots well before that time, watching the fishermen working in the dusk, tidying their boats ready for the morning sailing. Eight o'clock came, then half past. It grew dark, the fishermen went away and there was still no sign of Bobbie.

At a quarter to nine I jumped up, cursed myself for my idiocy and ran full pelt away from the harbour to the main road. I virtually commandeered a cab and told him to drive to the Hôtel d'Angleterre as fast as he could. At the hotel I thrust coins at him, didn't wait for change and rushed up the steps into the foyer, more than half expecting to see police and a stretcher party. Everything looked quite normal, with the sounds of an orchestra playing waltzes in the salon, people in evening dress coming and going, pages standing by the doors. It surely wouldn't have been so calm if somebody had attempted to kill one of their guests.

I went over to the reception desk and asked if Mr Chester was in. The reception clerk consulted a colleague. Yes, he was in the dining room with his wife. Would I care to send in a message? I said I must speak to Mrs Chester and it was urgent. By that point I was so worried that I'd have faced the man himself if need be, but I still hoped to deliver a warning in a way that would not lead back to Bobbie. I'd tell Mrs Chester point blank that there was a threat to her husband's life and she must make him go away at once, at all costs. A page boy departed with a note that I'd scrawled on the hotel paper. I stood with the curious eyes of the reception clerk on me, scrutinising every young man in evening dress in case he turned out to be Bobbie in disguise. Another thought struck me.

'Is Mademoiselle de la Tourelle dining here tonight?'

The clerk regretted that she was not, looking at me even more curiously.

A plump figure in a dress of olive green silk came towards me from the dining room, walking so quickly that she skidded and slithered in her evening slippers on the marble floor.

'Oh, thank goodness it's you. I've been wanting to talk to you, but I forgot to ask your name again, so I . . .'

'My name doesn't matter. It's about your husband. I'm afraid he's in danger, very great danger. You must make him go away at once.'

'Oh I know, I know. This dreadful place. You were quite right about it. I wish we'd never come here. Louisa is no better, no better at all, and now this. I simply do not know where to turn.'

'You knew?'

I was thunderstruck, marvelling at the disorder of her brain, that she could mention an assassination threat to her husband and a child's minor illness in the same breath.

'Yes, I read the letter. But how do you know about it? Are they all talking about it?'

By now some of her confusion was spreading to me. I suggested we should sit down and guided her to a sofa beside a potted palm. Waltz music drifted round us.

'Where's your husband?'

'In the dining room.'

'You say you saw a letter. What letter?'

'From that awful woman. I'd heard about women like her, but I didn't know they allowed them here, or I'd never have come. She's writing to David, actually writing. I can't believe anybody would be so brazen about it.'

If Bobbie had sent David Chester a letter saying she intended to kill him, I thought brazen was a mild word for it.

'She signed it?'

'Quite openly. Marie de la Tourelle, just

230

as if she were respectable.'

'Marie ... Your husband had a letter from Marie de la Tourelle?'

She nodded, eyes full of tears.

'And you saw the letter?'

'I was waiting for a note from the doctor about Louisa's medicine for the journey back. I opened it and ... oh dear.'

'What exactly did it say?'

'I can't tell you. Read it for yourself.'

She produced a small square envelope, I assume from the front of her corset. It was perfumed with a scent I remembered from the soirée. Trust Marie to send a perfumed murder threat. The writing was in a delicate italic hand.

Dear Mr Chester,
I am an admirer of yours and should very much like to meet you. I should be charmed if you could visit me at home at the Villa des Lilas tomorrow evening.
Marie

I stared from Mrs Chester to the note and back again, wondering which of us was going mad.

'But it's just an invitation.'

'Anybody would know what an invitation meant from a woman like that. To send it quite openly to my husband, and for a Sunday evening of all times. If he'd seen it, he'd have been so angry. It was my fault we came...'

'If he'd seen it. You mean he hasn't seen it?'

'Would you put a note like that into your husband's hands? He'd be so angry, so disgusted.'

I felt like laughing out loud from relief. I wondered, light-headedly, if Mrs Chester would be reassured if I told her that the note was simply an attempt on her husband's life rather than his virtue. I could have laughed, too, at the simplicity of the plot. Marie—no doubt suitably rehearsed as Delilah—was to entice the victim to her perfumed garden, then Bobbie would leap out from behind the oleanders with the family pistol. Then the urge to laugh dried up and all my anger against Bobbie returned. But at least I knew now that David Chester was safe for the night.

I said: 'I'd like to keep this letter.'

Her eyes had never left it. It had a fascination for her.

'I could show it to somebody in authority. I'm sure they wouldn't like to think that distinguished visitors were being subjected to this kind of thing.'

Since that kind of thing was precisely what some of the distinguished visitors came for, I wondered if even Mrs Chester would swallow so blatant a lie.

She looked anxious. 'I wouldn't want his name brought into it. Some people might think...'

'Of course not. But you do agree that this woman should be stopped?'

She agreed.

'And perhaps you should say nothing about this to your husband. If you think he might be angry, it would be best not to.'

She shook her head and dabbed at her eyes with a handkerchief, the large handkerchief, lace-edged but serviceable, of the anxious mother.

'Will he wonder what you've been doing out here?'

'I'll say it was the man with Louisa's medicine.'

I watched her pattering back to the dining room and put the letter away in my bag, hardly believing my luck at how Bobbie and Marie had played into my hands. I walked to my pension. There was a figure standing just outside the door, waiting for me.

'Nell Bray, I need to speak to you.'

'Bobbie, what are you doing here? I was waiting for you by the harbour.'

She was at least wearing women's clothes this time. Her face looked older, white and strained.

'I was looking for Rose. That's what I wanted to speak to you about. Since last night, I can't find Rose anywhere.'

'You mean since last night at the villa?'

'No, Rose didn't go to the villa.'

'Yes she did. She was there in the garden, looking for you. I talked to her.'

'She wasn't supposed to be there. What was she doing there?'

I'd never heard Bobbie so anxious.

'She said she had something to give you. She was upset, puzzled. You must expect that if you take up people and drop them.'

'I haven't dropped Rose. She knows that.'

'She didn't seem to know it last night.'

'Where did she go? You surely didn't just leave her there?'

I took a deep breath. 'The last I saw of Rose she was being followed by a secret policeman dressed as a satyr. I managed to draw him off, but I don't know what happened to her after that.'

Bobbie groaned. She looked more tired than I was, but I had no pity for her.

'As I said, I don't know what became of Rose after that, but I do know what became of the secret policeman. He was found knocked on the head and drowned. I saw his body in the morgue.'

I pushed past her into the pension and left her standing there, speechless for once in her life.

CHAPTER SIXTEEN

I woke as it was getting light, knowing that what mattered above all was to find Rose. I knew that she hadn't intended to kill the baggy satyr. He must have followed her down the garden to the cliff top, or somehow persuaded her to go there, and tried to question her about Bobbie or me. I could imagine her fear and anger, the desperate push that sent him staggering backwards over the cliff, her panic when he fell. Whoever's fault it was, it wasn't poor Rose's and she must not suffer for it.

I dressed hurriedly, let myself out and walked the streets and the seafront, trying to think of the places where a poor and frightened girl might take refuge in a rich holiday town. There was nobody but a snoring drunk in the seafront shelters, nobody on the sands apart from two fishermen down by the tideline, digging for bait against a pearl-coloured sky. It was a Sunday morning and soon the bells started to ring for early mass and men and women, respectably dressed in black, emerged from the fishermen's cottages by the harbour. It was still too early for the hotel guests to be up and about. I went inland, around the streets and the square where Tansy and I had gone shopping. The café was open and brown-faced working men sat over bowls of milky coffee and glasses of *marc*, but there was no sign of Rose.

I drank my breakfast coffee at the station buffet as soon as it opened, watched the first train pull out, then went round questioning ticket collectors and porters. I described Rose and asked if they could remember a girl like that leaving on the early train the morning before. The first train to Paris left at six fifty-two and I hoped she might have had the sense to take it and go straight back to England. No, nobody had seen her, either on the early train or later. In any case, I thought, she probably didn't have the four pounds she'd have needed for her ticket. As I was going round the station I kept an eye out for Bobbie in case she'd had the same idea. I was relieved not to see her. I had an account to settle, but that would have to wait until its due time in the evening, and I wanted to find Rose before she did.

Soon after ten o'clock I gave up the station and went to the Hôtel des Empereurs. The staff knew me by then and the man at the reception desk said good morning and nodded me towards the public lift in the foyer. I knocked on the door of Topaz's suite and Tansy's voice, sharper than ever, called: 'Who is it?'

'It's all right. Nell Bray.'

'What do you want this time?'

She was getting worse. She hadn't even opened the door to me.

'Can I have a word with you?'

'What about?'

'Tansy, don't be silly. It won't do any harm to let me in, will it?'

The door opened grudgingly. Tansy's eyes were red-rimmed, and it looked as if she'd slept in her black dress.

'Tansy, have you seen Rose?'

She plumped herself down in a chair, lips pressed together, and turned her head from side to side.

'She's in trouble, isn't she?'

She asked it flatly, as if she'd always known it would happen. I didn't answer.

'And it's all because of you, all the ideas you've been putting into her head. Isn't it enough for you, you've got Topaz's money and all her nice things? You want Rose as well.'

I said, as gently as I could: 'If she comes here, you will get a message to me, won't you? It's important.'

'Why should she come here? You've turned her against me.'

I didn't try to answer that. I stood by the door and she sat there, making no pretence of civility, waiting for me to go. The silence went on for minutes and she didn't move a muscle, then she said: 'Well, what else do you want?'

'I've been thinking about the day before yesterday, when you heard somebody in the lift.'

'Oh yes.'

'Do you think anybody could have been in here before? You remember when we went shopping, you came back and found the window open.'

'I must have just left it open and forgotten about it.'

'You didn't think so at the time.'

She burst out: 'Stop going on at me. What else am I supposed to do for you? All the time you've been nagging at me with questions, not helping me. I'm sick and fed up with it. Get out.'

'Tansy . . .'

I went over and laid what was meant to be a calming hand on her shoulder. She shook it off and drew herself up to her full five foot two, face red and eyes bright.

'Get out. What right have you got to come in here asking me questions? I told you, get out, get out, get out.'

She was shouting and actually pushing at me. It must have looked like an angry bantam trying to see off a heron. I tried to reason with her, but without success. In the end, I walked to the door and left her there in the middle of the room railing at me. As I closed the door behind me I heard her yell: 'And don't come back.'

By early afternoon, with no sign of Rose, I decided reluctantly that it was time to visit the consul again. For all I knew, Rose might already be in a prison cell. I could hardly ask the consul about that outright, but if it had happened I should surely hear something from him. On a Sunday I could not expect to find him at his desk, but my luck was in. As I got to the consulate he was just coming out of the front door with hat and walking cane, set on an afternoon stroll. He invited me to take a turn with him round the garden.

'I was intending to get in touch with you tomorrow, Miss Bray. We had a long telegraph message from Scotland Yard last night about this man of yours.'

'Not my man. Did they know anything about him?'

'Nothing whatsoever. I hope it's not too serious a blow to your self-esteem, but he wasn't following you.'

'I'm quite certain that he was.'

'Not on behalf of Scotland Yard, in any case. They inform me that none of their men is currently in France and they have no interest whatsoever in your movements, provided you keep away from the Prime Minister's windows. In fact, the commissioner hopes you are enjoying your holiday.'

It was precisely the tone of joking

superiority that most annoyed me, but I couldn't afford to be annoyed.

'The description you sent meant nothing to them?'

'Nothing. It fits nobody on their staff, or on their list of missing persons. It seems they are quite unable to help us.'

And yet there was an air of satisfaction about him that hadn't been present the day before. I feared for Rose.

'What about the French police? Have they found out anything more?'

He smiled. 'A little. In fact, they're following up what seems to be quite a promising line of inquiry.'

'What's that?' I tried to sound casual.

'They've found out where his costume came from, or part of it at least. You remember that he was wearing baggy trousers like a bear's legs? When the police dried them out and took a proper look at them, there was a name-tape stitched inside in indelible ink.'

'His name?'

'No, the circus's.'

I stared. 'Circus's?'

'Yes, there's a circus on a field just outside the town. I dare say they belonged to one of the clowns. So this morning the police chief came back to me and asked if I knew of any British subjects working with the circus.'

'And did you?'

I was still trying to sound no more than

politely interested, but my mind leapt at once to Sidney Greenbow.

'As I told him, circus folk are hardly the kind who come and sign the book at the consulate. Still, it answers the question of what he was doing at Mademoiselle Marie's party.'

'Does it?'

'I expect the poor beggar decided to go and mingle and see what he could pick up. I dare say he was behaving shiftily and you jumped to the conclusion that he was following you.'

'Have you asked the people at the circus if they knew him?'

'We leave that kind of thing to the police. I suppose I shall have to see to conveying the remains home sooner or later, if there's anybody at home who wants the poor beggar, that is.'

Remembering what I'd come for, until this latest news had blown me off course, I sympathised with the difficulties of his post and said I was sure he must be kept very busy.

'Up to a point, though to be honest with you there hasn't been a lot happening with us lately. In fact, poor old bear's legs is the most exciting thing we've had for weeks.'

He surely wouldn't be talking so lightly if the police were holding a British girl on a murder charge.

'Have the police any more idea about how

it happened?'

'I shouldn't think so. It seemed to be pretty much an open and shut case of accidental death, apart from the problem of identifying him. Perhaps he'd managed to get hold of a glass of champagne or two and that made him unsteady on his hooves, or paws, or whatever. There was plenty of it around, by most accounts.'

He sounded regretful at not having been invited. Deciding there was no more to be learned from him, I left him to his stroll and, as soon as I'd made sure he wasn't watching me, turned down the road that led to the Champ de Pioche.

It was all I could do to stop myself breaking into a run. I'd been so sure that there were political reasons for following us that I hadn't thought about any others. If I could be wrong about that, then I could be wrong about other things too. It was that hope that sent me hurtling in search of Sidney Greenbow, with no very clear idea of what I'd say when I found him.

The circus field was busier and more purposeful than on my first visit because it was mid-afternoon when I got there, and the first performance began at five. In a far corner I saw four of Sid's white horses trotting round in a circle, their riders in ordinary shirts and breeches. Nobody challenged me as I walked towards them. Sid, on foot in the middle of the circle, didn't notice me at first, intent on the horses and riders.

'Keep his head up. No, don't jerk at his mouth. He's not a bloody seaside donkey. Use your bloody wrist, man.'

I moved closer. He saw me and gestured to me to stay where I was. After a few minutes he sent two of the horses and riders away and made the other two practise part of the sabre fight routine from their finale. Stripped of its brassy music and costumes it was, if anything, even more impressive, as carefully worked out as a ballet. He made them do the same movements several times over, cursing the men when they got it wrong, but never the horses. In the end, grudgingly satisfied, he let them go and walked over to me, wiping his hands on his breeches.

I said: 'Did you know that man who was drowned?'

'Bobsworth? The one the police were asking about this morning?'

'His name was Bobsworth?'

'I don't know what his proper name was. Bobsworth was what our English lads called him.'

I was watching his face carefully and could read nothing on it, not even curiosity. He was polite enough, but his manner would have been the same if I'd been asking about the price of hay.

I asked: 'Was he a friend of yours?'

243

'No. He was just a hanger-on. You get them with circuses.'

'One of your team?'

'Not likely. I wouldn't let just anyone touch the Dons. No, he helped with the tent and the cart driving and so on, a bit of ticket selling. He joined us in Paris in the winter and moved on with us when we came down here.'

I looked hard at him and he stared back, hands on hips, head on one side.

'What's your interest in Bobsworth?'

'He was spying on me. Before that, he might have been spying on Topaz. Do you know anything about that?'

He shook his head. Behind him the two white horses were being led up and down. He turned to call an order to the men with them, and I had the feeling that at least half his attention had been on them all the time.

'You're sure?'

His eyes came back to me. 'Of course I'm sure. You're not accusing me of anything, are you?'

At least I'd stirred up some reaction. 'It's a coincidence, isn't it? You were a friend of Topaz. You work with this man. He spies first on her, then on me.'

'I told you, I never worked with him. He was just one of the rag tag and bobtail. Besides, why should I want anybody to spy on Topaz, or you either, come to that?'

I said: 'Was there anybody here who knew him well?'

'Nobody seemed to like him that much. I suppose Joe was the nearest thing he had to a friend, and even Joe wasn't what you'd call close to him.'

'Could I speak to Joe?'

'He'll be over in the men's van. I'll take you over there, then I'll have to go and get ready.'

He walked with me across the field to a pair of old green-painted railway carriages under a tree in the far corner.

'The police kept him talking half the morning, so he's probably fed up with it all by now. Anyway, he won't be able to talk long because he's got to change for his act.'

There was a babble of voices in several languages inside the first van. Sidney beat on the door with the flat of his hand and yelled for Joe.

'He'll be out in a minute,' he said. 'I'll leave you here. I've got to go and see to Grandee.'

He loped off across the grass, leaving me standing beside the steps to the van. After a few minutes the door opened and a young, lugubrious face looked out. It had red-brown curls, a wide mouth and the expression of a man who hopes for the best but expects the worst.

'Are you Joe?'

'Yes. Who wants me?'

'My name's Nell. I wonder if you can tell me anything about the man they call Bobsworth.'

He blinked several times, very quickly.

'Are you his wife?'

I couldn't help laughing. 'Certainly not. Did he have a wife?'

'I don't know.'

Joe emerged cautiously and shut the door behind him. As he stood at the top of the steps his feet were at the same level as my eyes. He was wearing green socks, with the big toes sticking out. Above them were a pair of moleskin trousers and a Russian tunic, much like the one the baggy satyr had been wearing. He sat down on the steps, curling his feet out of sight behind them.

I said: 'I think I might have known him. I'm not sure.'

He shook his head slowly, apparently bewildered.

'What do you want to know?'

'Whatever you can tell me. For instance, what was he doing before he joined the circus?'

'I don't know. I never asked him. In January, when we were in Paris, one of our men broke a leg. I met Bobsworth in a bar and got talking, the way you do when you meet somebody who speaks English, and it turned out he was down on his luck, so I said why didn't he see if he could pick up a bit of work with us, so he did.'

'Did he talk about his life, where he came from?'

'He didn't talk about anything much, not even when we'd had a drink or two. The more he drank, the quieter he got.'

'Did he have any other friends?'

'Not what you'd call friends. He had this manner, as if he was a bit above the rest of us, if you see what I mean. The lads don't like that.'

'Did he have any friends outside the circus?'

'I don't know. He'd go off by himself sometimes. That was one of the things the lads didn't like about him, going off by himself.'

'When did you last see him?'

Joe said, very promptly: 'Round about midday, last Thursday week.'

'You're sure of that?'

The day Topaz was found dead.

'Yes, I had to work it out for the police this morning. I knew it was a Thursday because that's the day the hay wagons come. We're all supposed to be there to unload them, and he wasn't, then about midday up he comes and says will I see they send on his pay to him, because he's leaving.'

'Did he say where he was going?'

'I didn't ask. We were all annoyed with

him over not helping with the hay, and I thought good riddance. He was pleased with himself, though. He said something had come up, all important and mysterious like, and he was wearing a coat and hat I hadn't seen him in before. Anyway, I said I'd see about sending his pay on, then the shout went up that the soup was ready, so I went off and left him to it.'

'And you didn't see him again?'

'No.'

'Did he take the bear's legs with him when he went?'

'He might have, I suppose. They were kept in a trunk in our van, along with a lot of other things, but we didn't notice they'd gone because we hadn't used them in the act since Christmas. Seems a funny thing to take.'

'Were they yours?'

'Yes. I was the bear. I'm not what you'd call a proper clown, you see. Haven't got the training for it. I run round a bit in various costumes and fall over when they hit me.'

Somebody shouted from inside the van. Joe uncurled his feet and stood up.

'I've got to go and finish getting dressed. I'm sorry I couldn't help you more, Miss, but nobody knew much about Bobsworth.'

'You've been very helpful. Just one more thing: you said he wanted you to have his pay sent on. Where were you supposed to send it?'

The surprise on his face showed the French police hadn't asked him that question. Perhaps they'd been handicapped by having to talk through an interpreter.

'He gave me this piece of paper. To be honest with you, I'd forgotten all about it till you asked. I meant to do something about it, only . . .'

'Have you still got it?'

'Wait there.'

He bolted back into the van and emerged clutching a grey, much-folded piece of paper.

'May I keep this?'

'If you want to. He won't be needing his pay where he's gone, poor blighter.'

I thanked him. He wished me good afternoon and shot back up the steps. From the laughter as he closed the door behind him I guessed that poor Joe was being teased about his assignation with an older woman. I unfolded the paper. The writing on it, in block capitals, was surprisingly neat and even for a circus labourer:

MR ROBERT WORTH
C/O HOTEL COQ D'OR,
RUE DES NAUFRAGES, BIARRITZ.

I managed to seize a cab just outside the circus field, as it was delivering a group of children and their parents. Rue des Naufrages, I told the driver, and as quickly as possible.

The Hôtel Coq d'Or turned out to be a mean little hostel in a street not far from the old harbour. Paint was flaking from door and window frames, cracked glass in an upstairs window was held together with paste and brown paper. On the way, I'd prepared a story about being related to Mr Worth, but I could have saved my time. All the drunken proprietor wanted was money. I passed over a fistful of coins and received a mumbled word, '*Huit*,' and a key attached to a block of wood by a dirty string. His lack of curiosity showed that the police had not been there before me.

Number eight was on the second floor, near the top of the stairs. I put the key in the lock and hesitated, remembering suddenly that it had last been turned by a man who was now lying in the morgue. I told myself not to be a fool, turned the key and pushed the door open.

The blind was up, so he'd left by daylight. The sun came in weakly through a dirty window but the room itself was surprisingly tidy. I thought at first that I was too late and that somebody had already come in to clear it, but it was simply that Robert Worth had been an orderly man. The bed, with its yellowed sheet and thin grey blanket, was as neatly made as one in a hospital, or a prison. A tweed jacket, old but well brushed, hung across the back of the room's one chair. Apart from that and the bed, the only furniture was a cupboard in the corner. I opened it and found a shirt, crumpled but clean, a pair of polished brown boots and a cheap canvas-covered suitcase with a strap round it.

I picked up the case, light to lift, and put it on the bed. When I'd unbuckled the strap I discovered that the two clasps were locked and I could see no sign of a key. Luckily the locks were as cheap as the rest of the case and a little implement from my manicure set made short work of them. My aunt had given it to me on my sixteenth birthday, saying a lady should always carry a manicure set because she never knew when she might need it. This was the only time I could remember my aunt being right about anything.

I lifted the lid and found a checked waistcoat, a clean, clumsily darned set of vest and combinations, a sponge bag containing soap and shaving kit. Apart from that, only a notebook covered in red cloth and a large brown envelope. I opened the notebook first.

Tall woman and short woman leave hotel 6.04 p.m.

TW and SW enter hat shop.

T & S enter 2nd hat shop...

And so on for two neat pages, a carefully itemized account of our eccentric shopping trip. I turned the page and found a new entry, with *Apr. 22* at the top, the date of Topaz's funeral. *TW arrives early. SW with foreign gent. 2 YW with wreath. One makes speech.*

Robert Worth clearly knew none of our names, yet he'd been providing a most detailed observation service for somebody. I rifled through the rest of the notebook, finding nothing but blank pages, then opened the brown envelope. It contained four English five-pound notes, looking quite new, and one letter in an unsealed white envelope, with no address. The letter inside was on the notepaper of a solicitor in Gray's Inn Road, London, dated November 1901 and headed, To Whom it may Concern. A reference.

Mr Robert Worth has been employed by us for six years, in the capacity of clerk. We have found him honest, sober and industrious and can recommend his employment in any similar capacity.

So, eight years ago, the plump man had been honest, sober and industrious. From the evidence of the notebook, industrious he'd remained to the end. Sobriety, judging by his complexion as I remembered it, probably hadn't lasted so well. As for honesty, there must be some reason why a solicitor's clerk falls to working as a circus hand. Possibly somewhere between 1901 and the present, Bobsworth had been caught with his hand in the cash box. But there was something pathetic in the thought that he'd carried with

252

him to his death this thin testimonial to his employable qualities. I replaced it carefully in the case with the rest of his things, did up the strap and returned it to the cupboard as neatly as he'd left it, apart from the broken locks. Downstairs the proprietor was asleep over his counter, mouth open. I put the key to room eight down beside him, and let myself out.

CHAPTER SEVENTEEN

I'd asked the cab to wait for me. It was past six o'clock by then, only just enough time to do what was needed before eight.

Within a quarter of an hour I was in Jules Estevan's studio.

'Mr Estevan,' I said, 'I need a man.'

'I admire your directness, Miss Bray, but doubt my capability.'

'You'll do perfectly well. In fact, practically any presentable man would do.'

It struck me that he looked a little alarmed. I tried to reassure him.

'It won't take long, perhaps no more than two hours of your time. And there's no need to change, you could just put on an overcoat.'

'Miss Bray, perhaps you'd be good enough to let me know exactly what it is you have in mind.'

'Bobbie Fieldfare and Marie de la Tourelle are about to do something extremely stupid. I want to be there, to show them how ridiculous the whole thing is.'

He blew out his cheeks and sat down heavily on the couch. He seemed to be losing some of his poise.

'Miss Bray, I understand your concern about this. If you think Miss Fieldfare and Marie are bad influences on each other, I might even agree with you. But in matters like this, surely it's anybody's right to go to the devil in his or her own way.'

I knew it was his affectation never to be excited about anything, but this was going too far.

'I'm afraid I can't take such an Olympian view of attempted murder.'

He sat up. 'Murder?'

'From the way you were talking, I thought you knew about it.'

'Of course not. I've no idea what you're talking about.'

'Then what did you think I meant?'

He hesitated, then smiled. 'I'm afraid I'd assumed that it was your intention to surprise them in ... so to speak, Sapphic dalliance.'

'Good heavens, no. I can assure you I've far more serious things to worry about than that.'

Jules started laughing and I couldn't help joining in, both of us, I think, more than a touch hysterical. Our laughter resounded off the polished floor, the painted pagan figures on the wall, the tailor's dummy with its china head, until it scared me. I wondered whether I'd chosen the right ally, but as I'd told Jules, I needed a man, and my choice was limited. When we'd sobered down I told him as much as I intended to. Bobbie and Marie, I said, were plotting to assassinate somebody for political reasons. I preferred not to tell him the name of the victim. The point was to break up their plot in a way that gave me enough hold over Bobbie to hustle her straight back to England. At first he was incredulous.

'Even Marie wouldn't be such an idiot.'

'I'm sure Bobbie's been playing on her over-developed sense of drama. And Marie wouldn't be the one who actually fired the pistol.'

'Pistol, is it?'

'I'm afraid so. But it's all right. The man they're expecting won't be there. The letter inviting him was intercepted, only Bobbie and Marie don't know that.'

'So who exactly will Bobbie be firing the pistol at?'

'Well, you in theory, only . . .'

'I see. And do I only get shot in theory?'

'It won't come to that.'

'I wish I shared your confidence.'

'All I need you to do is to act as a guide. You see, Marie will have told her servants

255

that she's expecting a male visitor at eight o'clock but I doubt very much if she'll have told them his name. If you arrive at eight, the servants will assume you're the man she's expecting, and they'll show you to the room where she is. Bobbie will already be hiding somewhere in the room. I follow you, catch Bobbie red-handed with the pistol and bundle her off by the next train.'

'There seems to me to be one small flaw in all this. Supposing the enterprising Miss Fieldfare takes a shot at me as soon as I walk in the room.'

'That's not their idea at all. The plan is that Marie decoys the victim into a position that will give Bobbie plenty of time to take aim. I'll be through the door long before that.'

'Can you give me one good reason, Miss Bray, why I should do this?'

I considered pointing out that Marie was a friend of his, but suspected he'd find that banal.

'It will at least be a new experience, Mr Estevan.'

'Here lies a martyr to experience.'

He collapsed flat on his back on the couch, then got up, left the room and re-appeared in white gloves and an opera cloak, carrying a top hat.

'Where is the tumbril?'

'I've a cab waiting outside.'

Horse cabs in Biarritz cost two francs an

hour, so I'd already spent three shillings of the Union's money, but that was the least of my worries. I'd more than half expected Jules to refuse, but he'd agreed so I was committed. I wished I could understand Bobbie Fieldfare. Jules, silent on the seat opposite me as the cab lurched its way uphill, must have been thinking much the same thing. He said suddenly:

'A vote must be very important to Miss Fieldfare.'

'It is to us all.'

'Not to me. If one knows the majority of the population is invariably wrong about anything, how can one accept a political system that assumes it's always right?'

'What's your preferred system?'

'To avoid systems. The point is, Bobbie Fieldfare is, by your own admission, a determined young woman who would kill if she thought it would help get her this precious vote. Has she done it already?'

It was almost dark in the cab but I think he sensed, if not saw, the way my muscles tensed.

'What do you mean?'

'I've suddenly understood the point of one of your questions to me. You wanted to know if Bobbie could have known about Topaz's legacy while Topaz was still alive.'

I said nothing.

'And the answer was that she could have

257

known—could very well have known.'

He waited. 'Well, Miss Bray, did she poison poor Topaz?'

'Even if she knew, that's no proof against her.'

'And that's no answer. I sense there are some things you haven't told me.'

That was all too true: Bobbie's visit to the doctor complaining of sleeplessness, Bobbie in men's clothes walking up and down in the street outside Topaz's door.

'And then,' Jules said, 'we have this strange business of the opal pendant.'

It was as if he'd been reading my mind. He sat back in the seat, but didn't relax.

'I can see why you're so anxious to get her out of the country.'

The cab slowed down as the road climbed. I looked out of the window and saw we were negotiating one of the sharp bends not far from the Villa des Lilas. It was dusk already, with the sunset no more than a long golden smudge over violet-coloured sea.

Jules said: 'Does the fact that you've recruited me mean I'm not under suspicion any more?'

I could see no point in lying to him.

'No, not entirely. But something I found out today makes you less likely.'

'What was that?'

'There's been a man spying on me and Bobbie. Before that, I think he was spying on

Topaz. He was an Englishman, and I think he'd been paid in English money.'

'Was?'

'He's dead.'

A silence.

'So how does that make me less likely?'

'You're at home in France. If you needed a man as a spy you'd probably choose a Frenchman and pay him in French currency.'

'Not necessarily. If I needed a really efficient spy I'd choose you and pay you in my unwanted votes.'

I said I was flattered.

We were rounding the last bend and, in the dusk, I could see the high garden wall of the Villa des Lilas ahead. It was about a quarter to eight. The difficult point, I knew, would be finding out where Jules was taken after he'd been let in by one of the servants. I suggested that he should ask where Marie was, then pretend he'd left something in the cab and come out and tell me. The likelihood was, I thought, that she'd be in the salon where her performance had been staged, or her bedroom. Jules disagreed.

'No, they'll be in the temple. Much more convenient for an assignation, or an assassination.'

'Temple?'

'Marie's Temple of Venus. It's a pavilion in the garden. If I'm right, we'll see the lights as soon as we're inside the gate.'

The cab turned through the gateway and into Marie's gravel drive. In contrast to the night of the party, house and garden were silent and apparently deserted, although there were lights on in some of the downstairs rooms. As the cab came to a halt Jules touched my arm and pointed.

'Look.'

I could see a lighted window glowing about a hundred yards away, from a white building on a little hill surrounded by bushes.

'That's where they are.'

Close enough, I thought, for them to hear the wheels of the vehicle on the gravel and believe David Chester was driving into their trap. I wondered how Bobbie felt and imagined her giving a last check to the pistol. Marie would be striking some appropriate attitude.

I whispered to Jules: 'You go to the house and let the servants know you're here. I'll go straight down there and wait outside.'

We both got out. I told the cab driver to wait and watched Jules as he went up to the house. When I heard him ringing the bell I walked down some steps on to the sloping lawn and cut across it towards the pavilion.

The ground was soft and I made no sound. The building was sideways on to me, the light coming from a small semi-circular window near the top of the wall. As I came closer I could smell woodsmoke. I pushed my way through harsh-leaved bushes as carefully as I could, freezing when I disturbed a roosted bird and sent it clattering away. There was no sound from inside. I waited for a minute, then moved on. It was completely dark by now and I had to feel my way carefully up the slope. When I came alongside the wall I found that the bottom course of stones projected out further than the rest. It gave me the foothold I needed to pull myself up and look in at the window.

The room inside was like a stage set, a white rectangle dimly lighted, with a fire burning in a wide marble fireplace, an armchair covered in apple green velvet, modern tapestries on the walls showing gods and goddesses in athletic poses. The centre piece was an enormous couch covered in tawny furs. Marie was on the couch wearing a pale-coloured dress that poured itself over her like a jug full of cream. For once, though, she wasn't posing. She was sitting there like a schoolgirl at a dormitory feast, bare feet burrowed into the furs, knees drawn up under her chin with an arm clasped round them. Her long dark hair was hanging loose and she was eating something, a plum I think. Bobbie was perched on the edge of the couch. Unlike Marie she looked worried and kept glancing towards the door. She was wearing an ordinary jacket and skirt and I could see no sign of the pistol. I guessed it might be behind the great bank of ferns and lilies in pots at the end of the room facing me. As a floral arrangement, it was overpoweringly large for the room. As a screen for an assassin it would probably do very well.

I waited, my fingers hooked on the windowsill, toes braced against the wall. If Bobbie had looked up she'd have seen me, but she was intent on Marie. I think, though, that she heard Jules' steps on the path almost as soon as I did. The servant was guiding him along the gravel path parallel to the wall, carrying an oil lamp. The first part of my plan had worked, with apparently nobody questioning that Jules was the visitor Marie expected. Bobbie said something to Marie and at once the plum was skimmed into the fire and Marie's bare feet wriggled out from the comfort of the furs. She crossed her ankles and leaned back, resting on one elbow and facing the door. Two practised flicks of the hand sent her heavy hair into obedient rivers on either side of her, framing her from pale forehead to white feet. Bobbie meanwhile had disappeared behind the ferns and lilies as smartly as a rabbit into its burrow. By now Jules and the servant were level with me, down on the path to my right. I saw Jules' face in the lamplight. He looked worried and I wished there was some way of signalling to him that I was so close. The servant stopped, pointed to the door and said something to Jules, then went back along the path, taking the lamp with him. I willed Jules to go on. He hesitated for a moment, then I heard his footsteps on the gravel and a firm knock on the door. From inside, Marie called to him in English to come in. When I heard him push the door open I jumped off my ledge and hurled myself down the slope towards the sheet of light coming through the open door. I got there in time to hear Marie's exclamation of surprise and anger.

'Jules, what are you doing here? Go away.'

Then there was a second's silence, followed by a flash as bright as lightning, a sharp crack, a man cursing in French and the sound of a heavy body falling into foliage. Marie screamed. From up the path the servant shouted something and came running back. Cursing myself for my idiocy I ran through the open doorway and saw Jules' elegantly trousered legs threshing among shattered ferns and lilies in what I took to be his death throes, and Bobbie shouting, whacking a stick up and down on his shoulders like a boy killing a rat. I flung myself at her, conscious as I dived through the air of Marie's screams and the scent of lilies combined with a hot metallic smell, struck her with all my weight and knelt on her, wrenching the stick away from her. Its end was a mass of splinters. I was shouting at Bobbie, calling her a fool and a murderer, as if one were as bad as the other, and all the time I could feel Jules' body twitching beside me. She was yelling back at me, but I couldn't hear what she was saying for the noise Marie was making. When Bobbie went on struggling I pushed her head against the floor, wincing at the crack it made. It didn't knock her unconscious, but at least it quietened her enough to let me get at Jules. I picked a hart's tongue fern off the back of his neck and turned him over as gently as I could on to his torn cloak. His face was set in a painful rictus, his chest heaving as he fought for breath. I put my arm round his shoulders and let his head rest against me.

'Jules, I'm sorry, I'd no idea...'

He struggled to say something.

'...wrong, you were wrong.'

'Yes, I was wrong. But that's not what matters now. The thing is to get a doctor for you and...'

The servant was standing there, staring down at us.

'...don't need a doctor.'

Jules managed to force the words out. His breathing was becoming less laboured, but that might not be a good sign.

'...wrong ... not a pistol at all ... a camera ... oh gods.'

He took a gulp of air and sat up and before his words hit me I realised what was wrong with him. It was nothing but laughter, a

264

shaken, hysterical laughter that wasn't far away from pain.

'A camera?'

I repeated the words, still not understanding them. I looked at the splintered stick Bobbie had used to hit Jules and slowly recognised it for what it was: the broken leg of a camera tripod. The other two legs and a splintered stump were there in the wreckage of the ferns, scorched by the remains of the magnesium flare. Behind them was the camera itself. Bobbie had pulled herself into a sitting position and was staring at it, as if wondering how it and she had got there. She looked at me and said, quite quietly: 'You didn't have to do that, Nell. Even if you disapproved, you didn't have to do that.'

I stood up. My legs felt weak, so I sat down beside Marie on the fur-covered couch. She'd stopped screaming and begun glaring at me instead. The servant picked up Jules and helped him to the armchair. Bobbie, still looking dazed, began to disentangle herself from the foliage.

I said: 'Of all the half-witted ideas I've ever encountered, this was one of the worst.'

Bobbie's head must have been aching, but there was still fight in her. 'It would have worked perfectly well if you hadn't interfered. It might even work now if you'll only go away.'

'No it won't. The camera's broken and Mr Chester won't be coming. Your invitation to him was intercepted.'

'By you?'

I said nothing.

'It was you, wasn't it, Nell? You've been spying on me. I know we have our differences, but you might have gone on doing things your way and left me to do mine.'

'Including blackmail? What would you have done with your compromising photograph if you'd got it?'

'Sent copies to every newspaper editor, every bishop and every High Court judge.'

Marie told the servant to go away. It struck me as the first sensible thing she'd done for days. He left without a word or a backward glance, making me wonder if this kind of thing was routine in Marie's household.

'Even if it had worked,' I said, 'it would have been a squalid way of fighting.'

'Unladylike?'

'Ungentlemanly.'

She stalked over to the fireplace, beating her clenched fist against her thigh.

'Nell, I can't tell you how much you annoy me. You think if we go on fighting by their rules, they'll invite us in the end to join their nice cosy gentleman's club and we'll all be happy. They won't. They'll hold that door shut with all the brute strength, all the dirty tricks, they can manage. The only way we'll ever get in is by battering it down.'

'And this was the best battering ram you could use? For goodness sake, what made you think David Chester would walk into this in the first place? I dislike the man every bit as much as you do, but as far as his private life goes, he's a model of domestic duty.'

'There's no such thing.'

Marie said: 'He'd have come to me. If he'd received the letter, he would have come.'

She was warming her feet at the fire and putting her hair up, as efficiently as a musician putting away his instrument when a concert has been cancelled.

'Why?'

'Because they always do.'

Jules said, from the armchair: 'You both have a touching faith in male lust.'

'No,' Marie said. 'In male vanity.'

Bobbie said: 'It was a question of finding the right bait.'

Marie winced, but Bobbie was too angry with me to notice.

'You've studied the subject, have you?' I said.

'You know very well what I've done. It was probably you interfering the first time. In fact, I'm sure it was.'

It was the first I'd heard of another attempt, but I didn't admit that.

'I thought at first it was assassination you

had in mind.'

She snorted. 'I wish it had been. It would have been over and done with by now.'

'It is over and done with. The best thing you can do now is take the next train back to England. I've a cab waiting. You've done enough harm.'

'I'm not going without Rose.'

'That's the harm I'm talking about. You must go without her.'

'You know where she is, don't you? You're hiding her from me.'

I didn't reply. At that moment, there was nothing I wanted to share with Bobbie.

'You tricked her into telling you all about this, didn't you? You accuse me of squalid behaviour, but you've been using your position in the movement to bully poor Rose.'

'There's no question of bullying. You've brought Rose into very deep trouble. The best thing you can do now is go away and leave me to deal with it.'

Bobbie turned her back on me, staring into the fire.

Jules said to her back, in a quiet conversational tone: 'Miss Fieldfare, did you kill Topaz Brown?'

Bobbie turned round to him, her face blank with shock.

'What did you say?'

'Did you kill Topaz Brown?'

We were all frozen, Marie with her arms

behind her head, putting a pin in her hair, Bobbie like a statue beside the fireplace, myself staring at her, feeling as if I'd laid a gunpowder trail and Jules had chosen to put a match to it. In the silence you could hear the logs crackling and the earth trickling from the pot of an overturned fern.

'Why should I kill Topaz Brown?'

The words, when they came at last, were as quiet as Jules' question. His reply was equally calm.

'For her money. Not for yourself, naturally; for votes.'

'How could I?'

I said: 'Did you know before Topaz Brown died that she'd left her money to us?'

She nodded. She seemed relieved to have a question she could answer.

'Yes, the evening before. It was all round town. Everybody knew.'

'The night Topaz Brown died, there was a young man walking up and down outside her private hotel entrance from ten o'clock until after midnight. That young man was you.'

Only Jules' sudden movement in the chair showed his surprise. Marie gasped. The blank expression on Bobbie's face had given way to anger, a cold determined anger.

'Yes, he was.'

Marie began to say something. Jules put up a hand to stop her.

'Your witness, Miss Bray.'

269

I said: 'There was the fire opal pendant. It was seen in Topaz's possession the day before her death. Later, it was in Marie's possession. I believe you gave it to her.'

'Yes, yes, she did.'

At last Marie had been given a cue she recognised. She registered horror with all the force of her great dark eyes, hand flying to her throat, released hair cascading down her back. With the other hand she pointed at Bobbie, an unnecessary action since she was only a matter of yards away.

'She gave it to me. She told me it had been sent by somebody who admired me. She is a murderer. She betrayed me. She murdered my friend...'

Jules stood up, grabbed the long rope of her hair and gently but firmly wrapped it round her protesting mouth. She tried to bite him, but he was clearly stronger than he looked. Then he sat himself down beside her, right arm round her shoulders, left hand holding the hair tight against her cheek. From the back, they might have been a close pair of lovers looking into the fire. He soothed her with his voice, the way Sidney Greenbow might have calmed a nervous horse.

'Marie, *ma mignonnette*, save it for the ticket holders. Sit and listen.'

Bobbie hadn't moved.

I said: 'Then there was your visit to Dr

Campbell. He wouldn't tell me what he prescribed for your sleeplessness. Was it laudanum?'

I could see Jules' arm tightening on Marie's shoulders. Bobbie looked puzzled, then angry. I sensed a change of balance, as if in the last question I'd somehow blundered, giving her back the initiative, although I couldn't see how.

'Laudanum? No. Besides, I wouldn't have taken it. There was nothing wrong with me.'

'Of course not. So why did you go to see the doctor?'

I waited for her answer, and as I waited she began to smile, first to herself, then a wide, mocking grin. She looked me in the eye.

'Oh, Nell Bray, you're a fool after all, and I was almost a worse one. You don't know after all, do you? You were bluffing.'

'It isn't a bluff. Did you kill Topaz Brown?'

'No,' she said. She began to walk towards the door. 'I didn't. I don't know who did, if anyone did.'

Jules let go of Marie and stood up. We both moved towards Bobbie.

'Are you going to stop me? Are you arresting me for the murder of Topaz Brown?'

She took another step, daring me to come between her and the door. I could have stopped her, but what would I have done

271

after that? I let her pass. In the doorway, she raised a hand to us all.

'I'm sorry, Marie. It wasn't my fault. Happy hunting, Nell Bray.'

We heard her footsteps going away up the path, jaunty footsteps. Then Jules and I had to turn our attention to Marie. She'd decided that it was the opportunity to register rage and betrayal, modelled loosely on Queen Dido of Carthage. It took some time.

CHAPTER EIGHTEEN

It was almost midnight before we were able to hand Marie over to the care of her Spanish maid to be put to bed. By then Jules and I were almost too tired to speak. The manservant showed us out to the porch—and we discovered that Bobbie had taken our cab. I suppose I should have expected that. Contemplating the walk back to town, I wondered if my boots would stand the strain. Jules, who seemed to be developing a taste for decisiveness, simply informed the servant that we'd be staying the night. The man didn't seem in the least put out, not even when Jules informed him that we'd also be needing some supper.

'Are you sure Marie won't mind?' I said to Jules.

'Why should she? Anyway, it's her own fault.'

We followed the man back inside and were shown into an intimate dining room with pale green walls and curtains the colour of seashells. I thought I was too tired to be hungry but changed my mind when supper arrived, cold chicken in mayonnaise and aspic, decorated with slivers of black truffle. A green salad came with it, glossy with olive oil, and the man brought champagne as a matter of routine, but Jules told him to take it away and bring Muscadet instead. Jules pulled out a chair for me, sat down and helped us to chicken and wine.

'I'm afraid Marie's cellar is undistinguished. In that respect, Topaz won easily.'

I thought of Marie upstairs, with her maid brushing her long hair, then of the bowing white horse in the churchyard. The chicken was good, and I found myself eating hungrily. Jules poured more wine.

'Was Miss Fieldfare telling the truth?'

'About not killing Topaz? Yes.'

'You seem certain.'

'I don't think she'd lie to me.'

'But you believed her capable of murder.'

'Oh yes, capable. Bobbie Fieldfare is capable of anything, but I don't think she murdered Topaz. There's something I've missed, though, and I can't think what it is.'

'Her plan to discredit this politician you dislike so much, would it have achieved anything?'

I took another piece of chicken from the plate he was holding and thought about it.

'If he'd have been the kind of man who'd have walked into a trap like that, if she'd taken her precious photograph and used it as she intended to, yes it might. But Bobbie got one important thing wrong.'

'What was that?'

'She has very romantic ideas about sexual attraction. She over estimates its force. For a young woman, she has some rather old-fashioned notions.'

Jules choked on his wine. 'Old-fashioned?'

'Yes. She's inexperienced. She thinks it's some great wild force like classical legends or the Old Testament, Mars and Venus, Salome and Kind Herod. She imagined that all she had to do was expose him to this force, and the job was done.'

Jules was looking at me in a way I found disturbing.

'What about you, Miss Bray? You don't see it as a great wild force?'

'I'm afraid the great forces aren't wild at all; they're all too tame. Vanity and ignorance, mostly.'

'You said Miss Fieldfare was inexperienced, implying that you...'

'Implying nothing whatsoever, Mr Estevan.'

I should have been annoyed, but I found myself laughing. It was late, very late, and I'd drunk my second glass of wine.

'I think you're a wild woman, Miss Bray.'

'Then you're a wild man. Whatever possessed you to take a leap at Bobbie like that?'

'I saw something move, and instinct took over. It's unspeakably commonplace to follow one's instincts. I should be ashamed of myself.'

But he didn't sound ashamed.

The manservant came in, cleared the empty plates and brought a great bowlful of pears and hothouse peaches. Jules peeled a peach carefully, drawing off the skin in long regular strips.

'So Bobbie Fieldfare, you say, did not kill Topaz. Do you still believe that Topaz was killed?'

My mouth was full of pear. I nodded.

'Then who did?'

I swallowed and said tentatively: 'Have you wondered about Sidney Greenbow?'

'El Cid? He was one of her oldest friends. Why should he kill her?'

'The horses, his Dons. Did you know she lent him a lot of money to buy them? Suppose she was pressing him to pay it back because she needed it for her vineyard.'

Jules looked doubtful.

275

'That wouldn't have been like Topaz. I never heard of her pressing anybody for a debt. Is that the only reason?'

'No. I told you that somebody had been spying on Topaz, then on Bobbie and me. He was an Englishman who worked for the circus.'

'And you say he's dead.'

'You remember the baggy satyr at Marie's party? That was the man. He was found drowned the next day.'

I'd no intention of telling Jules about Rose. I was already feeling guilty for taking my ease there when I should have been down in the town, looking for her.

'And you think El Cid paid this man?'

'I can't prove it, but he certainly knew him.'

Jules suddenly looked tired and miserable.

I said: 'That bothers you, doesn't it? Is Sidney Greenbow a friend of yours?'

'Not particularly. I met him a few times in Topaz's company and found him amusing, in his way. Only . . .'

'Only what?'

'I suppose I don't want to think of anybody murdering her. When we know who it was, if we ever do, she'll seem so finally dead. It will be like killing her again.'

I shivered. I felt as tired as he looked.

'Time for bed.'

Jules pressed an electric bell by the

276

fireplace and the man came back to show us upstairs. At my doorway, Jules said goodnight with a formal little bow. I supposed it was meant ironically but I was too weary to care. I undressed completely and slid between sheets of finest satin, smooth as diving into a dream. Topaz would have slept like that many nights of her life. I fell asleep wishing that, just once, I could have talked to her.

Next morning Jules was deeply unhappy.

'It really is the worst of feelings. My whole skin is trying to crawl away from it.'

He'd woken up to realise that he had no clean shirt.

'And I didn't change before you carried me off yesterday evening. Do you realise that means I've been wearing the same shirt for twenty hours?'

He seemed to blame me for it, and yet he hadn't been in the least angry when he thought I was close to getting him killed. I mentioned unsympathetically that in Holloway they allowed us one change of blouse a week and he closed his eyes and shuddered. The camaraderie of the night before seemed to have ebbed away, or perhaps it was simply Jules retreating to his usual distance from the rest of the world. He only permitted us one quick cup of coffee before hurrying out to the porch where Marie's coachman was waiting for us, with

two grey ponies harnessed to a light
barouche.

'Shouldn't we wait to say thank you to
Marie?'

'Good heavens, no. She won't be up before
midday.'

As we bowled along the Avenue du Bois de
Boulogne at a brisk trot, Jules sat miserably
in the corner of the seat, shoulders hunched
as if he were trying to keep as much distance
as possible between himself and his shirt.
Pitying him, I suggested that we should ask
the driver to put him down at his home first,
then take me on to the town centre. He made
no serious objection to that, and hurried
inside with only the briefest of goodbyes. I
imagined him tearing the offensive garment
off as soon as the door closed behind him.

The driver asked me where I wanted to go
and I said anywhere on the promenade. It
seemed high time to get on with the search for
Rose, though I had no idea where to start.
Then, on the steps outside a hotel, I saw a
dumpy woman with two children waving at
me, almost jumping up and down in her
eagerness to attract my attention. My heart
sank. Mrs Chester. I neither wanted nor
needed to talk to her any more, but it would
have been a snub to trot on past her. I looked
quickly round to make sure her husband was
nowhere in sight, then told the driver I would
get down there. She came bustling across the

pavement towards me, her two little girls trailing behind. She was, as usual, so absorbed in her family worries that she didn't seem to find it surprising that a supposed governess should step out of one of the smartest carriages in Biarritz.

'Oh my dear, I'm so glad to have seen you. You know we're going away tomorrow? I did want to see you and say goodbye.'

Marie's carriage turned and drove away. I tried to look interested in what Mrs Chester was telling me, but now I knew that her husband had never been in danger from Bobbie's pistol it was no concern of mine whether they stayed or went. I pretended a decent interest in the health of the coughing child, Louisa.

'Oh, she's glad to be going home too, aren't you, dear? Poor David was up with her nearly all night again. I'd stayed with her the night before and he insisted I must get my sleep.'

The two girls, taking no interest in what their mother was saying, were edging her to the kerb.

'Mama, can we look at the boats?'

Abstractedly, still talking at me, she let them take her across the road to a telescope mounted on the promenade railing, fumbling in her bag for coins. I was impatient to break away, but the stream of domestic inanities went running on and she seemed determined not to let me go. When the two girls were

279

safely occupied, quarrelling over the telescope, I understood why. Her voice sank to a whisper.

'That awful woman, the letter, did you do anything?'

'I can assure you, Mrs Chester, that the woman involved now very much regrets sending it. I'm sure your husband won't be troubled by a repetition of anything from that quarter.'

'Oh. Oh, I'm so grateful.'

Standing there among the strolling people she grabbed my hand and pressed it between both of hers. There were tears in her eyes.

'So grateful. He's so good and thoughtful, it makes me miserable when anything upsets him. We women can't understand the burdens on a man in public life like him. All we can do is try...'

This was altogether too much. I drew my hand away.

'I assure you, Mrs Chester, you have nothing to thank me for. Now I see somebody I must speak to over there. I hope you have a pleasant journey home.'

I left her with her mouth open at the abruptness of my going, telling myself not to feel guilty. It was a pitifully small world of hers, and I'd done what I could to make it safer for her. When I'd pretended to see an acquaintance over the road it had been a lie to get away from her, but it turned into truth before I was halfway across. On the hotel forecourt was Lord Beverley, in motoring coat and cap, standing beside his motor-car. He recognised me and waved.

'Good morning, Miss Bray. We're going off this morning, back home.'

The fashionable world was gathering for its migration from the shore of the Atlantic back to the parks of London and Paris, driven by instincts as mysterious and reliable as those of the swallows. Trunks and suitcases were piled outside the hotel doorway. The engine of Lord Beverley's motor-car was open and he was holding a spanner.

'Doing a few adjustments. The guv'nor thinks she won't make it. He's promised if I get us back to London in her, he'll buy her from me.'

I asked him what he thought the chances were and he said about five to one, given reasonable going. He began to explain to me in great detail what he was doing to the vehicle. The whole world seemed to be in a conspiracy to waste my time that morning. He insisted that I should look into the engine to see something called a fuel feed. When our heads were almost touching over pipes and cylinders, in a haze of petrol fumes, it became clear what he really wanted. He whispered to me:

'Any news about poor Topaz?'

'What sort of news?'

'You seemed to think somebody might have murdered her. Has all that blown over?'

'Nothing else has happened.'

That was true in the sense that nothing had happened to bring me closer to finding Topaz's murderer. I had no intention of telling him about Bobbie or the baggy satyr. Lord Beverley blew a great sigh of relief into the motorcar's giblets.

'Suicide after all, then?'

'That's still the official verdict, yes.'

'Thank the Lord for that. I've had enough trouble calming down the guv'nor as it was. If he thought I'd been mixed up in a murder case...'

A gruff, bad-tempered voice yelled from the hotel steps: 'Charles, the man says we didn't order a picnic hamper. I told you to be sure to order a hamper.'

Lord Beverley sighed, stood up and put down his spanner.

'The guv'nor. Excuse me, Miss Bray, I'll have to go and see to him. I won't introduce you, if you don't mind. He's not one of your warmest supporters.'

I waited, leaning on the motor-car with my back to them, while father, son and hotel manager sorted out the question of the hamper. In a few minutes Lord Beverley returned.

'Sorry about that. So it's all over, suffragettes get her money and everybody satisfied. Pity though.'

He asked me if I'd be staying long. I'd just started to reply when the thing happened. Somebody gave a scream and a long black lash hissed out of nowhere like a snake's fangs and thudded against the shoulder of Lord Beverley's leather motoring coat.

A man shouted: 'That's for her, you bastard.'

I turned round and there a few yards away was Sidney Greenbow, standing quite at ease in boots, shirt and breeches, legs astride, coiling the slack of a long ringmaster's whip back into his left hand. All round him the people who'd been chatting in the sunshine had drawn back, thunderstruck.

For several seconds Lord Beverley just stood there, staring at Sidney. He put his hand to his shoulder where the whiplash had struck, looking not so much angry as puzzled. If he'd heard what Sidney had shouted it didn't seem to register with him. He said plaintively:

'What was that for?'

'You know damned well what it's for.'

Sidney drew back his right arm and this time there was a whole chorus of screams. I was standing a few feet from Lord Beverley but it didn't occur to me to move away. Like everybody else, I couldn't believe it was happening. The lash hissed out again, so close that I could feel the wind from it on my cheek, but this time Lord Beverley wasn't there when it landed. He yelled something incoherent and threw himself sideways, landed on his knees but was up in an instant, hurling himself at Sidney before he could coil up the whip for a third attack. The speed of it caught Sidney off balance. Lord Beverley was several inches taller and perhaps two stone heavier than he was. The two of them went thumping down on to the gravel of the forecourt, Sidney underneath still keeping tight hold of his whip, Lord Beverley kneeling on him and trying to pull it away from him. But Lord Beverley's advantages of height and weight weren't much use against Sidney's circus muscles. After some panting and heaving the positions were reversed, with Lord Beverley's head on the ground and Sidney's knee braced against his chest. Lord Beverley could hardly speak, but had just enough breath left to ask Sidney what he was supposed to have done. Sidney kept repeating: 'You know, you bastard, you know.'

One of the worst things about it was that nobody did anything to stop them until I walked over to them.

'Sidney, what do you think you're doing? That's Lord Beverley.'

'Hello, Miss Bray. Yes, I know damned well who he is, and I don't care if he's Lord Muck. The police might not be able to touch him, but there's nothing to say that I can't.'

'Let him up. You're hurting him.'

'I'll let him up if he promises to make a proper fight of it. I don't want him running off to his daddy.'

Lord Beverley, thinking Sidney's attention was distracted, made another attempt to throw him off. After more grunting and writhing they ended up much as they'd been before. But by then somebody had sent for help. It arrived in the shape of four burly hotel porters and Lord Beverley's father, the Duke. When he saw what was happening his face went red and he shouted:

'Charles, what the hell are you up to this time?'

Lord Beverley had just enough breath left to say it wasn't his fault.

'Well, what are you all standing there for? Get that man off him.'

The porters closed in. Sidney looked up at them and rose slowly to his feet, taking his time about it. Lord Beverley followed his example, rather shakily, but seemed more concerned with his father's reaction than anything else.

'I promise you, guv'nor, I've no idea what it's all about. This man just came up and started laying about me with a damned great horsewhip.'

'Horsewhip? Why were you trying to horsewhip my son?'

One of the porters had picked up the whip. Sidney just stood there, arms folded. The Duke looked round the faces in the crowd, trying to make sense of it, then, unluckily, noticed me. I saw recognition dawning and his face went an even more alarming shade of red.

'I know that woman. She's one of those damned suffragettes. Good God, it's not enough for them now attacking people on the streets of London. They come out here and lie in wait for you while you're on holiday.'

I tried to protest that the attack had been nothing to do with me.

'She was talking to the man with the whip,' somebody from the crowd said. 'Urging him on. She organised it all.'

Lord Beverley tried to help.

'I don't think it was Miss Bray's fault, guv'nor. She was just standing there talking to me when this maniac arrived. Nothing to do with her.'

'Distracting you, that was what she was doing, while he crept up on you. Part of the plot. You're my son and that's enough for them. Nothing they won't stoop to. Prison's too good for them.'

Sidney tried to say something and the Duke told him to keep quiet. The woman who'd said I was urging Sidney on suggested we should call the police. Lord Beverley looked thoroughly miserable. I said to him:

'I promise you, I had nothing to do with this.'

'She didn't, nothing to do with it,' said Sidney.

I hope Lord Beverley believed me. At any rate, there must have been enough doubt in his mind on my side to make him do what he did. He said: 'I don't think that's a very good idea, guv'nor. The gendarmerie, I mean.'

'Why not?'

The Duke's respect for his son seemed to have increased now he thought he'd been the victim of a suffragette outrage.

'We'd be held up here for days talking to the police, then a court case. Not worth it. Besides, I gave the man a good thrashing for his pains.'

That was not strictly true, but in the circumstances I didn't blame him.

'What about her? We can't let her off scot free.'

'I honestly don't think Miss Bray had anything to do with it, guv'nor.'

The Duke snorted. 'Of course she did,' but the argument about a French court case clearly weighed heavily with him. He was the sort of man who'd regard anything foreign as sinister. He turned to me, cheeks bulging, chewing his rage like underdone beef.

'Let me tell you and all those other unnatural harpies of yours, you can do what you like, you can break every window in

287

Downing Street and attack us with bricks or horsewhips or anything else you can lay your filthy talons on, but we're not going to give in. As long as there's a man left in England who's worth the name, we'll never give in.'

I said nothing. He wasn't worth it. He glared at me for a while, then turned away and put his arm round his son's shoulders.

'Come on, Charles. Somebody go and get him a brandy.'

As they went, Lord Beverley looked back at me over his father's shoulder. It was a look that mingled apology and puzzlement.

I watched as father and son went inside, then turned my attention to Sidney Greenbow. He was still surrounded by porters. Two of them had grabbed him none too gently by the arms as he tried to follow Lord Beverley, another was still holding the whip.

'You can let him go,' I said. 'He can't do anything now.'

It would confirm my status as Sidney's accomplice in crime, but I could hardly leave him there. I think the porters were quite glad to let him go. He held out his hand for the whip, but the man holding it shook his head and put it behind his back.

'Come on,' I said. 'You can't blame them.'

He came reluctantly, grumbling that the whip had cost five pounds. The crowd drew back to let us go, muttering and looking askance. I could see no sign of Mrs Chester and hoped for her sake that she'd been safely on the beach when it happened. As soon as we were away from the fashionable area, I steered Sidney into a café and ordered coffees. He was surprisingly biddable, in the state of reaction, I think, that comes after you've screwed yourself up to some violent deed. I knew what it felt like.

I said: 'Why are you so convinced that Lord Beverley killed Topaz?'

He stared at me. 'He was the last one, wasn't he?'

'That's the only reason, because you thought he was her last lover?'

He leaned towards me, shirt-sleeved elbows on the metal-topped table. I could smell the perspiration on him, and the sweet hay from the stables.

'Look, Miss Bray, I told you a girl in Topaz's line of business takes risks, whether she's doing it up back alleys or where she'd got to. One of the risks is that someone will expect to be given it for nothing and he'll kill her if she doesn't give it to him.'

'But Lord Beverley didn't expect to be given it for nothing, as you put it. He'd spent a lot of money on her.'

Sidney nodded. 'All of it. The last of the money he won, he spent on her. That's when it happens. They come up the stairs one night, kidding themselves the girl loves them for their own sakes because they've bedded her a few times. She tells them it's no ticket, no show, they get annoyed and that's it.'

It was a horrible enough summary, but its naivety surprised me. I'd taken Sidney Greenbow for a quick-witted man. If, on the other hand, a quick-witted man wanted to turn suspicion from himself, the morning's little display might have done very nicely. The coffees arrived.

I said: 'I don't think Lord Beverley would feel like that. He was quite matter of fact about having no money left. That was why he came here—to spend it all.'

'But he'd fallen for her.'

'I don't think he had. He liked her, yes, but that was all. Anyway, if you really think he murdered her, why don't you go to the police?'

He made a derisive noise. 'What would they do, me against him? Anyway, I can't prove it. But I owed her something, and that was it.'

He drank his coffee thirstily, hot as it was. I wondered whether to show some of my cards and decided I had nothing to lose by it.

'What makes you so certain that Lord Beverley was the last one?'

'I asked around. I know a few people.'

He had a trick of looking into your eyes, very directly. I gave him back stare for stare. 'Yes, you know a few people, and you had some paid help as well, didn't you?'

He blinked. 'What do you mean?'

'The man they called Bobsworth, Robert Worth. Somebody paid him to keep a watch on Topaz. Then, after she was dead, he started following me and some people connected with me. I think the person who hired Bobsworth was you, Mr Greenbow.'

He shook his head. 'Not me. If I'd ever wanted a spy I'd have done better than Bobsworth. But I didn't.'

'Robert Worth was quite an educated man. He hadn't always been a circus hand.'

'Oh, they'll all tell you that. We've got two college professors and a prince of the blood putting up that circus tent, if you listened to their stories.'

'He wasn't so ambitious. But he had worked in a solicitor's office up to eight years ago.'

'Did he tell you that?'

'I never spoke to him.'

'How do you know then?'

I said nothing. For some reason the information seemed to interest him more than anything I'd said so far, but I couldn't understand why. For the next couple of minutes he said nothing at all, and when he broke his silence at last the question was unexpected.

'London was it, where he worked?'

'Yes.'

'Eight years ago?'

'It was eight years ago he left his job. He must have been working for the firm for some years before that. They gave him a reference.'

A long silence again, then he said: 'I wonder...'

'Wonder what?'

'If I tell you what I'm thinking, I suppose you'll say I'm jumping to conclusions.'

'You jumped to conclusions when you tried to horsewhip Lord Beverley.'

'Yes.' This time he wasn't looking me in the eye. 'What you've just said makes me wonder if I might have been wrong about that.'

'What I said about Bobsworth?'

'It's a long shot.'

'Long shot or not, you'd better tell me.'

So he did, sitting forward with his elbows on the table, eyes back on my face to see how I was reacting.

'We have to go back ten or eleven years, while Topaz was still on the Halls, but starting to do all right with her business on the side. I saw her now and then, when we happened to be on the same bill, and she told me about this man she had who was something in the legal business.'

'A client?'

'No, that was the point. This time the boot was on the other foot. He was working to pass some kind of examination, but he didn't have

292

enough money to live on and Topaz was looking after him.'

'Why?'

'Because she liked him, I suppose. It was putting on side a bit too, showing she could afford a man for herself. Him being in the legal business was a kind of step up for her. Of course, later on she could have had all the judges in the High Court if she'd fancied them, but that was how it was at the time.'

I could see where this was leading, but wanted to make him say it.

'What has this got to do with Bobsworth?'

'Well, when you talked about him spying on her, then said he'd worked in a lawyer's office, I started putting two and two together.'

I was putting two and two together as well, with a speed and exhilaration that left me breathless, like walking in the wind: seeing the young clerk of ten years ago, poor but ambitious, working his way as he saw it from clerk's stool to solicitor's desk. Then the same man sinking in his world as Topaz rose in hers, stealing from his employers to try to impress her, falling to utter ruin. Then years later, by a cruel coincidence, finding himself a hired hand living with apprentice clowns in a circus wagon, while she slept on gold sheets in the same town. *I.O.U. for one career.* I could see from the brightness in Sidney's eyes that he sensed my excitement.

'Supposing it was Bobsworth,' he said, as softly as an endearment.

I thought of Bobsworth asking for a meeting with Topaz late at night after his circus work was finished—and Topaz replying with the note that began *Too late*. Too late for Bobsworth, altogether too late. I tried to fight the current.

'Wouldn't he have been working at the circus that evening?'

Sidney smiled. 'It wouldn't have been any novelty to anyone if Bobsworth had gone bunking off again.'

The waiter had brought more coffee. Sidney drank his slowly this time, like a satisfied cat.

'And Bobsworth's dead?'

'Drowned. I've seen his body.'

We sat for a while, not talking, as the café began to fill up with people coming in for an early lunch. Sidney sorted out a franc and some centimes and piled them on the tablecloth.

'So that's it then.'

His jauntiness seemed quite restored. We went out into the sunshine together.

'I suppose I took my whip to the wrong one then?'

'Yes.'

'Serves me right, losing it.'

He wished me good morning and walked away, swinging along past the strolling holidaymakers with the air of a sailor among landlubbers. So that was it, then.

CHAPTER NINETEEN

I needed calm. I walked up and down along the parade with the great sweep of the Atlantic beside me, but for all I saw of it I might as well have been back in a prison cell. If Sidney had been speaking the truth, I knew the name of Topaz's murderer. If, on the other hand, Sidney had not been speaking the truth I surely still knew another name for Topaz's murderer, because what other reason could he have for inventing this legal lover? Every wave that broke repeated, 'Bobsworth, Bobsworth, Bobsworth,' thumping in on the 'Bob' and hissing out on the 'sworth'.

There was an irritation that came with it like grains of sand, a thoroughly unworthy irritation, but there it was. If Bobsworth killed Topaz, then Bobbie Fieldfare was a much better detective than I was. Almost from the time Topaz died she must have suspected the man. Take, for example, the matter of the fire opal pendant. On Tansy's evidence, it arrived with a card on the morning before Topaz's death. She seemed pleased and amused by it, quite likely reactions if it had come out of the blue from a

295

lover of ten years ago. The card might have carried Worth's plea for a meeting with her late at night, after his circus work was over. How a poor circus hand would acquire an opal didn't need much explaining on the assumption that he'd committed theft to impress Topaz at least once before in his career. The only mystery was how Bobbie had managed to guess the significance of the pendant and get it into her possession. Then, having got it, she passed it to Marie, apparently on a whim. That needed explaining too, unless for some reason it had ceased to matter.

I walked along the road beside the Grande Plage, towards Cap St Martin and its lighthouse. Perhaps the pendant had ceased to matter because Bobbie knew there was stronger evidence against Worth, the card in his handwriting, re-introducing himself to Topaz, asking her to see him. Suppose Bobbie, or possibly Rose, had somehow managed to get into Topaz's suite and taken both pendant and card. Suppose, further, that Bobsworth had found out they had evidence that could send him to the guillotine. That might be why he had followed Bobbie to the party in his hastily assembled satyr's outfit, to try to get it back. Then, failing to corner Bobbie on her own, he might have turned his attention to the two people he'd seen with her, myself and Rose.

When I thought of that I wanted even more to find Rose, to apologise to her for not understanding soon enough and protecting her. If Rose had killed the man in her panic, it was my fault, and Bobbie's.

Bobbie had been clever, cleverer than I was, and yet neither of us had been clever enough. I'd gone to Biarritz to claim Topaz's fifty thousand pounds for our cause. If we could prove murder rather than suicide, that would strengthen the claim that Topaz was of sound mind when her will was made. But with Bobsworth dead, we were in no position to prove his guilt without incriminating Rose.

By the time I'd come that far, the very cries of the seagulls sounded derisive. I sat down on an upturned rowing boat. All this assumed that Sidney was telling the truth, that there really had been a lover with legal ambitions about ten years ago who might have been Worth. There was only one person I knew of in Biarritz who might help me, and that was Tansy. The legal lover would have been before her time, but she'd been Topaz's confidante. It was likely that at some time, in those woman-to-woman sessions that Topaz seemed to enjoy with her maid, the existence of the man had been mentioned. I needed to talk to Tansy. The difficulty was that the last time we'd met she'd ordered me out of the room. Well, if she wouldn't let me in we'd have to speak outside. Surely at some time of the day she'd venture out of the hotel for fresh air.

I waited in the side street outside Topaz's private entrance from mid-afternoon until after six o'clock. I collected some suspicious looks from cab drivers and once Demi-tasse sauntered past and wished me a polite good afternoon. The sun was low down over the sea, sending a wash of gold light up the street and setting the pigeons cooing on the hotel ledges, when the side door opened and Tansy walked out, carrying a shopping bag. She locked the door and walked quickly down the street away from the seafront, the way we'd gone together on our hunt for underwear. She hadn't seen me so I walked some way behind her, not wanting to scare her into bolting back inside. When she came to the small square with its shops she made a beeline for the grocer's. I crossed over and stood outside the shop and when she came out ten minutes or so later, shopping bag bulging, she nearly bumped into me.

'Oh, Miss Bray, you did give me a fright. What are you doing here?'

She was nervy, but less angry than she'd been in the hotel suite.

'Strolling around. I see you've been shopping.'

She clutched the bag to her as if I had designs on it.

'More than I wanted. They don't

298

understand when you ask for a pound.'

I fell into step beside her. 'I'm sorry if I annoyed you the other day.'

'I'm sorry if I was snappy, only they fray at your nerves, all those questions.'

We walked on in silence and she stopped when we came to the side door.

'I'll be saying goodbye to you then, Miss Bray. I suppose you'll be leaving soon, like all the others.'

For all the world as if I'd been on holiday. I hadn't wanted to show my hand so soon, but there was nothing else for it.

'May I come up for a minute please, Tansy. There's something I think you'll want to hear.'

She hesitated. 'What's that?'

'I think I may know who killed Topaz Brown.'

Her face was blank. 'Who?'

'It's a long story. I think we should go upstairs.'

She turned the key in the lock, didn't hold the door for me but made no protest when I walked in behind her. We went up in the lift together, still in silence. Only when we were standing outside the door of Topaz's suite she began complaining loudly.

'I'm not asking much, just a bit of peace and quiet to get her things in order. That's all I'm asking from you, Miss Bray, just a bit of peace and quiet.'

Since I was standing behind her, she hurled the words at the closed door and made a great business of finding her key, asking herself out loud what she'd done with it, then clattering it into the lock as if it had done her an injury. The big salon looked untidy. In the twelve days since Topaz's death it had taken on the air of a luxurious waiting room, impersonal and unrestful. A tray of used tea things stood on a small table near the spirit lamp. Tansy dumped her bag down.

'Well?'

'Well what?'

'Who was it then?'

'Tansy, I'm not going to tell you just like that. Take your coat off and sit down.'

I sat down myself on an armchair. After a second or two she followed my example, but still as tense as a spring.

'Who was it?'

'I'm afraid there's one more question first. I hope it will be the last one.'

'I thought you were going to tell me something for a change.'

'Yes, I am. But please, Tansy, answer this question first. It's desperately important.'

'They're all supposed to be important.'

But she waited, hands locked tight in her lap, feet pressed together in her dusty, sensible boots.

'Did Topaz ever talk to you about the men she knew before you came to work for her?'

300

She glared. 'I told you. I never gossiped about her business, and I'm not going to start now.'

'It wasn't business, Tansy. It was a man she was fond of and trying to help in his career. This man had something to do with the legal profession. She knew him about ten years ago.'

'That was three years before my time.'

'Did she ever talk about anybody like that?'

She was silent. At first I thought it was the old stubborn silence, but then I saw that the expression on her face was not stubbornness but misery and her locked hands were gripping each other so tightly that the bones showed white. A fight was going on between her loyalty and the need to know what I could tell her. I tried to make it easier.

'It's all right, Tansy, you don't even have to tell me his name. I know that already. But there was a man, wasn't there?'

The nod she gave was only the faintest movement. If I hadn't been watching her very closely I'd have missed it.

'She talked to you about him?'

Another nod.

'Often?'

'Once.'

The word came out like the creak of a hinge on a chest unopened for years.

'What did she say about him?'

'She'd helped him and he'd been

301

ungrateful. It just came up one day when we were talking about men not being grateful.'

'Came up recently?'

'No, a year or two ago. Only I remembered it because she didn't usually criticise people. She'd liked him, you see, liked him quite a bit.'

She said 'liked' in the way most women would have said 'loved'. She sat there, eyes on my face.

'Well then, what have you got to tell me?'

I took a deep breath. 'I think he killed her, Tansy. He was here in Biarritz. He probably sent her that pendant asking her to see him again. She let him come to her. She even went out and bought cheap underwear and cheap wine to remind him of the time they'd spent together, before she had much money. And the fish—I expect they used to eat fish and chips together. She wanted to surprise him, and he killed her.'

'I see,' she said. 'I see.'

We sat in silence, with no sound in the room but our breathing. The noise of the evening traffic, hooves and car horns, came up to us from a long way below. I remembered what Jules had said about feeling that Topaz would finally have died for him when he knew who killed her, and guessed that Tansy was feeling the same.

As we sat there I wondered if it would help her to know that Robert Worth was dead, and that her own sister had accidentally avenged Topaz. I decided that it wouldn't. The silence drew itself out for minutes on end and the light in the room changed from gold to copper red as the sun went down over the sea. I was tired, but I had to leave Tansy to her grief and go on looking for Rose. There was only one thing I could do for her before I left, pitiful enough but not to be neglected.

'I'll make us some tea, Tansy.'

I went over to the table with the unwashed cups and the spirit lamp.

'No, leave those alone. I don't want tea.'

Her cry came just too late to prevent me from seeing it. I went back to the door and switched the light on, revealing a tray with two used cups.

'A visitor, Tansy?'

'Yes, my friend Janet.'

But she wasn't a good liar. I remembered her haste to get me out of the suite on my last visit, the bulging food bag, the fumbling of her key in the lock. I walked over to the big double doors leading to the bedroom and opened them.

'I should come out, Rose,' I said.

CHAPTER TWENTY

She'd been sitting there in the darkness, curtains drawn, on a chair beside Topaz's bed.

'You stay there, Rose. Don't take any notice of her.'

But Rose ignored her sister and came out, blinking in the light. She was wearing the same skirt as when I'd seen her in Marie's garden and one of her sister's striped blouses that was too small for her, straining across the bust, showing her wrists. Her face was pale and the skin below her eyes dark and sunken.

'Hello, Miss Bray. Don't worry, Tansy, it's probably just as well. I couldn't stay there forever.'

'Have you been here all the time?'

'Yes, I'm sorry. After what happened in the garden I was . . . I was scared and didn't know what to do. I came to Tansy.'

She sounded weary, defeated. The younger sister had gone to the older one like a child in trouble. I wondered whether she'd told Tansy about the death of Robert Worth and decided probably not.

'I didn't know what Bobbie was doing any more, what she wanted me to do.'

Her eyes were on me and there was an

appeal in them. No, she hadn't told her sister.

She asked: 'Does Bobbie know I'm here too?'

I was about to say that she didn't when there was a thunderous knocking on the outside door of the suite and a familiar voice, breezy and sure of itself.

'Tansy, Tansy, have you got Rose in there? I want to speak to her.'

Tansy shouted back: 'She's not here. Go away.'

'I don't believe you, Tansy. I'm going to stay here until Rose comes out, even if it takes all night.'

There was a sliding sound and I imagined Bobbie taking up a sitting position, back against the door.

'She won't go away,' Rose said.

There was still a touch of pride in her voice. I knew she was right and that Bobbie would stay there if necessary until the cleaning maids came in the morning.

I said to Rose: 'If you don't want to see her you can go out by the side door. I'll give you the key to my hotel room.'

'No, I do want to see her. I want her to know I didn't just go away and leave her.'

Tansy said: 'I'm not letting another of them in here. One's more than enough.'

It took me a while to realise that she meant more than enough suffragettes.

I said: 'I think we might let her in, Tansy.

She owes Rose an explanation.'

And me an explanation too, I thought. I was still smarting about Bobbie's superior detective powers and wondering how she'd found out about Worth so soon.

In the end, although Tansy refused to unlock the door herself, she made only a token objection when I said I'd do it.

'On your own head be it.'

It was a small, unworthy satisfaction to me when Bobbie fell into the room backwards when the door opened, but she rapidly recovered her dignity.

'I've been looking for you all over the place, Rose. We're leaving by the six fifty-two train tomorrow morning. I've got our tickets.'

From her manner, she might have been making the most routine holiday arrangements.

Tansy said: 'She's not coming with you.'

Bobbie ignored her and me and spoke to Rose. 'I was worried about you. I suppose I should have guessed that Nell Bray had kidnapped you. That's exactly her style.'

When I'd let Bobbie in I'd intended to be calm and reasonable, but as usual one minute of her company was enough to change that.

'Of course I didn't kidnap Rose. I've only just found her myself.'

Bobbie stopped short of calling me a liar, but she gave me a disbelieving look and plumped herself down on a sofa. In spite of the failure of her ambush, she still had the air of being pleased with herself. I hated to add to it, but I wanted to know how she'd guessed about Topaz and Bobsworth.

I said: 'I think I owe you an apology, Bobbie. In one respect at any rate you were ahead of me.'

She looked surprised, but took it as her due.

'I'm glad you see it that way, Nell.'

'Yes. I don't know how you immediately grasped the significance of that opal pendant.'

'Oh, that wasn't very difficult. In fact, it was the obvious thing to do.'

'What was the obvious thing to do?'

I was mystified, feeling as so often when dealing with Bobbie that things were slipping out of my control.

'Steal it back, of course. We needed it, didn't we, Rose?'

Rose said nothing. She was perched on the edge of a chair looking from one to the other of us like a spectator at a game of lawn tennis.

'Steal it back? What do you mean, steal it back?'

'It may have seemed disrespectful to do it so soon after she was dead, but it was no use to her and it wasn't as if I had pockets full of pendants. We had to have it to try again with the next one.'

Tansy said to me: 'What is she talking about?'

I was on the point of admitting that I had no idea, but I stopped myself. Bobbie was talking as if I knew all about it, and I wasn't going to disillusion her. I wished, though, that I had more time to think. It was like skidding down a mud slide, being carried faster than I wanted to go, but with no power to stop.

I said, struck by a moment of clarity: 'She's saying that it was her own pendant, that she sent it to Topaz herself.'

'It used to be my grandmother's. She left it to me. I'd heard men sent necklaces and such like to them when they wanted to spend the night with them, so I had to send something or I knew she wouldn't invite him.'

Tansy was still looking as if Bobbie were talking in a foreign language, but for me the moment of clarity had broadened into certainty. I remembered what Bobbie had said when I spoilt her plot with Marie: 'It was probably you interfering the first time.' The words made sense to me now. I didn't look at Bobbie, but explained it for Tansy's benefit as if I'd known all along.

'Bobbie had a wild idea that it would be to our advantage if we could put one of our political opponents into a compromising situation. Being in some respects an unworldly young woman...' (a gasp of protest from Bobbie) '...she decided to do it by arranging an assignation for him with a prostitute.' (Another sound of protest, this time from Tansy.) 'She made a few inquiries around the town, then she sent Topaz that opal pendant you saw, implying somehow that it had come from the man in question. The hope was that Topaz would invite him to come and see her, and that he'd be unable to resist.'

'Well, of all the wicked...'

I shushed Tansy. 'In the event, the plan failed. Whether Topaz would at some time have invited the man we shall never know. But we do know that she had other plans for that evening. Those other plans led to her death.'

I had to abandon the attractive idea that Bobsworth had stolen the pendant and sent it to her. His note, pleading for a meeting, must have come by the same post.

Bobbie, I was glad to see, was looking considerably less pleased with herself. Rose was biting her lip, staring out of the window at the darkening sky.

'Bobbie, of course, knew nothing about Topaz's other plans for the evening. In fact, she spent two hours walking up and down outside the side door, in the hope that the man she was trying to trap would come in or out. She didn't give up hope until after midnight.'

Rose looked across at Bobbie.

'When Bobbie heard that Topaz was dead,

309

she decided to reclaim the pendant for use a second time—this time with Marie de la Tourelle as the bait in the trap. How she managed to steal it I don't know...'

Bobbie said: 'If you must know, I watched the two of you go out, then I came up in the public lift and bribed the maid to let me in. I had to go out over the balcony when I heard you coming back. That's when you saw me mountaineering, Nell.'

Tansy said: 'Stealing from a dead woman.'

'I wasn't stealing it. It belonged to me.'

I said: 'I have to admit that there's still one thing in all this that puzzles me.'

'What can possibly puzzle Nell Bray?'

'I still can't understand why you made that visit to the doctor.'

Bobbie laughed. 'Oh that. Did she ask you about that, Rose?'

Rose said nothing.

'It was part of my reconnaissance. I needed to learn how things were done here, and everybody said the doctor was a gossip. A snob, too. Did you notice all those cards on his mantelpiece? I saw one I knew would come in useful, so I pocketed it while he wasn't looking. You can guess whose it was, Nell.'

'David Chester's. He wanted to see the doctor about his daughter.'

She nodded.

'So you sent his card to Topaz with the

pendant. Did you use the card again for Marie too?'

'No. I couldn't find it. It wasn't with the pendant and you came back while I was still looking for it. I suppose it's in this room somewhere.'

Rose said something so quietly that I couldn't hear her at first. She repeated it.

'It's here. I found it this morning.'

Tansy fired up again. 'I told you not to touch her papers.'

'I couldn't help it. A pile of letters fell off that table over there and I was picking them up. I knew it would only cause trouble if anybody else saw it, so I took it.'

She slipped a hand into the pocket of her skirt and passed me a visiting card, crumpled by now, with the gloss rubbed off it. I didn't even look at it, too worried about Rose. She looked near to tears and I was afraid she'd break down and talk about Bobsworth in front of Bobbie and her sister.

I said quietly: 'That's the whole story then. You'd better go now, Bobbie. You'll have packing to do.'

To my surprise, she stood up.

'I suppose so. Shall we go, Rose?'

Rose got up and took a step towards her, looked at her sister, stopped.

'Come on, Rose,' Bobbie said. 'It's not the end of the world. There's plenty to do back at home.'

311

'She's not going,' Tansy said. 'She's had enough of it.'

Rose looked daggers at her, took another step, stopped again.

I said: 'You go on ahead, Bobbie. Rose will follow later if she wants to.'

Bobbie couldn't in any decency oppose that. She stood in the doorway looking at me, then suddenly smiled and raised her hand.

'Goodbye, Nell Bray. See you at the battle front.'

When the door closed behind her, Tansy let out an explosive sigh of relief. Rose stood halfway to the door, where her two steps had taken her.

I said: 'I want to talk to Rose on her own.'

I took her by the arm, guided her gently into Topaz's bedroom and closed the doors on Tansy's protests.

CHAPTER TWENTY-ONE

I sat Rose down on the chair beside the bed and switched on the lamp. The light reflected off the golden sheets making a warm cave round us with the rest of the room in darkness. I wondered if it had been like that on the evening Topaz entertained her last guest. There was no other chair, so I had to perch on the side of the bed, my feet on the step of the dais. This meant I was looking down at Rose's pale face and resentful eyes.

I said: 'Rose, you should know I don't blame you for what happened, and neither would any other fair-minded person.'

She sat stiff and upright: 'I'm not having that. It may have been Bobbie's idea, but I agreed with it. I'm not putting all the blame on her.'

'If you insist on sharing the responsibility for that idiotic plot, I shan't deprive you of it. I'm talking about something else, about what happened in the garden the night Marie gave her party.'

'Oh that.' She looked away from me. 'I was silly to be so upset about it. It caught me off balance, I suppose.'

Even though I believed she had no cause for guilt about Robert Worth's death, this seemed a little too casual.

'I thought it was the other party who was caught off balance.'

She disregarded that, which was probably just as well.

'I didn't know what was happening. I heard the man following you and I waited behind a shed at the side of the house. Then everything went quiet so I went to look for you. I couldn't find you.'

'I was up the magnolia tree.'

'I went right to the end of the garden. I could hear the waves and I guessed it was near the top of the cliffs. I still couldn't see anyone, but I heard him saying something.'

'Him? You mean the man who was following us?'

'Who else could it have been? He sounded angry and I thought he was talking to you. But he wasn't, it was another man.'

'You saw another man?'

'No. It was dark. I couldn't see either of them.'

'Heard another man, then?'

'No.'

'Then how did you know it was another man?'

'A woman's voice would have carried, especially your voice. They were having an argument about a key.'

'What did they say?'

'The one I could hear said if the other one wanted the key back he'd have to pay him a hundred quid. He kept repeating, "a hundred quid" and he said if he didn't get it he'd know what to do with the key.'

'An educated voice or a working man's voice?'

She hesitated. 'In between.'

There was silence inside our cave of light. Outside it I could hear Tansy moving things around in the other room to remind us she was there.

'Rose, you would tell me the truth, wouldn't you? Whatever happened, I can't help you unless I know about it.'

'Of course I'm telling you the truth. Why shouldn't I?' She seemed genuinely puzzled.

'All right. What happened then?'

'I went back towards the house. I wanted to find you or Bobbie.'

'You simply left them there?'

'Why not? Whatever they were arguing about, it had nothing to do with me.'

The picture of Rose frightened by Worth, pushing Worth, had been so clear in my mind that it took me some time to replace it with what Rose had told me.

'You didn't find me. Did you find Bobbie?'

Another hesitation. 'In a way.'

'What does that mean? Either you did or you didn't.'

'I saw her. I didn't speak to her.'

'Why not? You'd come all that way to find her.'

'She was with somebody.'

'Who?'

'Marie. They came out of the house together and stood on the terrace talking. Some of the torches were still burning so I could see them. Marie was wearing a long black fur cloak. Then Bobbie picked up a torch and they went down the garden.'

There was stark misery in her voice.

I said: 'Hadn't Bobbie told you what she was planning with Marie?'

She shook her head.

315

'After Topaz, she didn't tell me everything. She knew I'd talked to you.'

I owed Bobbie nothing, and I was beginning to believe that we both had debts to Rose. I told her about the trap and its ludicrous end. She listened without saying a word, then sighed: 'Poor Bobbie.'

'Nonsense. Let's come back to you. You saw her and Marie together and decided not to speak to them. What did you do then?'

'Came here.'

'Straight here to Tansy?'

'No, I walked around for a long time, trying to decide what to do. I didn't know what I was doing any more. You all had your plans, but nobody had told me.'

Her eyes were bright with hurt and anger.

'You did the right thing to come to your sister.'

'I don't think so. We argue all the time. She wants me to give up the movement, and I won't, whatever happens.'

I thought the poor girl was being torn apart and it was high time we took her away from the conflicting influences of Bobbie and Tansy. When all this was over I'd find her a place in a teachers' training college and persuade one of our richer supporters to pay for her keep. But there was something that must be settled first.

'Rose, will you swear to me that all you did was listen to that man's voice, then go away?'

'Yes. It's true. But why...?'

'You didn't speak to him?'

'Of course not. I didn't want him to know I was there.'

'You didn't go back there later to speak to him?'

'No. Why should I?'

I believed her. The account of Marie in her sable cloak and Bobbie with the torch compared exactly with what I'd seen. I said, as gently as I could:

'The man who was following us, the one you probably heard—he's dead.'

She stared blankly.

'He was found in the sea the next day. He'd been knocked unconscious and drowned.'

Her hands went to her mouth. Two scared eyes stared at me over her bitten nails. She lurched forward from the chair and I managed to catch her before she fell. The noise brought Tansy bursting in.

'What have you been doing to her? Can't you leave the poor girl alone?'

Rose was saying weakly that she was all right, that we mustn't bother.

I wanted her to lie down on Topaz's bed but Tansy, either from respect or superstition, pulled her away from it as if it were live coals.

'She wants to come and lie down in my room, don't you, Rosie? Don't worry, my love. Her and her questions. If she tries to ask

317

you any more she'll have me to deal with.'

When I tried to help support Rose as far as the door, Tansy gave me a withering look.

'You stay here. We'll be better off on our own, Rosie and me, won't we, my duck?'

The look of appeal that Rose gave me over her sister's shoulder showed she had her doubts about that, but I was bone weary and knew when I was beaten. I sat in my chair, turning over in my hand the visiting card that had cost so much trouble. 'David Chester MP' embossed in copper plate. Then underneath, *May I call at 11 p.m.?* When I held it close to the light I could see that the 'p.m.', though cleverly forged, was in a slightly less glossy black ink than the rest. Bobbie's hand, of course. I was even angrier at the stupidity of her plot now I knew the harm it had done to Rose.

Then as I sat there, half dozing beside Topaz's bed, something connected in a way that would never have happened in my waking mind. I came bolt upright and awake, feeling as if some great catastrophe had happened. I went through to the salon for my bag—luckily Tansy was still occupied with Rose in her bedroom—brought it back to my chair beside Topaz's bed and rummaged for what I wanted. All the time I'd been carrying round with me Topaz's note: *Too late. 8 p.m. Return of I.O.U. for one career. Vin Poison.*' I held the visiting card in one hand and the note in the other, feeling as if each throbbed with an electric current and the consequences of completing the circuit by bringing them together were too dangerous to be faced. I must have sat there for a long time. I heard Tansy closing the door of her bedroom, coming back into the salon. She called through the door to me:

'Are you staying there all night? You can't sleep on her bed.'

I heard my own voice promising not to sleep on Topaz's bed, then Tansy moving around next door. I think she must have been making up a bed for herself on the chaise longue. Then she settled, switched off the light and the room fell quiet. I sat there, conscious of the sounds of a hotel also settling itself for the night, lifts ascending and descending with metallic creakings that I never noticed by day, pipes suddenly gurgling. I heard a clock outside striking midnight, then I must have dozed again because I was jerked back to consciousness by the sound of Tansy's voice whispering urgently from the other side of the door. My first thought was that she was checking to make sure I wasn't profaning Topaz's bed and I told her, rather impatiently, that she need not worry, it was all right.

'No, it isn't all right. I'm coming in.'

The light was still off in the salon. She closed the door behind her and came into my circle of lamplight. She was in stockinged feet, still wearing her black day dress.

'Somebody's coming up.'

Her voice was a scared whisper.

'What do you mean?'

'Coming up in her lift. Listen.'

When I listened I could hear the sound of the private lift on to the landing creaking up its shaft, but I still didn't grasp the significance of it.

Tansy said: 'Whoever it is must have her key. Nobody could use that side door otherwise.'

Then the fear in her voice ran into me and I felt icy cold. Only one person was likely to have Topaz's missing key. Topaz's last visitor.

The lift stopped on the landing. At first nothing happened. The silence stretched itself into ten, twenty heartbeats, then I heard the lift doors opening.

'Tansy, the man she said was ungrateful, you must . . .'

She shushed me. There was a metallic scraping sound at the outside door of the salon. I stood up and instinctively we moved closer together.

I mouthed at her: 'Is it locked?'

She nodded, but no more than a minute later there was a click and the sound of the door opening. Even grand hotels may be catchpenny in the matter of inside locks, and

320

that one had put up little resistance. There was now only the width of the salon and one set of unlocked doors between us and whoever had broken his way in. We could hear him now moving round the salon. A thin beam of light from a hand lamp came through a crack in the door, went away, cut back from another angle. Tansy was so close to me that I could feel her heart thumping. I put my arm round her and she didn't resist. The soft steps moved closer to our door, then away again. Tansy's heart thumped harder. She mouthed at me: 'Rose.' I nodded. He couldn't be allowed to wake up Rose. I led Tansy firmly to the chair, made her sit down in it, then walked to the double doors between Topaz's bedroom and the salon. I waited for a second, feeling the porcelain doorknobs smooth under my hands, just as months before I'd been very conscious of the roughness of the half brick in the second before I threw it. Then I took a deep breath and pulled the doors open.

'You'd better come in,' I said.

CHAPTER TWENTY-TWO

I think he was dazzled for a moment by the golden light pouring in from the bedroom because he stood there blank and staring, not focusing on me. When he moved it was not so much a conscious step as an overbalancing. He caught himself up in the doorway, inches away from me. I stood to one side and again invited him to come in, surprised to hear my own voice so level. He came, his eyes on me, not noticing Tansy in the chair. I shut the doors and leaned against them. I said to Tansy:

'That was the name you wouldn't tell me, wasn't it?'

She nodded, staring at him transfixed. When he saw there was somebody else in the room I thought he was going to turn and run. He looked at Tansy, then at the golden bed with its newly plumped pillows.

'Is this a trap of some kind?'

His voice was calm and low, but with a threat in it, just as I remembered from court.

I said: 'If it is a trap, you've taken some trouble to break into it.'

A barrister learns to control his expression. He gave me the same level stare he'd given me in the dock.

'I've come to recover a piece of my property which was stolen.'

The card and the note were on the floor by Tansy's feet. I'd dropped them when I fell asleep. I crossed the room, picked both of them up and handed him the card.

'This?'

That look again. 'May I ask how you came by it?'

'Do you confirm that it's your property?'

'It's a moot point whether a calling card left with one's doctor remains one's property, especially if it is subsequently stolen. I suppose that was your doing, Miss Bray.'

'Certainly not. Do you recognise it as your writing?'

'All except the last two letters, which are a palpable forgery. A forgery with malicious intent.'

He'd moved to a position in the middle of the room, trying to dominate it as if it were a court. I noticed that, after the first glance, he didn't look towards the bed.

I said: 'Exactly what malicious intent?'

'I'm sure that's clearer to you than to me, Miss Bray.'

'I doubt it, but let me summarise.'

Two could play at the court game. I stepped up to the dais round Topaz's bed, turned to face him from the foot of it. Tansy stayed in the chair. Her eyes hadn't moved from him since he came in.

I said: 'You've confirmed that this is your card, stolen from your doctor's consulting room. You left it to arrange an appointment for eleven o'clock, meaning of course eleven o'clock in the morning.'

He nodded. The stare wasn't quite so confident now he had to look at me across the bed.

'It was, as we've established, stolen. We've

also established that it was subsequently amended.'

'By forgery.'

'Indeed. I can tell you that it was stolen by one of your political opponents—and believe me that gives a very wide field of suspects—who forged the letters "p.m." to make it appear that it was a request for an assignation late at night. It was then sent, along with an opal pendant, to Miss Topaz Brown.'

He winced a little. 'You accept, Miss Bray, that I knew nothing of this, and to put it in the mildest terms, would have protested most strongly if I had known.'

'I accept that.'

'Then do you accept that it was a wicked attempt to harm my reputation by implying an association between myself and a common prostitute?'

Tansy stirred in her chair. I gave her a glance.

'I should describe it as stupid rather than wicked. Apart from that, I accept what you say.'

Tansy muttered something.

'Very well then. You can hardly be surprised that I should wish to recover my card.'

'No indeed, I'm not surprised.'

He seemed taken aback by my reasonable tone. He slipped the card into the pocket of his evening jacket.

'In the circumstances, since it is to nobody's advantage that such a squalid attempt should be made public, I'll refrain from any immediate legal action against you or your misguided supporters. I need hardly say that if any of this should become public knowledge I should immediately take the most serious steps to defend my reputation.'

He gave me another stare, held it for a count of three seconds, then turned and stepped towards the door. I waited until his hand was on the knob, then I said:

'Are we also supposed to be quiet about what happened next?'

He turned. 'What are you talking about?'

I held out Topaz's note but didn't move from where I was standing. He stayed by the door.

'What is that?'

'A note of invitation from Miss Brown.'

'I hardly see how that can interest me.'

He should have opened the door and walked out. He didn't move a muscle.

'She sets an assignation for eight o'clock in the evening. The note begins *Too late*. What do you suppose that means?'

'I can hardly be expected to guess.'

'I think it has a very simple meaning—that eleven o'clock is too late and she regards eight o'clock as preferable. A reply to the message on your card, Mr Chester.'

'If so, a reply to a forged message which you have already admitted was part of a plot.'

But his voice wasn't as level as it had been. If I'd been a rival barrister, I'd have sensed that the scales were tipping my way.

'But Miss Brown believed the card and the pendant came from you, so naturally the reply would be sent to you.'

'I received no such note.'

He took a step towards me.

'I believe that you did receive it, Mr Chester. And I believe that you brought it with you when you came to call on Miss Brown at eight o'clock that night to ask her what she meant by it, though I suspect you had a very good idea already.'

He wrapped his courtroom manner round him like a gown.

'In that case my behaviour surely would have been inexplicable. You are asking the . . .' (He almost said 'asking the court'.) '. . . You are claiming that I received out of the blue an invitation from a notorious prostitute to visit her and that I went in person to ask what she meant by it. Surely that would have been the action of a simpleton?'

'Indeed it would—if you'd never met Miss Brown in the past.'

'If you are implying, Miss Bray, that I'm in the habit of frequenting prostitutes, I can only say you have an even fouler mind than I should have expected from your activities.'

He was quite buoyed up by his indignation. I said: 'I wasn't accusing you of that.'

'Then what were you implying?'

'I believe that a normal relationship between a man and a woman like Topaz Brown is that he pays her expenses. In your case, it was quite the reverse.'

I read from Topaz's note, although I knew it by heart: *Return of I.O.U. for one career.* Your career, Mr Chester, your very successful career. And yet at the outset it depended on Topaz Brown's support and Topaz Brown's money.'

He made a pretence of turning away, but took only a token step to the door.

'Your brain's completely turned by your hatred of me.'

'There's a witness.' I gestured towards Tansy. 'This is Tansy Mills, Topaz Brown's maid. Tansy told me that Topaz once spoke to her about a man in the legal profession whom she'd helped early in her career. She said he'd been ungrateful. Tansy refused to tell me the name of that man. I'll ask her again now.'

'Yes, it was him.'

Tansy's voice was no more than a croak.

'We'll do this properly, Tansy. What was the name of the man Topaz said had been ungrateful?'

Another croak. 'David Chester.'

327

He took two quick steps towards her, then stopped himself.

'You've coached her. She's one of yours.'

'Oh no. If there's one person on the face of the earth who's more opposed to women's suffrage than you are, it's Tansy Mills. If there's one person who dislikes me more than you do, that's Tansy too.'

'That's a fact,' Tansy croaked.

He looked from her to me, utterly at a loss.

I said: 'The person who set that stupid trap for you had no idea how deadly it was. I swear to you that neither she nor I knew that you'd had any connection with Topaz Brown.'

'I don't believe you.'

'You received this note.' I walked across the room, let him look at it but didn't put it in his hand. 'Poor Topaz Brown meant exactly what she said. She was touched by the pendant that she thought came from you. She was prepared to forgive your ingratitude, to write off all that you owed her. She'd prepared a little supper to remind you of the old days when you were both poor; fried fish and cheap wine. She'd even gone out and bought underclothes of the kind she used to wear before she could afford better.'

His eyes flickered at the mention of the underwear.

'But you'd been making your preparations too, hadn't you? Topaz bought wine, but you

328

bought laudanum. You kept the appointment, poisoned Topaz and returned in time for a late supper with your wife and friends. You took the key to her private door away with you and used it at some time after two o'clock in the morning to make sure she was dead or dying.'

'Without my wife noticing my absence?'

He was trained to fight a hopeless case to the end.

'As far as your wife was concerned, you were sitting up with a sick daughter, with Louisa. You probably gave her a few drops of the laudanum on a sugar lump, to make sure she didn't wake up while you were away.'

He closed his eyes at the mention of his daughter's name. I think those few drops he gave his daughter caused him more guilt than the laudanum he'd poured into Topaz's wine glass.

I said: 'There was still a problem, though, wasn't there? When you met Topaz, she'd have thanked you for the pendant. You would naturally ask how she knew it came from you, and she told you your card was enclosed with it. The next morning it occurred to you that you couldn't afford to have your card discovered among her papers. You paid a man to try to get it back for you, first by impersonation. When that failed, you gave him the key and told him to steal it. That failed too. Worse, he kept the key and tried to blackmail you. And he knew quite a lot by then, because you were paying him to spy on us as well, in case we'd guessed anything.'

'Could you produce this alleged man to give evidence in court?'

'You know very well that I can't. He's lying in the morgue. I can tell you his name, though: Robert Worth. You'd met him in London more than ten years ago when he was working for a solicitor. You met him again here—probably when you took Naomi and Louisa to the circus.'

That had been a sudden guess of mine, but I knew from his face that I'd hit it. I'm sure it was my knowledge of his family affairs that broke him. He lurched towards me and I tensed myself for an attack, but he stumbled past me up the step to the dais and sat down heavily on Topaz's bed. For once Tansy made no protest at the desecration. He slumped there, head in his hands, long fingers pressed to his forehead. I remembered my hours in the dock and felt no pity—or only a very little.

'I'm sorry,' he said.

It seemed hopelessly inadequate as a confession, but that wasn't what he was trying to say.

'I'm sorry, I need some air. Is there a balcony?'

I signed to Tansy to stay where she was, led him out like a blind man through the dark salon and opened the French windows on to the balcony. A rush of cool air hit us, and the sound of Atlantic waves pounding the beach a hundred feet below. It was quite dark. The promenade lights had been switched off long ago and we were too high up to see the windows of other hotels. He stepped out on to the balcony, taking deep breaths. I'd guessed he had something to say to me that he didn't want Tansy to hear. I followed him, feeling as if I were treading on the broken fragments of something valuable, trying to tell myself that it deserved breaking. He had his back to me, looking out to sea. I waited.

'What do you intend to do?'

He asked the question without turning, his voice level again. It was the question I'd intended to ask him.

'What do you expect me to do?'

My voice sounded as calm as his. We might have been two colleagues discussing a difficult case.

'To name your price.'

'Price . . .' I was beginning to be indignant, then I realised he wasn't talking about money. 'What price were you thinking of?'

'A vote?'

'Our vote?'

'My vote.'

He was still facing out to sea, and the words were so quiet I hardly heard them. I moved closer.

'Your vote in Parliament?'

'It's not without influence.'

To hear him I had to stand close enough to touch him, but he still hadn't looked at me.

'Do I understand that you're offering to vote on our side the next time the suffrage question comes up in Parliament?'

His 'Yes' hardly moved the air on the balcony, but the stir it would make in London would be our biggest step forward for years. And he was right about his influence. He'd carry others with him, perhaps make the difference at last.

I said: 'And the price?'

I knew the price. To forget about Topaz, who'd never been a supporter of ours. To forget about Bobsworth, who'd been part of the world's small change.

He murmured something so quietly that I had to move closer to hear it, but as I moved something happened to my body. My ribs crushed in so that I could hardly breathe, the sky spun round and my back came up against something hard. It took a second of blackness and panic before my mind grasped what was happening, that he was trying to throw me over the balcony. But my body knew what to do and, even without instructions, was going into the routine for resisting attack. My feet kicked out, making contact with something solid, my left arm pulled itself free, grabbed for a handful of cloth. By the time my mind had caught up, my fingers were locked on his lapel and I was trying desperately to pull myself up, to take the pressure of the stone balustrade off my back. I heard myself shouting something, I don't know what.

He'd stepped back a little when I kicked his shin and I almost managed to pull myself upright. His face was inches away from mine, intent, eyes no colder than they'd been in court. A man doing a necessary job. I pulled my other arm free, jabbed my nails into his eye. He grunted with pain and I felt flesh tearing, but he didn't let go and I was still off balance, bent backwards. I felt the balustrade under my back again, my kicking legs being levered off the ground. All I could see was night sky and a constellation whose name I couldn't remember. I wondered if it would come to me on the way down. One foot, one toe was in contact with the balcony, and that was sliding.

'Stop that.'

Tansy's voice. She might have been speaking to a dog stealing the remains of the joint. He hadn't expected it. There'd been nothing else in the universe for either of us. He hesitated just long enough for me to get one foot back on the ground, to throw my weight forward. At the same time, Tansy simply grabbed his ear and pulled.

I think it was the indignity of it as much as anything that distracted him. He gasped as his head twisted round and I pulled upright and away from him. It looked for a moment as if he was going to attack Tansy, but by then I was standing beside her. He stared at us, chest heaving, one hand automatically massaging his mistreated ear.

'There's no sense in going on like that,' Tansy said.

The rebuke was directed equally at both of us, but Tansy and I had him boxed in now at one end of the balcony.

I said to Tansy: 'I'll keep him here. You go and ring for somebody.'

Then he moved, but not towards us. For a moment he was a shape on the edge of the balcony, black against the sky, then there was just sky. He made no noise as he went. Then, after a gap of silence worse than any scream would have been, there was a sound from the pavement below like a heavy door closing a long way away. When Rose came into the salon, blinking from sleep, she found me and Tansy clinging together like Babes in the Wood.

CHAPTER TWENTY-THREE

It was two months before I met Bobbie Fieldfare again. She and I found ourselves under arrest together in the same police vehicle, after the fracas in Parliament Square when Mrs Pankhurst was arrested for slapping a police inspector's face in the House of Commons. I was the first occupant and Bobbie landed on top of me, still shouting defiance at the two police constables who'd bundled her in.

'Oh it's you again, is it, Nell Bray?'

As the vehicle jogged along the familiar route to Bow Street police station she said:

'I suppose you're not going to tell me what really happened.'

'The verdict was suicide.'

'Like Topaz Brown?'

'Like Topaz Brown. There seems to have been quite an epidemic of it in Biarritz this year.'

'From her balcony?'

'He'd suffered a complete mental collapse from overwork.'

'That's what *The Times* said. If it was in *The Times*, it must be a lie.'

We slowed from a trot to a walk, caught in the queue of other police wagons heading for Bow Street with our supporters on board.

'You're protecting him, aren't you, Nell? Him of all people. Why?'

I said nothing. I could give no answer that would satisfy Bobbie. For a silly, plump woman who thought it was wicked to want votes, for a cold-eyed child who'd said ladies couldn't be in Parliament. For Tansy, who

335

wanted Topaz to rest in peace. Their worlds had been torn apart already. Should I shred them more to make a political point?

The crowd were shouting outside, but above the traffic I couldn't tell if it was support or insults.

I said: 'There's some good news about Topaz's will, anyway. It looks as if the brother may settle for half the money.'

'Half!'

'That still leaves us with twenty-five thousand. That's twenty-five candidates and a general election coming up any month now.'

An election that surely must make the difference at last, must give us what we deserved in justice and logic. And Topaz Brown, whether she'd supported us or not, deserved to be part of it too.

Bobbie said: 'Have you seen Rose Mills lately?'

She sounded a little less sure of herself.

'I rather think she may be in one of the police vans up in front. She was leading a detachment of garment workers who were trying to storm the Home Office.'

'That's good.'

For once I agreed with Bobbie. I was almost sure that I'd managed to secure Rose a place in the autumn at a teachers' training college that would not be shocked by a police record acquired in a good cause. Tansy might be pleased by that, and if Topaz's will were settled, she'd get her five hundred pounds for the cottage.

'And the ducks, of course.'

'I beg your pardon.'

Bobbie was staring at me. I must have spoken out loud.

'Cats, I mean. I was just thinking my neighbour will have to look after my cats again.'

The wagon had drawn to a halt. We could hear the heavy boots of a police constable stamping round to the back of the van to escort us up the steps to the police station. We both stood up at once, looked at each other, then laughed. Bobbie sat down again.

'After you, Nell Bray.'

It was as near as we'd ever get to a truce.

Photoset, printed and bound in Great Britain by
REDWOOD PRESS LIMITED, Melksham, Wiltshire